Cherem

Michael Paulson

BooksForABuck.com
2013

Chapter 1

On a rainy evening in early August Yu-tung Cheng's chauffeur-driven Mercedes rolled along *Carrer de la Barca* outside of Port Bou, Spain. In the dimly-lit rear seat, two men were conversing in Spanish. Mr. Cheng was a gaunt Chinese about sixty years of age. He had a shaved head, and sunken cheeks within a waxy face. His thick, round spectacles perched upon a broad blunt nose. He was dapperly dressed in a gray suit, gray boots and a white shirt. A gray pearl mounted to the head of a gold pin decorated the pink, silk cravat at his throat. The tainted sweetness of opium hung about him like rancid candy.

"You're asking a great deal of money, Shkarov." Cheng tilted his head back as he spoke, the words wheezing laboriously from his throat as if on a choking whisper. "A million Euros, by anyone's standard, is a fortune."

The other man was Mikhail Shkarov. He was a ruddy-faced Chechnyan with thick gray hair, cut in military fashion. Shkarov was tall, angular, fortyish and thin about the neck. His bulbous eyes constantly showed their whites, like those of a dog wary of an approaching boot. His mouth was a wide slit smeared across his mug in a crooked, permanently mocking expression. His protracted, narrow nose seemed to droop past his upper lip. His suit was dark blue. Several tiny links of gold chain, suspended between two ancient Roman coins, closed each white shirt-cuff. His tie was crimson.

"A bargain for the price," the Chechnyan said, in a sonorous voice. His bushy black eyebrows dipped slightly with annoyance.

Within the murky haze, that formed the skyline, lightening lashed out with purple claws. The resulting blaze silhouetted acres of surrounding trees. Then, thunder rumbled. It vibrated through the moving vehicle, sending tremors across each seat; a momentary backbeat to the tune created by the tires upon the rain-drenched highway.

"A seller always assumes he's offering a bargain," Cheng said.

"You know I am."

"That, most certainly, is my hope." The Asian addressed his boots, wearily. "But, expectations often fall short of realization."

"My information came at a great risk." Shkarov's nerves showed behind the irritated scowl he tossed his companion. "The price is not negotiable."

"The price is *always* negotiable."

"Not this time."

Oncoming headlights flashed through the windscreen and into the rear seat. Its blaze ignited Cheng's glasses, like a camera-flash striking a mirror. The resulting reflection hit the back of the chauffeur's dark head, and then dissolved into shadows.

"A traitor is, invariably, underpaid." The Asian's waxy hands spread like those on a posed figure in Madam Tussaud's museum. "The turncoat's untenable position makes him desperate. Thus, he's unable to negotiate fairly for his labor." Cheng studied his shiny fingernails. "Consequently *your* profit, in this venture, is very high." There were seconds more of thunder rumblings as the Asian lit a cigarette. He blew smoke towards the car's ceiling. Then he smiled thinly at the Chechnyan. "One must not let momentary greed override considerations of future business."

"The Russian troops and armament intelligence, in particular the missile systems between Irkutsk and Hohhot, is superior to anything possessed by your government."

Yu-tung Cheng laughed shortly, displaying his opium-blackened teeth. "If true, my superiors will be delighted."

Shkarov gritted his molars, barely controlling his impatience. He hated dealing with the Chinese. They were far too suspicious. The Americans were easy. Information passed. Payment passed back. The CIA never asked questions, never delayed.

"If you doubt my veracity, Cheng, I can take this business elsewhere."

"That would be a foolish mistake."

Mikhail Shkarov leaned toward the other man suddenly, his head tilted to one side. Despite the Chechnyan's growing irritation with the Asian, he anticipated success. Why not? He could see the pulse of self-indulgence beating steadily at Cheng's temple. He could hear the anxious workings of the other's overtaxed lungs. He could almost feel the million Euros, stuffing his pockets.

"Then, pay my price." There was certainty in Shkarov's voice.

"Are you prepared to make delivery?"

The Chechnyan leaned back, a satisfied smile tugging at the corners of his mouth. "Not yet."

"Your offer is speculative?"

"I expect to be in receipt of the material during the last week of September." Shkarov gave out a short relief-valve burst of laughter. The glint of exasperation in Cheng's eyes amused him. "Allowing another day for travel to Port-Bou..."

"Your time-frame creates a problem," the Asian cut in.

It was Shkarov's turn to flare with exasperation. "What do you mean?"

"I have certain business interests in South America. I plan to be there the first two weeks of October."

There was another session of silence with the exception of the tire-opera and thunder drum-rolls.

Shkarov spoke hesitantly, his words stilted. "I ... might ... be able to make delivery, before you leave."

"Rather than attempting to do so, which might hurry the progression of events to a risky level, I would suggest you await my return."

"The longer I hang onto this information the more dangerous it is."

"My trip cannot be delayed, Shkarov."

The Chechnyan crossed one long leg over the other and contemplated the gleaming, black leather of his left shoe. "I suppose a few more days will make little difference."

Cheng lit another cigarette using the burning end of the first. Then he snuffed out the latter in the ashtray embedded in the back of the front seat.

"There is still the price to finalize," the Asian said.

"I told you..."

The Asian cut in with, "So large an amount will require a review by my overseer's at the National Security Bureau." Cheng's mouth turned down at the corners. His eyes continued their veiled gaze. "This could lead to misgivings on their part. I might be suspected of profiteering."

"You've always filled your pockets at Taiwan's expense. Why should this transaction be any different?"

"I wouldn't mock me, Shkarov."

The Asian's tone had become harsh, threatening. It was true he did profit from each transaction with the Chechnyan. He did so with all who sold him information, intended for the NSB. Nevertheless, he did not like Shkarov's naked accusation.

"Assuming the approval for the expenditure is granted, by Taiwan, what assurances can you give regarding the *Glavnoye Razvedyvatel'noye*

Upravleniye? Have they tumbled to your ploy? I wouldn't like to find myself in their sights."

"If Moscow Center was aware of my actions, I would know, instantly."

"Hardly."

"Now who is mocking?"

"The GRU is the largest and most impenetrable spy organization in the world."

"Not entirely impenetrable." Shkarov made a vague gesture with one hand. "You see, I have a prescription for protection. It grants permanent immunity from detection."

The Asian's black eyebrows arched covetously. "You actually have a Mole within the GRU?"

Shkarov nodded. "One whose lair is deeply dug, placing my source beyond suspicion."

"Such protection must've come at quite a price."

"A mere trifle, considering its effectiveness."

"Effectiveness can be a razor in an unsteady hand." Cheng glanced at the smoldering cigarette stub gripped by his waxy fingers. "Traitors often serve two masters."

"There's no chance of a double agent."

"Hell and Chancery are always open, Shkarov."

"Not in this case."

"Taiwan wouldn't like to be the focal point for an international incident."

"No more than I."

The Asian sneered, his gaze locked upon Mikhail Shkarov's implacable face. "Yes, you and Innokenti Rakhmelevich are *dead*; aren't you?"

"A belief I would like to keep *alive*."

For the next several minutes, Yu-tung Cheng smoked while Mikhail Shkarov studied the crease in his trouser-leg. Then the Asian twisted into the corner of the rear seat, facing the Chechnyan obliquely; the former's eyes squeezed into bright slits behind his spectacle lenses, the thick glass magnifying the Asian's avarice.

"How certain are you of the Irkutsk Hohhot information?"

Shkarov smiled. "It is irrefutable."

"You've used this source before?"

"No. But, he's highly placed."

"Highly placed or not, how can you be certain this traitor is not playing you for a fool at my expense?"

"Because he knows the lengths I will go to retaliate."

"Do not misunderstand, Shkarov." A wicked grimace creased Cheng's gaunt cheeks, the ends of his mouth curling upward like a clown's painted leer. "I don't doubt your intentions. But, even an old woman can be fooled. I would hate to see our relationship compromised." He casually waved a waxy hand. "It would trouble me to seek reparations."

"There will be no need for that."

"The likelihood of two raindrops, descending from separate clouds, merging onto a single windowpane is immeasurable." The Asian paused. Then, with purpose, he flicked the ash of his cigarette onto the shiny toe of the Chechnyan's shoe. "But, it happens."

Chapter 2

221 Bd Renard Benoît in Épône, France has long been the headquarters of the Nabatov Imports Company. The offices for this little-known business occupy the second floor, above the Nin Bakery.

If someone were to climb the white, wooden stairs meandering up the side of this red brick building, he or she would confront, at the top, a massive steel door. Should that someone get beyond this door — not any easy task, except during business hours considering its equally massive locking system — he or she would enter a small reception area rigged with a plethora of cleverly concealed security cameras.

"Welcome to Nabatov Imports," would be the greeting offered by the young, pretty receptionist. Her full-figured form would be sitting primly behind a large, glass desk topped by a telephone and a brass nameplate bearing the inscription: *Anais Duras.* "How may I help you?"

Should a question arise concerning business operations, Anais' response would always be the same: Pasha Nabatov was its President; Kazimir Sokolof was its Senior Vice President in charge of Middle East Operations; and, Anitchka Nabatov was its Vice President in charge of European Operations. Whereupon, unless it was Tuesday, Anais would quickly add that everyone was unavailable. On Tuesdays, however, she would politely state that Anitchka Nabatov would respond to all inquiries — submitted in writing.

"Look at Anais' ass, Pasha. You could park a T-90 Tank between those luscious cheeks, and she'd hardly notice."

Kazimir Sokolof, speaking in Russia, was the source of the tactless comments. He eyed the receptionist in lustful abandon via one of several security monitors in Pasha Nabatov's office. Sokolof, a stubby man in a wrinkled brown suit, was about forty years of age, black-haired and bearded. An amiable fellow, he usually wore a leering half-smile on his round face. However, at that moment his mouth was agape and his normally sedate basalt eyes, glittered with unbridled adoration.

"You should be ashamed of yourself, Kazimir," Pasha Nabatov said, flatly. "Anais is our best employee."

Nabatov was stocky with the hardness of flint, about him. His rectangular, wrinkled and pitted face displayed, like a map, from sixty-years of personal and professional struggle. He sat at a large oak desk, his glinting black eyes staring at the other man with concern.

"Anais is our *only* employee, Pasha."

"Then she should be treated with the respect she deserves, and not viewed like some harlot."

The top of Nabatov's head was thick with short, white hair. He was clean-shaven. His eyebrows were long and gray. The corners of his orbs, being spider-webbed with wrinkles, imparted the illusion of grandfatherly benevolence. However, there was no foolish compassion in Pasha Nabatov's soul. He, like Kazimir Sokolof and Anitchka Nabatov, Pasha's daughter, were cold-hearted *Glavnoye Razvedyvatel'noye Upravleniye* soldiers, experienced in all phases of espionage and assassination.

"I don't have to treat her with respect," Sokolof grunted. "I love her."

"You don't know the meaning of love."

"I would die for her, wouldn't I?"

"You would die for a bowl of Basturma."

Kazimir tossed his boss a grin. "That would depend on who made it." Then his big hands worked the camera toggles to zoom closer on Anais' long and shapely legs. "How come I can't have monitors like this in my office, Pasha?"

"Because you would be doing just what you're doing and never get any work done — just like you're not doing. Come away from there."

Nabatov's nose was long and broad. His lips were thin. They formed a gash-like, perennially drooping, food receptor. His chin had a deep cleft. He was dressed in a blue double-breasted suit, a white shirt and a narrow black tie held in place by a silver stickpin. His thick forearms rested casually upon the desktop. These terminated into the large, square hands holding the *Moskovsky Komsomolets*, a national newspaper printed only in Russian. Beneath the desk, expensive black shoes encased Nabatov's large feet, luxurious footwear being his only weakness.

"Pasha, look. She's bending over. Have you never seen anything so beautiful in your entire life?"

Like Anais' reception desk, Nabatov's workspace was bereft of luxuries. Gracing it were two telephones, one black and the other red. He had acquired this Spartan view of living when he was a *Kapitán* in the *Voyenno-vozdushnye sily Rossii* flying a *Sukhoi Su-17* fighter-bomber, during the Soviet-Afghanistan war. In front of the desk were three, straight-backed, wooden chairs. Behind him, lining an otherwise bare wall, were seven military-gray filing cabinets.

"You're disgusting, Kazimir."

"Because I adore her?"

"You don't adore Anais. You lust after her."

"It is the same thing." Kazimir pushed a button on the toggle in his hand. Then in frustration, he pushed it several more times. "How come the camera no longer takes snapshots?"

Nabatov resumed reading the newspaper. "It no longer works because you've worn it out — yet, again."

"When are we going to get it fixed?"

"What in hell are you doing with all those photos of Anais?"

"I paper the walls of my bedroom. She's the beacon of light to my dreams."

Nabatov looked up, impatiently. "You're doing this at GRU expense?"

"Her image is imperative to my mental well-being, not to mention my fantasies." Kazimir scratched his head, still leering at the screen. "I'm sure it's covered by the National health plan."

"Questions are being asked, Kazimir." The white-haired Russian shook a scolding finger at his subordinate. "We are the only GRU sector in the entire world who keeps wearing out its internal-security, photographic equipment."

"Pasha, I'm going to marry her."

"As you well know, Anais *is* already married."

"One curl of a finger could take care of that."

"Don't even think about it. Do you hear me, Kazimir?"

"I hear, Pasha, I hear. But, that doesn't stop me from wanting her."

The bearded Russian toggled a different camera to focus upon the receptionist, from another angle. Then he tilted forward toward the screen his eyes wide with longing.

"Look at Anais in profile, Pasha. That woman is a living, breathing dairy." Kazimir let go a soft moan. "I would cut out my own heart for her."

"I shall mention your vow to Anais." Nabatov took fresh interest in the newspaper. "Perhaps, she will provide the knife and a great deal of practical assistance — thus, salvaging my fiscal responsibilities to Moscow Center."

A short, stooped, middle-aged man with graying-blond hair came into view on the screens, as he entered the outer office. He spoke briefly to Anais while picking a piece of lint from his dark suit. Then he strode past her desk, moving off-screen.

"Dr. Popovitch is here, Pasha."

Nabatov gave his white head an exasperated wag as he set aside the newspaper.

A moment later the office door opened, and the stooped man entered. "*Dobraye ootro*, Pasha."

"Good morning, Doctor. What brings you here?" Nabatov said.

The physician, Dmitri Popovitch, closed the office door and sauntered over to Nabatov's desk. With each step, his eyes darted around the room; landing briefly on each monitoring screen before drifting across each yellow wall.

"Anitchka telephoned." Popovitch took a perch on the edge of the desk. He cradled his Gladstone bag in his lap. "Apparently Anais is having emotional difficulties."

Nabatov tapped his yellow teeth with a thumbnail while offering Kazimir a scathing glare. "Has something happened to Anais' husband?"

"It wasn't me, Pasha," Kazimir Sokolof said in protest. Quickly, he left the monitors and rushed over to Nabatov's desk. "I swear on my dead mother's eyes I had nothing to do with it."

"I spoke with you mother only yesterday, Kazimir," Nabatov said. "Has something happened between then and now?"

"Would it help if I said 'yes'?"

"It is nothing as serious as that, Pasha," Popovitch said, with a laugh. He looked across the desk into Nabatov's all-seeing eyes. "Anais and her husband are going through a difficult period." His palms splayed, casually. "It happens with all couples; especially the young ones. During their courting days, they do not see each other's faults. Then, after marriage when these shortcomings appear, they become disappointed."

Kazimir jerked out a handkerchief and daubed at the sweat pouring from his forehead. "Disappointed, young couples with whom I have absolutely no murderous involvement or intent."

"We all have disappointments, Doctor," said Nabatov. "However one cannot help but wonder if certain people would leave other people alone, such problems might resolve themselves without the need for medical assistance?"

"I barely speak to her, Pasha." Kazimir stuffed the handkerchief back into his pocket, not daring to look at the angry expression on his superior's face.

"Not three days ago, Kazimir, I saw her hit you in the head with the telephone. She dropped you to the floor like a pole-axed bull."

The bearded Russian shrugged. "That is what Anais does when I speak to her."

"I don't think Kazimir is the problem, Pasha." Popovitch's solemn face relaxed into a slight smile.

"Nevertheless, Doctor, if Anais is not feeling like her old self very soon a certain person will find himself back at Moscow Center explaining…"

The harsh trilling of the red telephone broke in, instantly silencing the three men. It rang again. Pasha Nabatov reached over with one hand and gripped the receiver, but he did not lift it from its cradle. The corners of his wide mouth tilted down as he waited for the third ring. When the trilling repeated, he raised the receiver to his ear and listened.

For a moment, the white-haired Russian winced as if he was having trouble understanding the caller. Then, like a soldier ordered to stand at attention, Nabatov jumped to his feet. He spoke quickly but softly, his words inaudible to those around him. After several more minutes of listening and brief comments, he rang off. His grandfatherly face had become wary, with concern.

"Trouble, Pasha?" asked Popovitch.

"A small matter."

Pasha Nabatov turned to the filing cabinets and opened the second to the last one. Quickly he rummaged through the binders within the third drawer. Selecting a rather fat folder, he withdrew it and resumed his seat; setting the manila container upon the desk. Across the folder's front was an age-yellowed label bearing the name, *Alexi Kalandarishvili*.

"Smuggling?" persisted Popovitch, curiously studying the name.

Nabatov shrugged, not speaking as he opened the file.

Dr. Popovitch left his perch, one hand gripping his bag. "I'd like to take Anais away for a few minutes." He glanced over at the bearded Russian. "I think it will be more productive if she and I discuss her situation, privately."

"I have done nothing," Kazimir said. "Her husband is an idiot. He is having an affair with the sex-mad pastry filler in the Nin bakery. Who, by the way, I barely know and how she got my name tattooed across her big beautiful ass is beyond me."

Nabatov made a barely perceptible movement of his head. "Do what you think best for Anais, Doctor."

Pasha Nabatov waited until Popovitch was out of the room before speaking about the telephone call. "We have trouble, Kazimir." Then he took an 8 by 10 photograph from the open folder. "That was Moscow Center on the scrambled line."

"With Moscow there's always trouble," Kazimir Sokolof said in a choked voice. He dragged his hands across his sweating face, looking terrified; his voice becoming a whimper. "What in hell have I done, now?"

"It is not about you — *for a change*. Do you remember Alexi Kalandarishvili?"

Kazimir turned his head to stare at the monitors again. A lusty smile formed upon the bearded Russian's face as Dr. Popovitch escorted Anais out of the office.

"I would kill a thousand men for one night with her, Pasha."

"Alexi Kalandarishvili, Kazimir!"

"No need to shout, Pasha." Kazimir quickly faced his superior. "What about Kalandarishvili?"

"He has become *our* problem." Nabatov set the photo on the desk in front of his subordinate.

The bearded Russian picked up the print and studied it. It showed a dark-haired, bloated, middle-aged man seated at a table outside a cafe. The fellow wore a wrinkled, gray suit. TA tall, partially filled, beer stein sat on the table beside him. In his mouth smoldered a fat cigar. The man had crossed his legs in casual relaxation. The surrounding, sunlit buildings suggested a German location.

"That is the latest photo we have of Kalandarishvili," Nabatov said. "It was taken ten months ago, at a café in Berlin. There he met with an unidentified American." The white-haired Russian took another photo from the folder. This one was partially faded, parts barely visible. It showed an incomplete view of a young man with dark hair and a good physique, wearing casual clothes. "The camera failed while taking this snapshot. Unfortunately, no others are available."

Kazimir picked up the second photo and compared the two. "I recognize Alexi Kalandarishvili. However, this other man — the one in the leather jacket — is new. He could be American. His clothes and physique suggest it." The bearded Russian hesitated. "He looks Jewish."

"Our people followed him to the American Embassy. We assume he's CIA."

Kazimir set the two photos on the desk and gave his boss a questioning look.

"What do you remember about Kalandarishvili?" Nabatov asked.

"He worked as an operative for Mikhail Shkarov. But, that was before Federal Security Services Branch killed Shkarov and his lieutenant, Innokenti Rakhmelevich, in a shootout outside of St. Petersburg." The bearded Russian's eyes rounded in momentary thought. "For several months, after that, Kalandarishvili went into hiding. But, recently, he's been suspected of doing freelance work for various crime families. So far, however, nothing has been proven."

"It would seem you do one or two things besides ogle Anais."

One of Kazimir Sokolof's furry eyebrows shot up hopefully like a stretching, well-fed caterpillar. "Does this mean I'm ready for promotion?"

Pasha Nabatov said, dryly, "Let us not get into that, again." He returned the photos to the file and then closed the folder. "According to Moscow Center, Kalandarishvili has been selling our military secrets to the East — China, North Korea, and elsewhere."

"Kalandarishvili doesn't have the brains for that." Kazimir batted the air with one hand. "He has no expertise in establishing contacts within our military ranks, let alone with foreign buyers. How can Moscow Center make such foolish assumptions?"

"It is probably because Moscow suspects Kalandarishvili of having attended some of your foolish weekend parties."

"I have never invited him!" The bearded Russian's eyes bugged. "What did Moscow say?" Then he fanned the air with both hands. "I deny everything, Pasha. Tell them I have never invited Kalandarishvili to nowhere."

"But, you admit to knowing the man more than casually?"

"Only slightly and with great reluctance due to a mutual intolerance."

"Reluctance? I know for a fact that during your last annual leave you and his oldest daughter were inseparable."

"The daughter who has since married and whose location I do not know and who refuses to have anything to do with me, even if I should ask her if she would like to get together, which I don't."

Nabatov rolled his eyes. "If Moscow Center's information is accurate — and it always is — Kalandarishvili has not been working alone. Someone with the necessary expertise to interface with the traitors in our military has helped him."

"Pasha, I swear on my dead mother's eyes…"

"Let's not rehash your mother's demise, Kazimir."

Kazimir Sokolof slumped into one of the chairs fronting Nabatov's desk. "All right, I confess."

The white haired Russian started out of his chair. "You have been helping Kalandarishvili?"

"Of course not!" Kazimir let go a whimper, making a pleading motion with both hands. "But, maybe once or twice I did say a little too much to that pastry filler from the Nin Bakery."

"*Vot gde sobaka zaryta*," Nabatov sighed, resuming his seat. "So, that's where the dog is buried."

"It was only because she's extremely beautiful, her vodka is spiced with cayenne, and at the time I was under the impression that she did not understand a word of Russian." His broad shoulders rocked up and down as he sniffed. "How could I know she was bisexual?"

"I think you mean bilingual."

"Whatever she is, Pasha, I knew nothing about it."

"What did you tell her?"

"Just that I'm an American spy working for the CIA who is undercover pretending to be Russian."

"Did she believe you?"

Kazimir hesitated. "What would be the best answer? Yes, or no?"

"Kazimir…"

"I will never see her again, Pasha! I swear."

Nabatov's his pale fingertips drummed on the desktop, next to the folder, as he gave his head an exasperated shake. "No, that is impossible."

"What is impossible?"

"That you're the Mole."

"What Mole?"

"Never mind." The white-haired Russian took a deep breath and continued with, "According to Moscow Center, Kalandarishvili spent the last two months lurking around Irkutsk. Do you understand the implication?"

"He made a terribly wrong turn during his holiday?"

"No, you idiot, Irkutsk is one of our military outposts on the Chinese border!"

"Ah, that Irkutsk." Kazimir winced under his superior's harsh gaze. "I get it confused with the other one that is more or less a shit-hole."

"There is no other one, you, you…" The white-haired Russian stopped, filling his lungs and then letting go a long sigh. "As expected, our people became suspicious of Kalandarishvili's presence. Therefore, they detained and questioned him. According to Kalandarishvili, he was planning to marry and was merely evaluating the real estate market prior to moving to Irkutsk."

"What real estate market? In Irkutsk, for two pigs and a goat you get a mud pile. And who would marry him? He smells like a manure pile and he has the table manners of a chimpanzee."

"The man you barely know?" Nabatov asked, dryly.

"You know how rumors get around."

"Curiously, a young blond woman by the name of Galina Vishnevskaya came forward to substantiate Kalandarishvili's claims. She identified him as her fiancé."

Kazimir Sokolof tilted across the desk. "Young, you said?"

"Twenty. Why?"

"Kalandarishvili must be nearly fifty. Is she a real dog?"

"What difference does it make?"

"Does she have a great big…"

Nabatov cut his subordinate off with, "Documents produced by Galina, in the form of a marriage license, lent a certain amount of credibility to Kalandarishvili's story. Consequently, he was released."

"Kalandarishvili is old enough to be her father. He should be ashamed of himself." Then Kazimir became philosophical. "Why can't I find a desperate young woman like that?"

"To be your adoptive daughter, I suppose?"

Kazimir grinned crookedly. "That would be my second choice."

"Our people quickly determined the marriage license was a fraud. This, of course, prompted our organization to assume, and rightly, there was more behind Kalandarishvili's movements than looking for a home. Our field officers followed him, day and night. This produced results. Sometime last week, Kalandarishvili met with Kirill Semyonovich Moskalenko, a Colonel in the *Raketnye voyska strategicheskogo naznacheniya Rossiyskoy Federatsii*. Although their meeting was not sinister, such an unlikely joining of souls was suspicious. Therefore, our people attempted to detain both men. According to Moscow Center, Colonel Moskalenko unsuccessfully attempted to flee. Kalandarishvili, however, escaped during a heated gun battle. Under a hail of GRU bullets, he fled to the outskirts of Irkutsk. There, he disappeared."

"He probably slipped across the Chinese border and took refuge in Hohhot." Kazimir stared up at his boss. "I think his youngest daughter works there as a prostitute."

"You dated her, as well, I presume?"

"Only briefly, because her fees were exorbitant. What about Galina Vishnevskaya? Could she not help find Kalandarishvili?"

"From what Moscow Center just told me, she has since disappeared. Our agents, of course, are searching for her."

"Disappearing happens a lot in Irkutsk." Kazimir nodded, thoughtfully. "Those Chinese have so few women that anything with the usual equipment, or nearly so, is kidnapped and sold into marriage. A twenty-year old, even if she was mud-wall ugly, especially if she had a great big…"

"Under rigorous interrogation," interrupted Nabatov, "Colonel Moskalenko confessed to selling Kalandarishvili the complete defense plans for the Irkutsk-Hohhot region. As you can imagine, Moscow Center was horrified by this revelation."

"Should I plan to attend Moskalenko's trial?"

"It won't be necessary." Pasha Nabatov brushed the air with one hand. "Moskalenko died, quite unexpectedly, during a break from questioning."

"How many times was he shot during this otherwise uneventful respite?"

"Estimates vary. But, the general consensus is five bullets entered his skull." The white-haired Russian took a deep breath and quickly exhaled. "Moscow said it was a dramatic suicide."

"That's also happens a lot, and always with multiple bullets during a breather from questioning."

"Based upon Moskalenko's admissions, our people put out a worldwide pickup order on Kalandarishvili. Fortunately, our Dover sector spotted him yesterday. He was traveling under the name: *Klaus Schmidt*. Unfortunately, attempts to capture him failed. Moscow suspects that Paris is Kalandarishvili's destination. When he enters France, we are to pick up the chase, determine Kalandarishvili's contacts and identify the intended recipient of those plans. Once this is accomplished, we are to detain all concerned. Understood?"

"Pasha, those defense plans Moskalenko gave Kalandarishvili… They will be in what form?"

"That is an excellent question, Kazimir. Perhaps you're promotional material, after all." Nabatov offered one of his faint, economical smiles. "The documents were photographed using a digital camera. This took place over several months. In each instance Moskalenko gave Kalandarishvili the camera's memory-stick." His heavy shoulders twitched. "Kalandarishvili, it is presumed, combined the various sticks onto one for ease of transportation. But, this has not been confirmed."

"Kalandarishvili is an idiot. He will have a stack of memory-sticks shoved up his ass."

Nabatov allowed himself another private smile. "As much as I would like to dwell on the prospect of a pot calling a kettle black, I want you to get out your *Direction Générale de la Sécurité Extérieure* identification. You will make contact with French Customs at the Channel Tunnel checkpoint." Then he frowned, woodenly. "And, for God's sake, remember to speak French when addressing them. I don't want another incident where I have to gain your release from jail by explaining to the *Préfet de Police* that you're a Russian lunatic, who I will be sending back to Moscow, who somehow got hold of French Secret Police identification papers."

"I won't forget this time, Pasha."

"If Kalandarishvili comes through the tunnel, you will have French Customs search him, as well as his vehicle, for the memory stick or sticks." Nabatov moved his thick eyebrows into a sharp wedge. "In the process, you will add a tracking device to his auto so he can easily be followed from a distance. Understood?"

"What if the memory sticks are not found?"

"In any case, you will order Kalandarishvili's release."

"But, Pasha…"

"There is no other way to document the route he takes, every stop he makes, everyone he contacts. Per procedure, you will keep me informed via our cellular phones."

"Where will you be? Here?"

"I will be with Airport Customs in case Kalandarishvili attempts to enter France there."

"What about the ferry from Dover?" The fingers of his one hand clawed at the palm of the other.

"I will send Anitchka to take care of that."

"And when Kalandarishvili reaches his destination?"

"When he stops for the night, whether it is you, Anitchka or I who are following, we will let the others know," Nabatov said with heavy articulation. "At that point we will join forces to discuss our next move."

Kazimir's eyes narrowed. "Shouldn't I confiscate the memory-sticks if he still has them?"

"Under no circumstances are you to do so."

"But, Pasha…"

Nabatov offered his subordinate a wintry smile. "Those are my orders."

Kazimir Sokolof took out a rather large and clumsy gray cellular phone. "My GRU issue satellite phone isn't working too well."

"What's wrong with it?"

"I keep getting wrong numbers."

"That's impossible. You get what you dial." The white haired Russian made a faint sucking noise between his teeth. "Tell me the truth. What did you do to it?"

"I accidentally dropped it."

"It doesn't look damaged."

"That's because I rinsed it off."

"What were you doing? Using it to take photos of some scantily clad woman, in your flat?"

"Of course not. I was in a café and the waitress wasn't wearing underwear."

"How, pray tell, did your foolish photographic efforts damage your phone?"

Kazimir made a feeble gesture. "I got so excited it slipped from my hand into a bowl of *béarnaise* sauce."

"And you wonder why you haven't had a promotion in eight years?"

"It wasn't my fault, Pasha."

"With you, nothing is your fault. The entire world could flush down the shitter because you pulled the chain, and still it wouldn't be your fault!"

"Pasha, please… Just in case… Where can I reach you should I need to use an alternative means of communiqué?"

"Leave a message at Ambrosii Golovkin's safe-house, in Paris. I will have Ambrosii relay all calls to me. As for you and your half-dressed waitresses…"

A tall, leggy, dark-haired woman of twenty-some years strode into the office. She was a shade taller than average, and athletically built. Her legs were shapely, her hands and feet narrow, and her body was very erect; insentiently elegant. She wore a pink, two-piece suit, a gold watch on a leather strap at one wrist and a gold charm bracelet at the other. As she passed Kazimir Sokolof, the woman glared at him with her large, smoky eyes.

Kazimir's head followed her movements step-by-step; his wide eyes locked upon the small video camera in her hand — the type used for concealed security observations. Repeatedly, Kazimir swallowed, like a hungry dog trying to consume its own tongue.

"I was just about to call you, Anitchka," Pasha Nabatov said in greeting to his daughter.

She thrust an accusing finger at the bearded Russian. "Poppa, you must do something about that — that disgusting pervert's obsession with women." Her voice had a sharp edge to it, like a freshly stropped razor.

"I don't know nothing about it," Kazimir said. "Especially that camera."

Anitchka dropped the camera onto her father's desk; her eyes narrowing to slits of gray thunder as she glared once more at Kazimir Sokolof. "I found this camera mounted to the modesty panel of Anais's desk, the lens directed right up her skirt. The coaxial cable from the camera leads under the reception-area carpeting directly into Kazimir's office. From there, it goes to that hideously huge television screen he has mounted on the wall across from his desk."

"It must've been the janitor," Kazimir said. Then he added in a drenched murmur, "You should see how he ogles Anais while doing absolutely disgusting things with his hand on the broom handle."

"His or your broom handle?" she demanded truculently.

"Never mind that, Anitchka," Nabatov interjected, impatiently. "We have a far more important issue to resolve." He focused his gaze, first on the bearded man and then on his daughter. "I want you to head for Calais. You will meet with French Customs posing as a French DSGE agent. We are looking for Alexi Kalandarishvili. I have already given Kazimir instructions for the Channel Tunnel. I will be at the air terminal, in case Kalandarishvili crosses there."

"What's Kalandarishvili done?" she asked.

Pasha Nabatov quickly explained the situation to his daughter. She hung on her father's every word, her excitement showing pink in her cheeks.

"Under no circumstances is Kalandarishvili to be detained or denied access to the memory-sticks," Nabatov summarized.

Anitchka remained silent for a moment, reflecting. Then her dark head wagged. "Letting Kalandarishvili keep the memory-sticks makes no sense, Poppa. Yes, it would be nice to arrest the miscreants who purchase the information. But, the risk of such sensitive data being passed on, is far too great to leave it under that traitor's control."

"It makes no sense to me either," enjoined Kazimir, with a demure nod. "But, your Poppa didn't like it when I said."

"I will not have my orders questioned!" said Pasha Nabatov.

Anitchka rolled her gray eyes in mild objection, as her arms folding across her ample chest.

Her father turned to Kazimir, who was watching a security monitor's view of Dr. Popovitch and Anais entering the building. "Why are you still here, Kazimir?"

"I'm going, Pasha." Then he pointed at the monitor. "Look at the way Anais moves. Her thighs must be like velvet to put such a beautiful swing in those magnificent hips."

"That is just the sort of remarks this pervert has been saying to poor Anais," Anitchka said. "Poppa, she's at her wit's end over him."

"If you don't get going, Kazimir, I will not be responsible for my actions," Nabatov said, his fist slamming down onto the desk.

"I'm going, Pasha, I'm going."

When Kazimir was out of earshot Anitchka turned to her father and said, "Is this another effort on Moscow's part to ferret out the Chechnyan Mole?"

"The problem will not solve itself, Anitchka." Then he shook a warning finger at her. "But, that is all I can say."

"Another of *your* orders?" she said, resting her hands on the desk, and tilting toward her father in defiance.

"I have my duty, Anitchka." His arms rose and fell with exasperation. "And even though I'm your father, I'm still your superior."

"That is not good enough." She stood erect, putting her hands akimbo at her hips. "Now, I want to know the real reason we are not to reclaim the memory-sticks."

"Why do you always assume you're above the others?" he asked, rising from his chair in frustration. "That you're entitled to special treatment?"

"I'm entitled because I'm your daughter. I'm entitled because I went into this filthy business to please you. I'm entitled because I'm incorruptible. I'm entitled because I'm better at what we do than any of the others — better, even, than you."

He slumped down at his desk, and ran his fingers through his white hair as if his scalp was on fire, reluctant to respond.

"Well?" she demanded.

"You give me such a headache."

She took a perch on the edge of the desk, staring at him. "Am I a suspect, Poppa? Has Moscow warned you against me?"

"Of course you're not suspect."

"Then who can you trust, other than me? Who can you call upon when there's trouble, other than me? There is no else, Poppa. Because we both know that in our business trusting a friend gets you dead."

For nearly a minute Pasha Nabatov considered his daughter's words. Then in a low voice he said, "The defense data on the memory-stick was concocted for the express purpose of deceiving whoever purchased it."

She stood up with a start. "Surely Kalandarishvili is aware of this?"

"He has no idea. The misinformation was mixed with accurate but benign data, to make discerning the fraud extremely difficult."

"Then Moskalenko wasn't actually a conspirator?"

"Of course he committed treason. Colonel Moskalenko was completely unaware of the fraud when he sold the plans to Kalandarishvili." Nabatov gave a derisive grunt. "That traitorous bastard got what he deserved."

"Yes, I read about his suicide. Nevertheless, how could Moscow Center know in advance about Moskalenko's betrayal so as to manipulate the data?"

"Colonel Moskalenko fell under suspicion early on. As a precautionary measure, Moscow transferred him to a position that excluded any contact with top-secret information, while the investigation against him continued. However, as the inquiry broadened, Moscow got an idea. Why not make his treachery work for us?" Her father made a series of satisfied sounds. "It was at this point, Moscow altered the plans Moskalenko photographed for Kalandarishvili." Pasha Nabatov leaned his head back and closed his eyes, then opened them locking upon his daughter's beautiful face. "At this point, to mollify Moskalenko's suspicions, the traitor was told that accusations had been made against him. However, those accusations had proven to be false. Moskalenko, as you can imagine, was relieved. In order to bolster his confidence further, Moscow rewarded him with a grade increase. Then Moscow Center transferred him back to his old job where, it was assumed, he would return to his treason." Nabatov put a cigarette in his mouth and dug in his pockets for a lighter. "Upon arriving at his old office, Moskalenko discovered a small but potentially profitable surprise. During his absence, military intelligence had performed a new assessment of the Irkutsk-Hohhot region." Nabatov lit the cigarette, dropped the lighter onto his desk and clasped his broad hands across his bulging belly. "As we anticipated, Moskalenko relayed this unexpected change to his confederate. The partner, who we later determined was Kalandarishvili, requested this data. Naturally, Colonel Moskalenko eagerly complied —

for an additional fee. Thus, the new information — *the false information* — made its way to the recipient, who promptly discarded the previously received and accurate information."

"So, it was at this point our people arrested Moskalenko?"

Pasha Nabatov nodded. "Once we knew he had passed the last of the data to Kalandarishvili, Colonel Moskalenko was no longer needed."

"Then, it follows, our fellow GRU officers purposely allowed Kalandarishvili to escape."

"Exactly. The mock gun-battle was necessary in order to convince Kalandarishvili that he had the real thing."

Anitchka's face tightened sharply. "But, if the information is essentially useless, why are we bothering to…"

Her father cut her short with, "We want the Mole to become an active participant in the theft by keeping the Chechnyans, who we believe employ Kalandarishvili, informed of our reclamation efforts."

"I don't like it, Poppa. This whole thing could backfire in our faces."

"I agree. However, the decision to proceed in this fashion was not ours. Further, Moscow is now convinced the Mole is in my sector."

"Nonsense! Everyone in our sector has been part of our team for years."

He looked away for a moment. Then his eyes came back to rest on hers, squinting with concern. Nabatov knew that it was not beyond probability that Moscow Center would do a complete purge of his sector, in order to terminate the Mole's activities if the Mole could not be identified.

"Moscow suspects Kazimir is the Mole?" she asked.

"Even Moscow Center cannot be that desperate for a scapegoat." He leaned back, letting go a long sigh. "I think it is far more likely that I'm suspect."

"You?" she gasped.

"Why not? I'm the one person, in this sector, who sees everything."

"But, they can't…"

"They can, Anitchka. And they will, unless we uncover the Mole."

She sat down on the edge of her father's desk, here brow furrowed in worry. "Why didn't Kalandarishvili simply transmit the stolen data to the intended recipient, with a computer?"

"Possibly because he's not computer literate or the intended recipient is not. Alternatively, it could be the volume of data. There are over 500 images and almost 200 documents on the memory-sticks. The process of emailing all that information would take at least a day, probably longer.

What is more, our governmental watchdog agencies might've intercepted his transmissions and tracked the secret material back to him."

"Surely, Kalandarishvili realizes we know he's involved?"

"Of course he does. However, he also thinks we do not know where he is."

"But, won't he become suspicious when we allow him to retain the memory sticks after he enters France?"

"Moskalenko included several pornographic snapshots as a blind, at the beginning of each memory stick. The assumption being that anyone who might examine the memory sticks would see the obscene material and pass off the rest of the sticks' contents as being the same." He raised a finger of emphasis. "But, there may have been another reason for physically transporting the memory sticks."

She stared at him, puzzled. "What?"

Her father opened the folder and took out the photo of the man who had met with Kalandarishvili in Berlin. "I think Kalandarishvili decided to go out on his own," he said, handing the print to her. "I think this American, who we have not yet identified, is the intended buyer. He met with Kalandarishvili in Berlin, a number of months ago, and was trailed to the American embassy."

She studied the photo a moment and then said to her father, "The photo is too blurry to be certain, but I don't remember coming across this man."

"Neither Kazimir nor myself could recall him." He put the picture back into the file.

"Kalandarishvili won't let us take him alive," Anitchka said. "He will know what happened to Moskalenko will happen to him."

There was a knock on the door.

"Come in," Nabatov called.

Dr. Popovitch stuck his head into the office. "I'm glad you're here, Anitchka," he said. "I've given Anais a prescription for a mild sedative. It should take care of her jangled nerves, for the time being."

"I don't suppose you can prescribe something to neuter Kazimir without him realizing it?" the young woman asked, pointedly.

The doctor laughed. "Unfortunately, that is beyond my province."

"Perhaps the solution to the problem *is* more along my lines, Doctor. I can always take him to the pistol range for target practice."

"I will follow up with Anais in a few days," Popovitch said. "Is there anything else I can do, Pasha?"

"No, Doctor. As always, I'm indebted for the care you provide to the people in my sector."

With a cheerful wave, the stooped physician closed the door.

Pasha Nabatov gave his daughter a warning look. "As you must realize, what we have been discussing cannot be shared."

"I know our business, Poppa."

Her father let go a sigh. "I'm not looking forward to the shame of being shot as a spy."

She went around to his chair, leaned down and kissed his cheek. "You won't be shot, Poppa. Our interrogators will let you commit suicide during a respite from questioning."

He nodded, grimly. "Whether I want to or not."

Chapter 3

"You're a Yank," the young redheaded woman proclaimed.

She stood behind Dover, England's *Tour-France* ticket counter. The afternoon sunshine dappled her red uniform and glinted from a nametag etched with: *'Sally'*. She was smiling at Harry Bronstein, showing more than a professional interest.

"Guilty as charged," Harry admitted, offering his pretty inquisitor a provocative wink. "I'd like passage on the Calais Ferry for the rental car and myself."

The sign above Sally's head proclaimed the ferry's virtues: The *Berlioz* was nearly 700 feet long and displaced 49,000 tons. Its draft was 21.4 feet with a beam of 103 feet. It had a capacity of 1,900 passengers and 700 cars. Accommodations were modern. It traversed the distance between Dover, England and Calais, France in just under 70 minutes; presumably with the help of a strong tailwind.

"Is this your first trip to France?" she asked.

From the expanded pupils in the redhead's green eyes, Sally clearly liked what she saw... Harry's tall, muscular build encased within blue denim; his brown eyes, his black hair, the easy smile on his handsome face; even the casual way Harry carried his leather bomber jacket over one shoulder. Sally closed her eyes trying to imagine what it would be like to wrap arms and legs about him, as they made love. In her imagination, Sally and Harry were in some remote, romantic spot; naked and alone. Harry was holding her close, about to kiss. She was moving her hands across his buttocks, scraping the firm flesh with her long fingernails.

"Not my last trip, I hope," Harry said.

Her eyes fluttered opened and Sally ran the tip of her pink tongue across her full lips. "That's my hope, too."

"It's huge."

She flushed, nodding. "I thought it might be."

He pointed to the sign. "I didn't realize ferries were so immense."

In spite of his remark, Harry had only a passing interest in the vessel's size. Harry Bronstein was far more interested in its passenger accommodations. On the Berlioz he hoped to enjoy a brief interval from driving. In so doing, he intended to unwind with the seedy novel he had just purchased. He could not recall its title. However, the half-naked harm girls dancing across the paperback's cover indelibly inked his mind.

"There's nothing like riding a big one," Sally said.

"So, I've been told." Harry twisted slightly to see if anyone had gotten into line behind him. But, he was alone. "Where can I find a bit of seclusion?"

"I get off at six," she confided. "You could be, by six-fifteen."

He laughed, surprised by her playful patter. "I mean on the ferry."

"Why bother with the ferry when my car has reclining seats?"

"As tempting as your car's seats sound, I was thinking more along the lines of having a drink or two and a quiet read on the way to Calais."

"Oh, that kind of seclusion," she said, in disappointment. "Try the lounge farthest aft on 'C' deck."

"Which one is 'C' deck?"

"It's second from the bottom. The aft lounge on that deck is called, *Tailspinner.*"

"I have to tell you…" he said, in teasing confidentiality. "I've never actually had my tail spun, before."

"That's only because you've never traveled with me." There was a nerve twitching one corner of the redhead's pouting mouth. "I'm an expert at all things tail."

"It sounds like I've been missing out." Harry glanced around, again, and was pleased to find he was still the only customer. "But, if this Tailspinner is such a remarkable spot, how come the entire passenger list doesn't perch there?"

"An aft ride tends to get a little bumpy."

"That's only to be expected."

"If you're not the type to beat a hasty retreat, as a result of sudden surges, you'll love it."

"Hasty retreats are completely foreign to me."

She eased back and cocked a rust-colored eyebrow. "Are you coming back to Dover?"

"Cumming is definitely in my plan. But, just so there's no misunderstanding, how does my plan fit with yours?"

"I think we'll mesh, perfectly."

"Meshing is good. Although I can't remember the last time I did so perfectly." Harry gave one more look around. However, he was still the only customer within earshot. "I feel I should warn you… I'm a little out of practice."

"I'd love to get you up to speed."

Harry Bronstein handed her a credit card. "I have no doubts about you being the woman to do it."

Sally quickly processed his ticket purchase. "I'm here Monday through Saturday." She wrote her name and telephone number on the back of his copy of the ferry ticket. "Most evenings I'm free. Sunday afternoons I'm open for anything."

He held up his ticket and gave her another cheek-pinking smile. "Pencil me in for a week, from this Sunday. I'm very partial to open Sunday afternoons."

She blew him a kiss.

Sally had a delightful personality, Harry decided, as he climbed back into the rented Range Rover. She was, also, a very pretty girl. Her eyes were her best feature. Large, green eyes a man could sink into; not that there was anything wrong with her mouth. Those pink lips looked delicious below her exquisitely formed nose. As for Sally's figure, there was a good deal to brag about, there, too. Yes, she was a very pretty girl.

However, as his mother had so often warned, *"Nit fun a sheyner tsurke vert a gute vayb."*

As usual, his mother was correct. A pretty face alone does not guarantee a good wife. However, who needed a wife? Especially a man who had just divorced the one he had married less than two years earlier.

Harry grimaced, thinking back over his brief but sad marital history.

Why do mothers always hate the women their sons marry? Was it some sort of rule? Admittedly, hate comes in degrees. Moreover, conflicts over religious convictions are often difficult to overcome. However, with a little patience and mutual understanding even the most intense disputes will resolve themselves.

Nevertheless, the strangling incident at his marriage reception had been a little hard to overlook. However, as Harry had tried to explain to his bride, Maggie: What seventy-year-old woman, when falling, doesn't reach out for a handhold on the bride's throat while screaming, "You anti-Semite bitch?"

"Marry the Rubenstein girl," his mother had urged him. "Her father's a butcher. That would mean beef at a discount."

There was nothing wrong with discounts, particularly on kosher meats. Unfortunately, the same could not be said for neurotic Naomi Rubenstein. Life with her would have meant paying full emotional freight for every ounce of flesh received.

"Mary Pushkin is perfect for you," his mother had suggested. "When her parents died, Mary inherited several luxury apartment buildings. I could move into one of those for half-rent."

Perfection had its place in real-estate. In fact, it was a plus in every aspect of life. However, Mary Pushkin was not what Harry could consider perfect. In fact, rumors abounded about her having actually been born a *he*.

"God will get you for Maggie, Harry."

Those were his mother's last words to him before she passed over. The not-so-loving dear had died shortly before Harry's divorce. Doubtlessly, her demise was part of a complex plan to punish him for his choice in a mate.

Harry drove the Range Rover to the vehicle loading area. After handing ticket and car keys to a swarthy man with a lean face and nervous green eyes, Harry slipped on his leather jacket and made his way up the companionway to the ferry's 'C' deck.

The ship seemed to be awash with blurs of reds and blues, plus all the other colors in the clothing rainbow. There were so many passengers that even breathing was an exertion. Harry headed aft, swimming through a sea of gin-slurred voices and morning-after bleary eyes.

A young, long-legged blond woman stepped in front of him, nearly causing Harry to trip over her heels. She had long hair, finely chiseled features and was heading in the same direction.

He let his eyes drift from her slightly mussed coiffure, down to her pink sweater with its torn shoulder-seam, to the pert outline of her pulsating posterior, beneath a gray miniskirt. Despite the tarnished state of her ensemble, the blonde had a fascinating stride. Each leg-movement caused her buttocks to flex. This, in turn, sent the hem of the skirt flitting upward, as if caught in a breeze, thus disclosing the narrow roundness of the naked flesh beneath.

Blondes were nearly as nice as redheads, he quickly decided; especially the ones who tossed caution to the winds and forwent the use of undergarments. Stride, flex, flit. Stride, flex, flit. There was no doubt about it. Her movements were more than tantalizing. Even a man with morals of steel would have to attest to the blonde's seductive powers.

As Harry studied the young woman's ongoing game of *buttocksian* hide and peek, the blonde made an abrupt left turn. Seconds later, she disappeared into a crowd. He was so caught-up in his blonde-driven preoccupation, that Harry nearly trampled a pair of nuns who abruptly crossed his path. The near entanglement got him a scolding cluck from the older penguin. The younger one offered up a grinning, "Bless you."

He apologized and continued his trek.

It was not the blonde's naked allure that had distracted Harry, during those last moments. It was the splotch of purple he had noticed on one side of her neck and the dried blood on her fingertips. Had someone tried to strangle the blonde? In her own defense, had she savagely clawed her attacker? Alternatively, had the blonde been the antagonist? Had she just butchered her lover on one of the ferry's lower decks? Perhaps redheads were safer, after all.

The *Tailspinner Lounge* was typical of shipboard accommodations. It offered an artificially cozy atmosphere that included a kaleidoscopic of molded plastic in the form of chairs, tables and even the bar. A grinning man wearing a white barman's jacket fixed Harry a Manhattan on the rocks: bitters, but no cherry. While Harry paid for the cocktail, a woman's voice rambled over the ship's loudspeaker-system announcing, in four different languages, the vessel's imminent departure.

"Slightly over an hour to Calais?" Harry asked.

The bartender nodded. "Unless, this leaking tub sinks."

"It leaks?"

"Like a sieve."

"But, is sinking likely during a twenty mile run?"

"I don't keep a life jacket behind the bar because I enjoy its company."

Harry glanced around. "I don't see any life jackets for passengers."

"That's because us worker-bees expect you passengers to flounder around, thus keeping the sharks in the channel busy while we wait for rescue."

"Something to look forward to."

Harry moved off, amidst wave after wave of pre-exodus vibrations rising up through the deck from the ship's engine room. Softly he muttered a prayer.

At the rear of the lounge, near a window, Harry found a table with two chairs. He glanced outside and was momentarily transfixed by the swirling water in the ferry's wake. Soon he would be in Calais, God willing. A few hours after that, he would reach Paris. A week after that, he would be in Berlin. After Berlin, he would be back in the United States — in the house he had inherited from his mother. Unless, of course, he took a brief but rewarding layover in Dover.

The vessel tilted abruptly. Then it tilted back. Harry's stomach lurched, and then lurched again. Sally had been right about traveling aft. It did have a queasy impact on the digestive system. However, he took the optimistic view that once the vessel was clear of port, it would stabilize. His sanguinity took a crash-dive as he recalled the barman's words about leakage and sharks.

How many times had news reports recounted the risk of ferry crossings? He could recall at least four, in recent months, which had failed to make port. In those instances how many had endured the seagoing ordeal successfully? In each occurrence there had been no survivors among the passengers. However, each ship's crew had managed to survive quite easily. Probably due to preplanning on the life preserver front. Harry made a mental note. Before he took the ferry back to Dover he would purchase a life jacket — just in case.

The ferry gave another lurch, dropping Harry into a chair facing the lounge entrance. It was going to be a long trip to Calais; long, and hopefully, uneventful.

Harry put his cocktail on the table, got comfortable and then withdrew the paperback from his jacket pocket. There was nothing like classic literature to take a man's mind off the prospect of being eaten alive in the midst of a ship-sinking.

Harry smiled as he studied the novel's lusty title: *The Rape of Randy Nell, Harem Girl Extraordinaire*. He eased forward, resting his elbows on his knees, and opened the book; holding it between both hands, his eyes glued to the page.

"Chapter One. 'Nell was one hot and bothered tomato with a sex-toy collection that could cross the eyes of a—'"

"Is all right?"

Who would be so rude as to interrupt a man reading about a near-virgin sexpot with eyes on an Arab Sheik who was suffering from excessive amounts of money, compounded by a temporary bout with erectile dysfunction?

"Is all right?" the words repeated.

Harry Bronstein looked up at the intruder.

Staring back was a short, balding, double-chinned man with the eyes of a pig, thick glasses, and a number of fresh scratches on his sweaty cheeks. Despite there being nearly a dozen empty chairs in all directions, the older man was pointing to the vacant one next to Harry.

"I'm sure you'd be far more comfortable elsewhere." Harry gave a bleak smile. He picked up his Manhattan, drained the glass, set it back onto the table and then resumed reading.

"'Despite the Sheik's dangling condition, Nell had to admit that she was looking at the biggest snake since…'"

"I know you," the other man said.

He settled into the adjacent chair amidst a flurry of guttural noises. The fellow was about fifty years of age. He had an oily complexion and a pursed mouth. From one corner of the latter jutted an unlit, stubby, black cigar. He was dressed in a badly fitting dark suit, a wrinkled white shirt and a dirty tie.

Harry looked over at the intruder in despair. Not only was Nell already in a crisis situation, but the sun coming in through the window over Harry's shoulder reflected from the dirty lenses in the other fellow's spectacles so brightly that shards of disruptive light danced upon the book-pages.

"I'm trying to read," Harry said, impatiently. "Go away."

The other man pulled the cigar from his mouth and grinned, showing an expanse of orange teeth. "I was worry you not make it."

"Don't concern yourself." Harry raised the book slightly. "Between the bawdy promises of the ticket seller and Randy Nell's forthcoming adventure, I'll get where I need to go."

"Klaus Schmidt." He offered his hand. "Berlin, remember?" Then he shifted to an angle that allowed him to face Harry circuitously. "We agree meet on ferry."

Harry winced; ignoring the hairy, outstretched paw, his eyes returning to the other man's bleeding face. "You've got me mixed-up with someone else."

"I have information you want."

Schmidt reeked of garlic sausage, beer, sweat and cigar smoke. And if that was not enough to make him distasteful, a droplet of blood from the deepest scratch dangled carelessly from his chin like a miniature, ripe pomegranate.

"Sie sind bleeding, Herr Schmidt."

"What say?"

"You are bleeding."

"I trip and fall." He wiped his sleeve across his face smearing the blood from his chin and onto his furry neck. "Big feet."

"Her big feet must've had long toenails. Those claw-marks are deep enough to require stitches." Harry inclined his head toward the lounge entrance. "You should get some antibiotic ointment before infection sets in. It might undermine your act as a German."

Schmidt stuffed the cigar back it into his mouth. There his pasty tongue lolled the black stick of tobacco around between his purplish lips, until it lodged at one corner. "You sure you not American I supposed meet?"

"I'm an American. However, I'm not the one you're looking for. I'd like to say it's been nice talking to you, but I'll simply bid you good bye."

"Sure you him. Same jacket. Same shirt. Same pants. Everything like Berlin."

"Berlin is another part of my itinerary."

"Sure, it you."

"Why would I lie?"

"Don't worry. No need secret spy stuff, big time."

The scratches dribbled more blood, but Schmidt did not seem to notice.

"Look, I'm not lying," Harry said. "But, you certainly are."

"No, I got what you want, hot stuff."

"I mean you're lying about who your identity. You may be using a German name, but you're a Russian, probably from Nenetsia."

Schmidt gaped a moment in surprise. "How you get that?"

"I'm fluent in four languages: English, French, German and Russian. I can also muddle through several others without getting my faced slapped, too often. My knack for linguistics is based upon an innate expertise in identifying different dialects. This little gift kept me in good stead during my senior trip with Army Intelligence." He gave the novel a waggle. "Now, if you'll excuse me. I'm trying to read a very tawdry book filled with historical farce portrayed as fact, distorted social mores and perverse sexual tension."

"Ah, you read biography of politician."

"Close. It's fiction written by a full-fledged degenerate with exceptional expertise at drawing the reader into every disgustingly deranged scene." Then Harry lowered his eyes to the book. "'With her heart racing, Nell reached out and grabbed the limp, but hotly pulsing…'"

"I guess, maybe, make mistake," Schmidt said. He let a long moment go by. Then he folded his hands into his broad lap. "What your name?"

"Harry Bronstein, Austin, Texas. And I would like to be left alone. Nell has just grabbed the big one and things are about to get sticky."

"Ah, Texas. I hear about, big time." Schmidt's breathing was heavy as if the exertion of speaking was more than his heart could bear. He chewed the cigar for a bit. Then he asked, "You on happy holiday?"

The American sat erect and faced the older man. "Herr Schmidt, or whatever your name really is, let me give you a piece of advice. Never interrupt a man who hasn't had sex in six months while he's in the midst of a pertinacious Arab proverb."

Schmidt shifted the cigar between his loose lips to the opposite corner. "Your first visit Calais?"

Harry, more than a little irritated by the other man's continuing intrusion, merely nodded as he resumed reading.

"'To her delight, Nell's gentle fondling proved to be a sure cure for...'"

"What business you got?" Schmidt asked.

"If you must know, I'm a computer programmer."

"Computer interesting, big time," the older man said, using the heel of one hand to brush away another droplet of blood.

"You are easily entertained."

"Computers hot stuff. Run world." Schmidt's greasy smile became seraphic. "Without computers world is nothing."

"Leave a forwarding address with the barman as you depart. With that attitude, you'd be handy to have around the next time I negotiate my consulting fees." Harry fingered-out a chunk of ice from his glass, dropped it into his mouth and then recommenced his read.

"But, at that moment, just before Nell could complete her impassioned resurrection, the Sheik's daughter..."

"I private inquiry agent."

"Like Sherlock Holmes, no doubt? Well, I'm glad to hear the Baltic world is a safe place for all who wear the golden sickle." Harry's face stretched outward expanded by anger-knotted muscles as he glared at Schmidt. "Now, don't let me keep you from other things."

Schmidt frowned in confusion. "Who Sherlock Holmes?"

"Holmes was a nineteenth century, fictional — oh, never mind." Realizing he was not about to escape the other man, Harry closed the book and gave a sharply sarcastic edge to his tongue. "You're not following me, I hope? My divorce isn't final, yet. But the papers have been signed."

The older fellow hesitated. Then he tilted toward Harry and spoke in a confidential tone, bathing the American's cheek with garlic fumes. "I not follow you, Mr. Bronstein."

"Are you certain? You're unexpected, and I might add hygiene-deficient, nearness is giving me cause for alarm."

"I finish case in London." Schmidt made a backward jerk of his thumb, as he eased upright in the chair. "Married woman. Have affair with married man — not husband, you understand?"

"I assumed there was illicit dallying involved when you mentioned the word: 'affair.'"

Schmidt paused a moment, sucking his teeth and thinking. "How long you stay Calais?"

"Just passing through. But, in case you're wondering, my time is fully booked. Now, if you'll excuse me the Sheik was about to send his daughter on a deadly mission so he could get his eyeballs rolled."

"You go Paris?"

Harry allowed himself a silence to take control of his fervent irritation. "Hopefully, very soon and without accompaniment. Is there anything else, Herr Schmidt?"

"Paris, me too. I go Montmartre Hotel." He fumbled through his pockets and took out a tarnished Zippo lighter. "Not fancy. But, clean, well-run. You stay there?"

"Fortunately for me, considering where you will reside, I have reservations at the Alessandra Hotel."

"Classy place, big time." The older man carefully looked around as if concerned he might be overheard. "You travel alone?"

"I had been until you showed up. I find I have fewer arguments that way."

Schmidt cocked one eye, striking the lighter several times trying to bring flame to its wick. "Then not married?"

"I'm divorced, also to reduce arguments. And if this less than subtle interlude is leading to a proposition I will find disgustingly amoral, despite my taste in perverse literature..."

"I married," the older man interposed, touching lighter-flame to the cigar. He puffed heavily as the fire put a glow to the tobacco quite near his nose. Then he doused the flame, exhaling a plume of foul smelling smoke. "Been nearly thirty years." He pocketed the Zippo and took another drag on the burning cigar. "Not same woman." With a grunt, he gripped the cigar between his teeth and brushed his hands across the knees of his dark trousers, as if trying to dust them clean. "That be too much any man. How long you married?"

"Sixteen months was too much for me," Harry said, with a short, derisive laugh. "Now, if we're through sharing pleasantries, I'd like to enjoy a bit of mental wickedness before I get back behind the steering wheel." Then he lowered his head and continued reading.

"'For a moment, Nell poised over the Sheik, prepared to take all the man had to offer. Her eyes glittering with unabashed...'"

"I wondering, Mr. Bronstein..." Schmidt drew a long, quivering breath. Then one hand went up and wiped away a mix of sweat and blood from his cheek. "How you like thousand Euros?"

Harry's grunt was impatiently disinterested, as his eyes quickly continued down the novel's page.

"'Nell gurgled with delight as she engulfed the Sheik's towering member, like a seal swallowing a...'"

"I worried 'bout customs," Schmidt said.

"So is the Sheik. He's never had so much happen so fast in so short a time from a self-described *virginette*."

Again the other man frowned with confusion. "What is virginette?'

"Someone who has had only one sexual experience. Now go away."

Schmidt squinted. "Are many of those in your country?"

"I wouldn't think so. But, it makes for great reading on a perversely fantasy level."

The older man tilted closer. "What you say to money?"

Harry rested his chin in his hand, and his elbow on his right knee, and fixed Schmidt with a repellent stare. "Did you miss the part about me, the Sheik and Randy Nell?"

"Man involved with woman is customs officer."

"That has nothing to do with me," flung out Bronstein, impatiently. He quickly gathered his limbs together, sitting upright. "Now, I don't want to sound erasable, unless doing so would get my point across more clearly, but I would like to be alone in my mental debauchery."

The older man's brows contracted for a second as if he were gathering his thoughts. "He know I photograph."

"How could he know?"

"He saw."

"Careless of you to get caught, wasn't it?" Harry crossed his arms; the muscles at the corners of his mouth twitching. "What with you being a *professional* private inquiry agent, and all."

"I not get caught, I caught him."

"But, you said he saw you take the pictures."

Schmidt wrinkled his nose. "He do."

"Well, if he do... If he knows you took the damn pictures... Look, doesn't your profession have some sort of code about never being seen?"

"He desperate man, Mr. Bronstein."

Harry waggled the book. "So is the Sheik. He's got three hundred women in his harem and he hasn't been able to get it up for the past year. Right now his only hope, not to mention mine, for a sexual rejuvenation is Randy Nell."

"He confiscate memory-stick holding hanky-panky pictures."

"You want to hear about desperate, Herr Schmidt?" The American's knuckles whitened in clenched frustration as he gripped the book. "My life is completely bereft of hanky-panky, except on a literary level. Despite that, I'm actually weighing the benefit of shit-canning this book, leaping into the ocean through the window behind me and swimming with the sharks to Calais, in order to end this conversation."

Schmidt dropped his voice a tone and looked round over the angle of his shoulder as he spoke, "How fifteen hundred Euros sound?"

"It sounds like I'm late for my swim with toothy friends."

"I pay. You carry memory-stick my hotel. No trouble, big time."

"I may not have the lineage of Israel stamped upon my face, but I still have a suspicious bent when it comes to strange smelling men offering money they don't have."

"I don't think you understand, Mr. Bronstein." Schmidt lifted an arm and sleeved away more blood and perspiration. "Nothing illegal involved, hot stuff."

"As may be, Herr Schmidt, but I'm still not interested."

The older man took from his shirt pocket a black memory-stick about two inches square, the large capacity type used in cameras. "You hide anywhere."

For a moment, Harry was tempted. There were no laws controlling the taking of memory-sticks through customs. In any event, it would be easy enough to get the stick across as part of his camera equipment. On the plus side, it would end the need for Schmidt to remain nearby, not to mention a tidy sum for walking-around money. On the negative side, there was a very big question: If the stick was so innocent, why would Schmidt pay someone else fifteen hundred Euros to smuggle it into France? Why not simply email the photos to himself?

"He not know you," said Schmidt, "so he not get suspicions, big time."

Harry's lips tightened, and then relaxed. Of course, there could be a great deal more to the stick than was visible. Well, a little more. It was only about an eighth of an inch thick. Nevertheless, what if there *was* something more to it? What if inside it was some sort of secret electronic circuitry — besides what memory-sticks use? What if it held a subminiature circuit, for medical research? Alternatively, what if it held secrets concerning space exploration? Corporate espionage was illegal.

"*Without* respect, Herr Schmidt," said Harry Bronstein, "wouldn't it be a lot cheaper for you, and a lot less dangerous for me, to shove it up your own ass?"

"Maybe you like see what on stick?" the older man suggested.

"My ex-wife had a cat like you," Harry said, with a sour grin. "It pestered and pestered until it wore me down. Finally, I would relent and pet it. Whereupon, the vicious little mouse-mugger would bite me with the ferocity of a rabid tiger. Each time I knew it was a bad idea to pet the damn thing. Each time I knew I would get bit. However, that lousy cat would wear me down and I would pet it. Well this time things are going to be different. This time, I'm not going to be suckered."

"Suckered?"

"I don't like being bit, Herr Schmidt. Nobody likes being bit — except under very special and private circumstance, between consenting adults which, I hope, is detailed at length in this novel."

Schmidt made a pleading gesture. "Who knows from biting?"

"I was trying to… Never mind. Just take your damn memory-stick, take your lousy fifteen hundred Euros and shove them where the sun don't shine."

Undaunted, Klaus Schmidt took out a digital camera and slipped the stick into its memory slot, and then turned the camera on. A moment later, the camera's viewing screen flickered to life. Schmidt turned it to face Harry, displaying a pornographic snapshot.

"See?" the older man said, giving a distant nod. "Her."

The photos showed a bleached blonde woman with a long face, narrow chin and large dark eyes. She was wearing a black, lacy thing that opened in the front and covered very little of the too much her maker had blessed her with and what mankind had surgically enhanced. Her hair was puffed up on the top. Her makeup was so thick it could be chipped with a chisel. Her eyebrows looked to be penciled on. She was well over seventy years of age but obviously enjoying what was, doubtlessly, a memorable moment.

Harry said, "Your client's wife certainly has a mouthful."

"She's used to it."

"As reassuring as it is to see a woman her age enjoying several pounds of tube-steak., I'm not going to be your mule."

"No need mule. Just stick in pocket."

Schmidt pressed a button and the camera went to the next photo, equally obscene. This time the male participant was clearly recognizable. He was dark, plump and very excited by what the blonde-haired woman was doing.

"Actually, I think I've seen him somewhere before," Harry said. "Not in the same vein, of course. But, his face looks familiar." Then the American heaved a theatrical sigh. "I'll give you six out of ten points for your photo-work, Schmidt. I'm deducting four points for getting caught behind the lens. Nevertheless, I must remain firm in my refusal."

After pocketing the camera, Schmidt produced a fold of bills. "Where else you earn all this for little work?"

As tempting as the sight of all that money looked, Harry shook his head in stern rejection.

"But..." Schmidt's eyebrows came together and he pushed his chin at Harry.

"Herr Schmidt, I've tried to be polite. All right. Maybe I was more acerbic than polite. And for that I'm very sorry. I'm usually a non-violent and understanding person. But, if you don't get the hell away from me with your dirty pictures and your lousy memory-stick, I'm going to bust your nose."

The older man's lips twitched. Then, his whole body began shaking and his face took on the pallor of a dead man. "We land in short time. I need help, big time."

An abrupt rush of rage overwhelmed Harry, and he jerked to his feet. "I'm going to count to three, like they do in the movies. If you're still sitting there, I'm gonna' put my fist right through your head."

Klaus Schmidt, frustrated by his lack of connection with Harry Bronstein, struggled onto his pins; jarring Harry with the effort. Then, the old fellow waddled off shoving his hands deep into the pockets of his trousers.

"Why do they always find me?" the American muttered as he resumed his seat. "I could be on a desert island ten million miles from anywhere. And some unwashed idiot with plans for taking over the world would show up and want my help." He looked at his watch. Then he opened the novel. "Now where was I? Ah, yes. 'Nell was ringing his bells while bumping her bangles...'"

Two disappointing chapters later, Harry was back in the rented Range Rover following a long line of cars leaving the ferry toward several French Customs Officers, who were checking passports and insurance cards. Quickly, he gathered the required documents and held them at the ready.

"Not only was the sex in that lousy book halfhearted," he said, as the vehicular procession crept forward, "But, I still don't know what bangles are." Harry maneuvered his car closer to the one in front. "It's all Schmidt's fault. He kept interrupting me. I pray to God the bastard gets strip-searched, orifice prodded, and his genitals introduced to a stun gun. Then, after that, I hope he's forced to eat his damn memory-stick, dirty pictures and all."

One of the Customs Officers suddenly blew his whistle. Then he motioned a rusty green Volkswagen off to one side. That left only two officers to deal with the hundreds of cars trying to get into France.

"Why isn't anything easy for me?" Harry complained. "At this rate, I'll be late getting to my hotel. The bastards will rent my room to someone else. Probably some horny over-the-hill local accompanied by his hot, tourist twist. The old bastard will end up having the time of his young life in what should've been my bed while I'm stuck here wondering why it's always the other guy who gets the mattress-motion?" He blinked, surprised at his own creative vent. "I should write that down. There could be a dirty book in that." Then Harry squinted over the steering wheel. "I'm gonna' die here of old age, you idiots. Hey, you. The yo-yo in the soon-to-be condemned Volkswagen. Why don't you pull both hands out of your spotted, fat ass and then…"

Harry's words hung in the air, as three Customs Officers rushed out of the nearby building over to the Volkswagen. Whereupon, the car's door was jerked open and the combined efforts of the officers dragged out Klaus Schmidt. In a trice, the trio had the middle-aged man pinned to the ground and handcuffed.

Harry gaped in total surprise. "Who says God never answers prayers?"

****

"Something's wrong," said Mikhail Shkarov. He shifted in his dark gray suit, watching the same scene, through a pair of high-powered binoculars. "Galina isn't in Kalandarishvili's car."

"That's because your blonde tart did a runner with our memory stick," Innokenti Rakhmelevich, Shkarov's companion, said.

Rakhmelevich was a big man, neatly dressed in a pale blue suit. He had a clear white skin. There was a black patch over one eye. He, too, was watching Alexi Kalandarishvili alias Klaus Schmidt being forced inside the customs office.

"Galina Vishnevskaya is committed to our cause," Shkarov said.

His voice was firm with conviction. But Shkarov was not entirely certain of Galina's loyalty. He frowned sharply, bringing his thick eyebrows close together. This movement made a ragged crease in the skin at the top of his nose. Galina was no angel. She had betrayed Moskalenko in order to seduce Kalandarishvili. She had betrayed Kalandarishvili in order to make a better deal with him, Shkarov. Why would she not perform another betrayal in order to accept yet a more profitable offer?

"With blind trust and five Euros, you can buy a cup of coffee," said Rakhmelevich.

The two Chechnyans were in a white Peugeot parked alongside E-15, just beyond the Custom's checkpoint, at Calais.

"Use your head for a change," Shkarov said. "It's obvious that something's happened to her."

"Something's going to, if she's crossed us."

Shkarov lowered the glasses and gave his partner a warning look. "I wouldn't act impulsively if I were you. There must be more to this than we know about."

"You're worrying about me being impulsive? When we've got the ass end of nothing after nearly a year of work and expense?"

"I'm worried about many things, including the memory stick."

Rakhmelevich gritted his teeth. "Your tart's probably hooked up with the American who met with Kalandarishvili, in Berlin."

"That American is dead."

"More crystal ball communication?"

"He's dead because I arranged it."

For a moment the two men sat and glared at each other. Then, Rakhmelevich shrugged his broad shoulders, and returned his interest to the Customs area.

"You should have let me handle Kalandarishvili, Shkarov."

"Like it or not, Rakhmelevich, you and I are supposed to be dead." Shkarov's lips spread back against his teeth. "Unfortunately, for both of us, you're a turnip in a tulip garden when you lose your temper. People tend to notice things like that."

Innokenti Rakhmelevich gave his companion's words some thought. In spite of Shkarov's womanizing weakness, he was right about one thing. It had been very nice to have the Russian GRU think they were dead.

"What happens if the French find the memory stick?" Rakhmelevich asked.

"If Kalandarishvili did his job, they won't."

The patch-eyed Chechnyan looked swiftly into the Shkarov's eyes and then away again. "Somehow I find that less than reassuring."

Shkarov raised the field glasses and resumed studying the scene.

After a few seconds he whispered, "Anitchka Nabatov." Then Shkarov handed Rakhmelevich the binoculars. "Look at the women squatting next to the Kalandarishvili's Volkswagen; yellow slacks and a white blouse."

Rakhmelevich put one lens of the binoculars to his unpatched eye. "Moskalenko must've known more about Kalandarishvili's plans than we thought. And what he knew, the GRU now knows." He lowered the binoculars, his mouth a hard white slit. "Well, that's that."

"You give up to easy. She's attached something to Kalandarishvili's car."

"A homing device?"

Shkarov's chin came down an inch, and he grinned. "If so, that means we're still in the game."

"How do you figure?"

"They intend to follow him, presumably to whomever he sells the memory stick. That gives us time to make our own moves."

"I'd prefer to write this off as a loss and begin again."

"Nonsense."

"They may have more than Anitchka working this. What if we're spotted?"

"We won't if we're careful."

"Why weren't we forewarned about this?" Rakhmelevich handed the field glass back to Shkarov. "Your Mole in Nabatov's sector must've known."

"Maybe. Maybe not. In any event, Kalandarishvili will panic, over this. He'll drive directly to the meeting place he arranged with the American." Shkarov's eyes became as black as the enamel on a Japanese fan. "When the American does not arrive, Kalandarishvili will correctly assume that something has gone wrong. He'll go to his hotel. Because he does not have our contacts, he will quickly realize that his only hope of a getting rid of the memory stick is to comply with the original arrangement he made with us."

"So you say."

"Stop worrying. When you arrive at his room, he will cooperate. He'll have no choice. Whereupon, you will bring him out to the car. Then you and I will take him to a secluded spot and you will kill him, for his treachery. You'll enjoy that, won't you?"

"With Anitchka following? I'm not about to be caught in her cross-hairs."

Shkarov smirked. "So there is someone who frightens you, eh?"

"Only a fool does not worry about the Nabatovs."

Shkarov looked back towards the ferry and his mood suddenly brightened. "There's my lovely Galina." A quick jerking smile of anticipation played across his face. "What a breathtaking sight she's."

Rakhmelevich shifted in the seat, not at all satisfied with Shkarov's handling of Kalandarishvili. The blonde tart was just another in a long line of women who had fouled up their operations. He and Shkarov had started their partnership intending to raise badly needed funds to arm the Chechnyan underground. As the years went by, less and less of their monies went towards Chechnyan independence. Shkarov claimed their cause was being badly mismanaged. Therefore funding the effort was a mistake. Rakhmelevich had not agreed. How could he? Unlike Shkarov, he was still a dedicated Chechnyan soldier.

Chapter 4

A thin slice of moonlight, cutting through black clouds, gave the *Alessandra Hotel* a ghostly appearance. The four-story white box was on Place-Boulnois, in Paris. From the outside, it looked like a pre-war hospital. Its roof was flat. Its walls were stone. Its windows were large, rectangular and evenly spaced. These, for the most part, were big enough for the inmates to leap from, should the whim take them. Lights shined behind some when Harry Bronstein arrived, nearly seven hours after arriving in Calais.

Harry parked the Range Rover in the lot behind the hotel, and then got out. The rain had stopped, making the night air stiff with a dank wetness thoroughly fouled by the stench of sewer gas. He dragged out his suitcase, camera bag and laptop-computer. After locking the rental car, Harry lugged his belongings inside the hotel. It had been an exhausting drive, rife with detours and wrong turns. All he wanted to do was eat and go to bed — assuming he still had a meal and bed waiting.

To Harry's right, in the hotel's rear foyer, was an ornate staircase. It led upward to a gallery encircled by a white wrought-iron railing. Near the base of these steps were several large, gray chairs with red plush seats. Straight ahead of him was a large, empty fireplace. Massive chunks of white marble framed the firebox. Flying cupids decorated the milky stone. Some of these mythical creatures blew flutes. The others strummed Lyres. All had notable erections. Above the fireplace's enormous, marble mantel was a large portrait of Louis XIV having a bad wig day. To his left, Harry spotted the main reception area.

Giving his luggage a determined heft he staggered off in that direction.

As he lumbered along, Harry could not help but wonder why his ex-wife had booked reservations at the Alessandra. Blood-red slate tiled the floor. The walls were military gray with gold-painted filigree. The ceiling was a collection of square copper panels embossed with naked cherubs, each blessed by obscenely large buttocks. And everywhere was the stench of stale tobacco smoke.

"Bonjour, monsieur," Harry addressed the reception clerk. "Je m'appelle Harry Bronstein."

"Welcome to the *Alessandra Hotel*, M. Bronstein," the reception clerk said, tonelessly. The nametag on his badly-fitting, brown suit read: *Sidoine Benoît*. "How may I help you, Monsieur?"

Benoît was tall. He was painfully thin and pale, with hunched shoulders. His black eyes floated in deeply shadowed sockets.

"My ex-wife, Maggie, made reservations about eight months ago." Harry's baggage hit the floor. "She requested a double room."

"Ah, yes, you American's always want a double room. Unfortunately, this hotel restricts itself to suites."

Harry's jaw muscles flexed with mild irritation. "As long as it has a bed, I don't care."

"It has a bed, Monsieur." The reception clerk made a sucking noise with his teeth as if trying to rid his mouth of something bad-tasting. "In fact, the entire accommodation is suitable for everyone; from the highest, who arrive timely, to the lowest — such as you Americans — who invariably arrive late."

A large, beaked nose graced Benoît's face. His grey hair smoothed straight back across his narrow head, like a greasy second skin. He had wide, thick lips. As he spoke, these rippled in the plastic pleasure required of his profession. A disgusting brown color, presumable nicotine, stained the thumb and first three fingers on his left hand. His shirt was tan. His necktie was yellow.

"There was construction on the A15," Harry said. "After taking the detour, I made a wrong turn. Before I realized that I'd gone the wrong way, I was nearly back to Calais."

"Ah, yes. You Americans always have an excuse."

"It's the truth."

"If you say so, Monsieur."

"Are you, in your own obscure way, telling me that my reservation has been cancelled?"

"Of course not, M. Bronstein. We French have come to accept the fact that American's are easily confused. This is why we urged your wife to guaranty a late arrival with her credit card."

Harry's heart sank as he considered the prospect of sleeping in the Range Rover. "Did she?"

"If she had not, you and your shabby accompaniments would be on the way back to your automobile on the end of my shoe."

"I take it you dislike Americans?"

"Ah, you are far more perceptive than first I thought."

"Listen, Froggy... If it weren't for us Americans, with our innate confusion and shabby accompaniments, Hitler would have become prime minister of France and you and I would be having this irritating conversation in German."

"You, of course, are entitled to your own opinion, Monsieur." There was another round of teeth sucking. Then he turned his attention to the computer screen. "Let me see what is still available..."

For many irksome moments, Harry listened as Benoît teeth-sucked, tongue-clucked and hissed during a laborious, keyboard-clicking check of computerized records. Finally, he nodded his sleek head in approval.

"Your wife requested accommodations on the top floor, M. Bronstein. However, the best I can offer is a suite on the floor, below."

"Why not the top floor? You've had long enough to arrange it."

"Because we rented the entire floor to a group of Canadian Shriners."

"I won't get a wink of sleep with a bunch of drunken Shriners above me."

"My apologies for any inconvenience this slight change in your lodging may create. But, as you Americans like to say, that is as good as it's going to get." Benoît glanced around. "Your wife is where?"

"Ex-wife. Maggie's back in the States."

"When are you expecting her?"

"I'm not."

"Why not?"

"Maggie and I divorced. Which is why I refer to her as my 'Ex'."

"How quaint."

"The only reason I'm here is because you people refused to cancel our reservation unless I paid a fee which nearly matched the price of the bloody room."

"Suite."

"Whatever!"

"But, if you're no longer married, how do you expect to use her credit card for the room?"

"I don't. I will use my own."

"Nevertheless, we based all our evaluation procedures upon her credit standing." He cocked his chin at Harry. "Now, I will have to begin again."

Harry smirked. "How delightfully inconvenient for you."

The reception clerk extended a hand. "I will need a credit card in good standing."

Harry took out his wallet and removed one. Then he placed the plastic on the clerk's palm. "Try this one for size."

Sidoine Benoît's long nose twitched a little as he placed the credit card next to the computer keyboard. Two minutes later, he returned the plastic and set a white registration card on the desk in front of Harry. In doing so, the clerk's onyx cufflinks glinted under the light above the desk like drops of ink dropped into molten gold.

"One person or two, Monsieur," Benoît said, "the room-rate is the same."

"No one in his right mind would expect the French to offer a discount on a room at a dilapidated hotel in the foulest section of Paris."

"There is nothing foul about this part of Paris, Monsieur, just the tourists who visit." The clerk set a pen down next to the registration card. "If you will fill this out and surrender your passport I will have someone assist with your luggage."

The hackles on the back of Harry's neck rose as he said, "You wouldn't also like my first born?"

"That will not be necessary, Monsieur."

Harry picked up the pen and then scrawled his name and address on the card. It was only then he realized the writing instrument leaked, leaving the flesh between his first two digits splotched with indelible purple.

"Is the café open?" he asked, discarding the seeping device.

"Our restaurant closes in less than thirty minutes." The clerk shuffled his feet a little, as he placed the pen back into its holder. "If you intend to dine here, I would suggest doing so before you unpack."

"Sounds reasonable. That way I won't have to repack should a bout of ptomaine take the fun out of my visit."

"We never joke about such things, Monsieur."

"I've dined in Paris, before. I wasn't joking."

Benoît took another look at the computer screen. "Ah, I see there was a telephone call for you, M. Bronstein." Quickly, he scrawled a line on a slip of pink paper. "M. Schmidt rang a few moments ago. He is staying at the Montmartre Hotel, a gruesome accommodation: much more suitable for a man of your limited intellect. M. Schmidt said he would appreciate a visit from you this evening." Then the clerk handed the note to Harry. "Your friend was quite insistent."

"He's not my friend."

Harry winced as he looked down at the slip of paper. On it was a telephone number. Why had Schmidt telephoned? Why would he assume that Harry would return the call, let alone visit? It's not as though they had become fast friends on the ferry.

"Did Schmidt say why he called?"

"It is not my province to interrogate the Bosch, Monsieur."

"This trip to Europe has become a bad dream," Harry said.

"Nightmares are part and parcel to life, Monsieur. As for me, I keep telling myself that retirement is not many years away and, with a little luck, the American tourist industry will soon collapse."

"I thought Schmidt would be in jail," Harry said, more to himself than an explanation to the reception clerk. He folded the note and stuffed it into a pocket.

"An unpleasant end of journey for many foreigners, I'm told." Benoît extended a hand. "To complete this unpleasant interaction, I will need your passport."

Harry dug out his passport and handed it to the clerk. "Just to satisfy my curiosity, what do you do if a guest arrives who does not meet your credit expectations?"

Benoît's eyes darkened a couple of shades. "That is when we take the first-born child."

After pigeonholing Harry's passport in one of the mail slots behind the counter, the reception clerk handed Harry a keycard. Then he explained that the suite, assigned to the card, was number 3111.

"I hope I won't have a disturbing night," Harry said. "I'm tired. So I don't relish the idea of a bunch of Shriners whooping it up."

"It is my deepest wish that your room shall be as quiet as I hope your tomb will soon be."

The clerk tapped a bell.

In response, a small man with a fringe of very dark hair sprouting clown-like from his otherwise bare skull, seemingly appeared out of nowhere. He was wearing a gaudy maroon bellhop uniform, sans pillbox cap. His age was sixty or close to it. He had black eyes as remote as an outside toilet in a sand storm. His skin was wrinkled and as white as boiled pork. He crept across the blood-red floor like a thief.

"*Par ici, s'il vous plaît, Monsieur,*" the bellhop said to Harry, when the little man reached the reception desk.

The dark gray curls of a large, downward-drooping moustache almost hid his purplish lips. Several windings of white, cloth tape repaired the bridge of metal spectacles. He picked up Harry Bronstein's luggage and staggered off.

As instructed, Harry quickly fell into line behind the Hop.

"Been at the hotel game long?" Harry asked the man's back, as they headed toward the elevators at the rear of the hotel.

"Longer than I like being reminded, Monsieur. What is your suite number?"

"Three-one-one-one. It sounds like you have reoccurring nightmares, too."

"Sadly, yes."

"Benoît, I assume, contributes to most of them? He's an asshole of the third water, if I'm any judge of character."

"As much as I would like to agree with, Monsieur, my dreams usually involve hotel fires."

Harry fell silent, slightly taken aback by the Hop's response. Then he asked, "Just to satisfy my morbid curiosity, do people die in your dreams?"

"What self-respecting nightmare does not include fatalities?"

"Does any hotel in particular burn in your dreams?"

"Just this hotel."

"I hope you're not a pyromaniac."

"It has been suggested, Monsieur."

"Just to assuage my growing paranoia, not to mention my rising sense of terror, when was the last time you had one of those dreams?"

"Last night. But, don't worry, Monsieur. In my dreams I'm always on vacation when this hotel catches fire."

"Planning a holiday anytime soon?"

"Not until after the end of my shift."

Less than a minute later, Harry and the bellhop stepped into the elevator.

"How far is the Montmartre Hotel from here?" Harry asked.

"About a forty-minute drive, Monsieur."

The American's stomach made an indignant growl. "I got the impression from Benoît that it wasn't a very nice place."

"I wouldn't want to die there."

"Meaning they charge at every turn, grave or otherwise?"

"I was thinking more along the line of rats feeding upon my rotting corpse."

The Hop punched the button for the third floor. The elevator doors shut. Then the car lurched upward with a loud squeal.

"Does this thing do that often?" Harry asked, his eyes suddenly wide with fright.

"Does your query concern the lurching or the squealing, Monsieur?"

Harry squinted at the other man. "Which one should worry me the most?"

"The squealing, I think. It occurs only when the cable suspending the car is in need of replacement."

"I take it a call has been made to head-off this potentially fatal problem, before something terminal occurs?"

"One can only pray, Monsieur."

"I'm already ahead of you, on that. Has the cable ever broken?"

"In my experience, at this hotel, only once." The bellhop shivered with revulsion. "That was a real mess, I can tell you. Blood and shit everywhere."

"This trip gets better and better."

Suite 3111 overlooked the street running in front of the hotel. It had a small sitting room furnished with a chair, a davenport and a desk. There was a separate *boudoir* fitted out with an ornately carved armoire and a double bed. The baroque bedposts rose like phalluses toward the ceiling. There was an *ensuite* bathroom: a bidet, toilet, pedestal sink and a hulking claw-foot tub accessorized it. The same floral pattern papered the walls of each room: Yellow and pink water lilies tangled amongst an endless green vine, set against a beige background. Polished parquet set in a geometric pattern covered the floors throughout the suite. The entire atmosphere reeked of insecticide.

"Invading roaches?" Harry asked, making an audible sniff.

"No monsieur." The bellhop dropped Harry's baggage onto the bed. "We are content to collar and leash the ones we already have. Will there be anything else?"

"Benoît was right. Things *are* as good as they're going to get."

"If Monsieur would like, I can arrange his menu selection for this evening."

Harry nodded, his stomach growling again. "I'll have a steak, any cut, medium rare." He went over to the other man, pulling out his wallet. With it came the memory-stick Schmidt had shown him; the device falling unnoticed to the carpet. "I'll take anything for sides. I'd like a small bottle of something red for beverage. But, I don't want dessert. Tell them to charge the meal to this room."

"You dropped this, Monsieur," the bellhop said, dutifully retrieving the memory-stick from the floor.

"Why that lousy..." Harry began, suddenly steaming over Klaus Schmidt's audacity. Then with a forced grin, he took the memory-stick and handed the hop several Euros as a tip. "On second thought, I'd like my meal brought here. I have to make a phone call. It's liable to take a great deal of time what with me translating American obscenities into Russian colloquialisms. Can you handle room-service?"

The hop's voice rustled. "Room Service is part of my *devoirs*, Monsieur."

"Well at least that's something to…" Harry began. Then his worries darted back to the bellhop's dreams. "You said your dreams are mostly about hotel fires. Have you ever had one about serial killers? The kind who use poison on unsuspecting, American hotel guests?"

"Only once, Monsieur. But, do not despair. In my dream, I used a fast acting poison. The pain lasted for only a few days. *Bonsoir.*"

After the bellhop left, Harry locked the door to his suite and tossed the memory-stick into the trashcan, next to the desk. Then he strode over to the television and turned it on.

"Schmidt, you fat, bleeding bastard. For two cents I'd call French Immigration and report you."

Harry paused a moment, fuming and thinking. The memory-stick, at least, explained Schmidt's telephone message. However, it did not clarify why he thought Harry would jump to deliver the damn thing. In fact, he should have assumed that Harry would do just what Harry had done – gotten angry over being used and tossed the stick into the trash.

"What I should do," he mused, "is get old Schmidt on the phone. Then for our mutual auditory enjoyment, flush his damn stick down the toilet." Harry started toward the telephone. Then he stopped. "Or better yet, erase the damn thing before mailing it to the bastard."

He giggled at the vindictive prank, changed directions and strode over to the bed. There he quickly unpacked his laptop computer.

"Let him try bargaining for payment with photos that no longer exist. Better yet, replace his snaps with some of my holiday pics. That series I took on British cheese making would be perfect. Especially those close-ups of the fulminating Stilton yeast."

But, as the laptop came to life another idea came into his head. He had done the job, albeit unknowingly. So, why not collect for it? He could get driving directions from the desk. Admittedly, fifteen hundred Euros was not a fortune. However, it would cover his Paris expenses. Better, still, he could demand a fortune for the stick's return. He chuckled, vindictively. It would be fun to watch Schmidt turn green with rage.

Harry retrieved the memory-stick from the trash. For a moment, he studied it. The fifteen hundred Euro offering still bothered him. From the cut of Schmidt's clothing, the Russian-come-German was not well-heeled. That, of itself, was not surprising. The typical detective barely made a living in the United States. European versions probably did not fare any better. So how could a poor man afford to pay such a large bribe? On the other hand, he had produced a thick pile of Euros as part of his efforts to garner Harry's cooperation. Why was smuggling this insignificant square of plastic worth so much money? Could it be the naughty pictures? Not hardly. The French were one of the earliest purveyors of pornography and photographs of an elderly couple having it off would hardly cause Customs Officers to wink, let alone blush.

What about the risk Schmidt had taken?

Secreting the memory stick in Harry's pocket was the act of a desperate man. Admittedly, their conversation involved names and hotel information. Nevertheless, what if Harry had lied about everything? There would have been no way for Schmidt to recover his property.

There was also Schmidt's arrest to consider.

Theoretically, at least, there may have been a grain of truth in his claim concerning the man in the photo being a French Custom Officer, at the Calais station. However, why would those other officers join forces with the photographed one, to arrest Schmidt? Friendship, after all, had it limits. Compelling Schmidt to give up those incriminating photos could have cost each of them their job.

Harry gave his dark head a shake. Schmidt's story was not quite kosher. For example, what about Schmidt's prior knowledge of the man in the photo working at the Calais crossing? It made no sense for Schmidt to risk taking that route into France when he could have shuttled his car through the tunnel and avoided the customs officer entirely.

His curiosity piqued, Harry stuck the memory-stick into one of the computer's photo-card slots.

Instantly, the hard-drive whirred as the computer automatically copied the contents of the stick to a subfolder. Then the library explorer popped open displaying a list of the new data. The presented inventory included about five hundred images and about two hundred text documents. This was far too much information for a simple case of adultery. In fact, the total disk space used suggested a memory-stick stuffed to capacity.

Harry adjusted the display properties of the new subfolder to show previews of the pictures. The screen flashed. Then miniatures of the images spilled into view. Curiously, there were only three photos of the sexual variety. The others looked like maps.

"So there was a surprise inside," he whispered, his excitement growing.

Harry double-clicked on the first image in the display. A few seconds later, the computer screen filled with the pornographic shot Schmidt had first shown him. Harry clicked the space bar two more times. With each pressing, another photo of the aged lovers came into view. Then he pressed the space bar once more to advance beyond the porn-shots.

A map popped open. For a moment, Harry was perplexed. He was looking at part of the border-region between Russia and China. But, this map contained unfamiliar icons and corresponding text written in Russian, hardly suitable data for the French or English travel markets.

He minimized the photo, then moused over to one of the text documents and double-clicked. A second later the document displayed. This, too, was a curiosity. It appeared to be a spreadsheet of numeric and text data. Like the map, the text was Russian.

As Harry translated Russian into English, he made a spine-chilling discovery. Not only did the document detail Russian troop movements and personnel counts, it identified the numbers and types of Russian defense armaments in that area.

"The blood-dripping bastard's a spy!"

No wonder Schmidt had been anxious to have someone smuggle the memory stick into France. Being caught with this information would have result in a lengthy detention while an international investigation took place. Then, there was the prospect of the miscreant being handed over to the spooks from the GRU. Those torture-experts would have spent several days beating a confession out of the smuggler, whether he had known what was on the stick or not. Whereupon the poor sod would be dragged to Russia for a quick trial culminating in a brief rendezvous with a Russian firing squad.

Harry's mouth went dry with fright. For the next several minutes, he paced the room trying to decide on a course of action.

He considered delivering the memory-stick to the United States embassy. His own country would probably take an interest in the stolen data. However, that seemed deceitful. The Russians had been hurt by Schmidt's espionage. So, in all fairness, they were entitled to receive their property back — at Schmidt's expense, of course.

How could Harry do the right thing without becoming the brunt of a GRU interrogation?

A grin tugged at Harry's lips and he stopped pacing.

The solution was simple. He would use a two-step approach. First Harry would make a copy of the memory-stick. Then, he would retouch the maps and edit the documents on the original stick so they would be useless to Schmidt. Afterwards, Harry would drive to the Montmartre Hotel and deliver the altered stick to an unsuspecting Schmidt. Then, tomorrow, he would drive to the Russian Embassy and hand over the untouched version of the stick. In so doing, Harry would get twofold revenge upon Schmidt. First, when Schmidt tried to sell the data, his intended purchasers would beat him within an inch of his life for trying to swindle them. Secondly, the unaltered memory stick would provide the necessary evidence against Schmidt to the GRU. Who would promptly go in search of him.

Harry hurried over to his camera case and found an unused memory-stick. Then he returned the computer and copied the contents of the subdirectory holding the original memory-stick's contents, to the new stick. Afterward, he removed the second stick from the computer, went over to his leather jacket and slipped it into a hidden pocket within the jacket's lining. This was a precautionary measure. Considering the data's sensitivity, there was a chance that Schmidt might invade Harry's room while Harry was on his way to the Montmartre. Then he returned the computer.

By the time midnight rolled around, Harry had devoured his steak and finished his computerized vengeance. He saved the edits. Then he uploaded the lot to the original memory-stick, overwriting its contents. Afterward he stuffed it into his shirt pocket, strode over to the telephone and dialed the number on the note provided by Benoît.

It took only a few seconds for the clerk at the Montmartre Hotel to answer. Harry asked to have his call routed to Klaus Schmidt's room. A few seconds later, the reception clerk came back on the line. He told Harry that Schmidt had not yet checked in. Nevertheless, he was still expected.

Harry muttered a curse, as he rang off. He started for the bath but stopped when the telephone rang. Harry turned and grabbed the receiver. A moment later, the oily voice he remembered from the ferry came across the line.

"That you Bronstein?"

"Herr Schmidt?"

"I try call early." Schmidt's voice wheezed with excitement and relief. "You not in. You get message?"

"I got it. Moreover, I have something of yours. Can you imagine my surprise when that memory stick you wanted smuggled into France fell out of my pocket?"

"Mr. Bronstein, I apologize for little ploy. But, had no choice. I arrested when reach Calais. Car and person search. Had been carrying memory-stick, would lost it."

"Yes," Harry said, "I saw the Custom's Officers shackle you hand and foot."

"You be wake short time?"

"What did you have in mind?"

"I come your hotel. I collect memory-stick. You collect thousand Euros."

"I'm thinking that my cut for getting the memory-stick into France — you know the Russian maps and their relevant documents — should be worth a great deal more, than that."

There was a long silence, except for Schmidt's erratic breathing, on the other end of the line. Then, sounding as if the words were coming from a very deep hole, Schmidt said, "Have you speaks 'bout situation with anyone?"

"No. I've been too busy planning what to purchase with the hundred thousand Euros you're going to pay me."

"Hundred thousand?" Schmidt's voice choked with fury.

"Too pricey?"

"We agreed thousand Euros."

"We did not agree on anything," Harry said. "You first offered a thousand Euros. Then you upped the ante to fifteen hundred. In both instances, I refused to help. However, since I did assist I think I'm entitled to an amount worthy of the risk I took."

Schmidt cleared his throat. "I got only thousand."

"Maybe, I should be cutting a deal with the Russian embassy?"

"Don't do foolish, Mr. Bronstein!" Schmidt shouted. "Your life hang with mine in balance, big time."

"Are you threatening to kill me, Herr Schmidt?"

"Right down to your tippy-toes."

"I might not die so easy."

"I not alone, Mr. Bronstein. People I work not be crossed. They find you no matter you go. They squash you like bug."

Harry's hands became clammy as he realized that Schmidt was probably telling the truth. "In that case, I'll settle for the thousand Euros."

"That being smart, big time. I drive over."

"No. Are you at your hotel?"

"Not yet."

"Wait for me at the Montmartre. I have enough trouble here without you and your cronies showing up. Meet me in the lobby — alone. We'll make the exchange there."

"When?"

"I'm on my way out the door. It will take me about an hour to get to the Montmartre."

"That work. I be there by then. Please listen, Mr. Bronstein. Even after finish business, don't discuss anyone."

"Or I get squashed like bug?"

"Big time."

As Harry rang off, he glanced over at the television which showed a short blurb on the new Paris Prefect of Police, including an excerpt in the form of a video clip. To his surprise, the Prefect was a dead ringer for the man in the porno snaps on the memory stick.

"You've got a doppelganger on the loose, Slick," Harry told the television persona, as he slipped on his jacket. "And from what I saw, he's having one hell of a good time with somebody else's bit of well-aged fun."

Down at the registration desk Sidoine Benoît gave Harry an irritated look. "Are you dissatisfied with your room, M. Bronstein?"

"I'm not dissatisfied. There was a mix-up on the Calais ferry. Schmidt, the idiot who left the message for me, wants what belongs to him brought to his hotel. I'm going to drive over there and straighten things out."

"I cannot return your passport until the room is paid."

"I didn't ask for it back." Harry took a small notebook from his jacket pocket. "Just tell me how to get to the Montmartre Hotel."

"Well, that hotel's proximity is not simple to explain." Benoît grimaced, as he made a throwaway gesture. "You will have to take Place Boulnois to Rue Bayen, and then make a right. After that you will take a sharp left at Avenue Niel. This will take you to Avenue des Ternes where you will go left again but only for a short…"

For another five minutes, the clerk continued with a long series of complicated directions. Each of which, Harry carefully wrote down.

"Wouldn't you prefer a taxi?" the clerk suggested, in conclusion. "It might be more convenient than driving all that way and back."

"The drive will do me good," Harry said. "I'm working on a little speech for Schmidt. The time behind the steering wheel will give me an opportunity to include obscenities I haven't used in years."

"You are a very odd person, M. Bronstein. Have you considered therapy?"

Harry smiled faintly. "I have to tell you… I hear that a lot."

***

"I don't like this," said Rakhmelevich. "First Kalandarishvili is arrested at Calais. Then he gives us a multi-hour tour of the French countryside, only to stop at a café to make a telephone call. When he finally gets to his hotel, he goes out before we can make a move. We're being set up, I tell you."

Mikhail Shkarov, Galina Vishnevskaya and Innokenti Rakhmelevich were in Shkarov's Peugeot, parked across the street from the Montmartre hotel.

"Kalandarishvili's nervous because of the incident at Calais." The other man gave a quick, tight laugh. "He wants to be certain he wasn't followed." Shkarov raised the binoculars to his eyes as a dark Citroën rolled into the parking lot. "That's Anitchka driving in, now." After a few seconds, he set the field glasses on the seat between him and Rakhmelevich. "She won't make a move until Nabatov gets here."

"She will if she spots me dragging Kalandarishvili out of the hotel."

"Stop thinking like a bully. " Shkarov twisted his mouth sardonically. "When you approach Kalandarishvili, tell him we want him for another job."

"You don't think he'll ask how we found his hotel."

"If he does, tell him the truth — we tailed him. In any event, what you must emphasize is the promise of double pay if he delivers the memory stick to Cheng in Port Bou. Tell him that I'm waiting in the car to pay for both jobs. He'll come willingly enough." He twisted to look over the seat at Galina. "Go back into the hotel. Find out if Kalandarishvili is back."

"If I go in, again, the reception clerk will get suspicious," she said. "Have Rakhmelevich do it."'

"Do as you're told," growled the patch-eyed Chechnyan.

"If Kalandarishvili has returned, don't forget to ask if he's put anything into the hotel safe," Shkarov told her. "Understand?"

"Why would the clerk tell me that?" she asked.

"He'll tell you anything you desire, my sweet, if you make use of your charms."

"Nearly getting killed wasn't part of the deal." Galina touched her bruised throat. "Neither is this."

"You'll be taken care of, my precious."

Amidst muttered curses, Galina climbed from the car and quickly crossed the street.

"I don't trust her," said Rakhmelevich.

"You didn't trust your mother, as I recall." Shkarov raised the binoculars to his eyes. "Anitchka's using her cell-phone. She must be telephoning Pasha." After a few seconds, he returned the field glasses to the seat.

"Kalandarishvili will realize he's done for as soon as he sees your tart."

"Galina won't be here. There's a taxi stand down the block." Shkarov frowned and looked down at his long white fingers. "I'll send her to our hotel in a cab."

"What happens when Kalandarishvili realizes we're not taking him to the rail depot?"

"By that time, it will be too late for him to do anything."

Ten minutes later, Shkarov pointed toward the moonlit figure of a woman hurrying toward the car. "There's Galina, now."

"Took her long enough."

"She had a great deal to accomplish."

A few seconds later one of the Peugeot's rear doors opened and the young blonde slipped inside.

"Well?" Shkarov looked over the back of the front seat at her.

"That creature is disgusting." Galina adjusted her clothing.

"Never mind that; is Kalandarishvili in?"

"Yes. But, he told the reception clerk he was expecting a visitor."

"Who?"

"An American. No name was said."

"C. I. A.," muttered Rakhmelevich.

"What about the hotel safe?" Shkarov asked.

"Kalandarishvili hasn't put anything in it."

The patch-eyed Chechnyan picked up the binoculars and pointed them toward Anitchka's car. A moment later he said, "Anitchka's getting out."

"Nabatov must be on is way," Shkarov said. "We won't have much time. Go in the back. Take the stairs up to Kalandarishvili's room."

"What makes you think Anitchka won't be headed there, too?"

"I know Nabatov. He would never send her after a man like Kalandarishvili, alone."

"That bloodthirsty bitch could devour a dozen Kalandarishvili's without working up a sweat."

"Nevertheless, Nabatov will insist that she wait for him. Anitchka's a good daughter. She'll do as her father tells her."

"I can't wait to see Kalandarishvili's face," Galina said.

Shkarov looked over the back of the front seat. "I'm afraid I'll have to leave you at the taxi stand down the block, my pet."

"But, I want Kalandarishvili to see that I'm not dead."

"As much as I know it would please you, my dear, I want Kalandarishvili to think all is well — at least until Rakhmelevich and I get the memory stick."

Again, her hand went to her throat. "Mikhail, I have a right to see him killed for what he did."

"I know you do, my pet, but business must come before pleasure. Do not despair. I shall make Kalandarishvili suffer for your injuries."

Rakhmelevich opened the door and climbed out. "Don't be long," he said. "I'm not convinced Anitchka will wait for her father."

"Frightened of a mere woman?" Galina taunted.

"Anitchka Nabatov is no mere woman."

Chapter 5

The Montmartre Hotel's lobby was up several steps from the street entrance and through an arch framed by a pair of plastic palms. To the left of the arch, a curving carpeted stairway led down to a bar. Half a dozen people smoked and chatted. Most were elderly. Two old women with haggard faces and blue hair were arguing over who was going to make the trip down the stairs to buy the next round of pink gins. One of the women wore enough face powder to dust down an elephant. Both of them smoked cigarettes stuck in long, black, plastic holders.

Farther along, in the lobby, was the hotel's reception area. A short, bald, plump man of middle years stood behind the check-in desk, his elbows leaning heavily on its shiny top. His black suit looked like it belonged to a chimpanzee. The garment was tight across the shoulders and far too long in the arms. His white shirt was open-collared, his necktie loosened just below his Adam's apple. He was speaking with a pair of middle-aged females dressed in tight blouses, and extremely short skirts. The women's nearly-exposed breasts seemed to captivate his spectacled, darkly-ringed eyes.

Harry Bronstein stopped a few feet from the chatting trio. The reception clerk's plastic nametag read: 'Charles Aznavour'. The women smelled of flowery perfume, and men. Harry looked around. Beyond the desk, not far from the elevator, was a stand of telephones. A leggy brunette in yellow slacks stood in front of one, punching buttons. Harry's eyes drifted further but he did not see Schmidt.

Irritated that his Russian-come-German problem did not keep their rendezvous, the American quickly strode over to the reception desk.

"Could you ring Klaus Schmidt's room?" Harry asked, looking at the clerk. "Tell him that Harry Bronstein is waiting in the lobby."

Aznavour's eyes reluctantly left the opulent field of feminine flesh and focused upon the unwelcome intruder. "Who do you wish to speak with, Monsieur?"

"Klaus Schmidt. My name is Harry Bronstein. I have an appointment with him. He was supposed to meet me in the lobby."

The reception clerk turned and eyed the wooden pigeonholes behind him before returning his attention to Harry. "M. Schmidt collected his mail, so I assume he's in."

"Can't you tell him that I'm waiting for him, here?" Harry asked.

"The elevator is just a little farther alone."

"I know that. I want him to come down."

Aznavour took off his glasses, laid them on the desk in front of him and pinched the bridge of his nose where the spectacle-pads had dug two shallow pits. "He is in suite 204, just one floor up."

"A trip, it should be obvious, I'm trying to avoid."

The clerk gave a despairing roll to his shadowed eyes. Then he put on his glasses, went over to the PBX box, stuffed two brass-tipped wires into a pair of holes and pressed the button directly below. After a few seconds, he turned the toggle, next to the button and spoke into a handset. After a brief verbal interlude, the clerk removed the plugs and returned to Harry.

"Well?" the American asked.

"Monsieur Schmidt requested that you come back tomorrow morning."

"Like hell I will!"

"I'm just the messenger, Monsieur." Aznavour tried to grin, but one side of his mouth tilted down unconvincingly. "There is no need to shout."

"I have half a mind to wring the fat bastard's neck."

Aznavour cleared his throat and started to speak, then said nothing.

Harry turned and strode to the elevators at the rear of the hotel. A moment after he pushed the call button, the doors opened and he quickly went inside the lift.

The dimly lit hallway was empty when Harry stepped out of the elevator. He sniffed the air. It was warm and dry. Then his nose wrinkled, as he picked up a whiff of something foul. Urine, possibly.

Harry moved off, checking room numbers as his feet creaked upon ancient parquet. At the far end of the corridor, Harry found a slightly-ajar door bearing the number 204.

"Schmidt? It's me, Harry Bronstein."

When Harry received no reply, he knocked. Then, after half a minute, when he still had not received a response, Harry knocked again; harder, this time.

"Dammit, Schmidt, I'm tired. Let's get this over with."

Still he got no response.

Angrily, Harry pushed the door wide and stepped inside. "I'm not driving back here in the morning. We settle up now, or I go to the Russian's."

The main room of Schmidt's suite was small by any standard, not much larger than a walk-in closet. The walls were an off-white plaster. Ancient stone tiles, in a mix of colors, covered the floor in soiled disharmony. A loveseat and a chair, with a low table between them, furnished the room. However, the cushions from each were scattered upon the floor as if someone had been searching for misplaced property. Across the room, from where Harry stood, was a terrace door. It stood open; the filmy, yellow curtains across it swished lazily in the night breeze.

"Damn it, Schmidt, I haven't got all night!"

There were two closed doors just a few feet to the right of the suit's entrance. Impatiently, Harry strode over to the nearest and knocked. As with the entrance door, he got no response.

"Look, we made a deal. I was to drive over. You were to meet me in the lobby. Stop stalling."

Harry turned the knob and pushed the door open. The room looked like a fight had been lost in there. The mattress tilted up against one wall. The armoire doors stood wide open, and clothing from the massive cabinet littered the floor. One corner of the room held a tangled pile of bedding.

He backed away from the door shouting, "Schmidt?"

A sudden chill laddered up Harry's spine. Had this apparent battle taken place before or after Schmidt's telephone call? More importantly, did it have anything to do with the memory-stick? Schmidt had warned him about having unpleasant partners. More important still, were the people responsible still there and, if so, what had they done to Schmidt — and what might they do to Harry?

The American started back the way he had come in, but stopped and turned when a groan from beyond the other door caught his attention.

"Schmidt?" Harry called, quickly moving over to the door. "Is that you?"

"Pa mawch."

In response to the Russian plea for help, Harry pushed the door open.

Klaus Schmidt lay just beyond, in a pool of blood. He wore blue striped pajamas and shiny brown slippers. The crimson of fresh blood stained the front of his pajama top. Within the center of the stain glinted the handle of what looked like a knife or letter-opener. Both of Schmidt's bloody hands gripped the cloth next to the handle.

"Dear God," Harry said. Then he rushed over to the fallen man, and knelt down; ignoring the spreading blood, soaking through his trouser leg. "What happened?"

"He kill me," groaned Schmidt.

"I'll ring for a doctor."

"No." he cried, extending his blood-covered hands toward Harry. "Get this out of chest, first. *Pazhalsta.*"

"Who did this to you?"

"Innokenti Rakhmelevich, the bastard."

The American gripped the letter opener and with a sharp jerk, pulled it from Schmidt's chest. "Why did he do this?"

"Memory stick. I kill him, next I see him."

"The memory stick?" Harry felt his cheeks turn pale. "Does that mean he knows about me?"

Schmidt nodded. "*Spaseeba.*"

"Try to stay calm. I'll ring for a doctor."

Harry started to rise but Schmidt reached out with one bloody hand and grabbed him by the shirt. "Wait."

"If I don't get a doctor here, quick, you're as good as dead."

"Where is memory stick? I need…" With a gasp the older man's eyes bulged and he sat up. "It worth million Euros. You give me…" Then Schmidt fell back to the floor, dead; his right hand in a death grip on the front of Harry's shirt.

There was the sound of movement from behind. Startled, Harry twisted toward it, struggling to get free of Schmidt's dead hand. A moment later, the reception clerk stepped into view. When Aznavour spotted the blood, he let go a cry of horror. Then he turned and raced away.

Harry shouted his innocence to the clerk's back. However, it was to no avail. Out in the hallway, he heard the frightened man screaming 'murderer'.

It took many seconds of prying on Schmidt's fingers to get free. Then Harry stood up and strode from the room. In the hallway, he saw a dozen or more people clustered around the clerk, looking terrified.

"*Meurtrier.*" shouted the clerk, pointing at Harry. "*Assassin.*"

Aznavour and the others retreated from Harry's approach, their eyes locked upon the bloody letter-opener still in the American's hand.

"You don't understand." Harry protested. "It wasn't me. I…"

"He still holds the dagger," someone shouted.

"We heard him shouting angrily," someone else said.

Yet another bleated, "Look at the blood on him."

"You've got it all wrong," Harry dropped the blood-smeared weapon. "Schmidt was dying when I found him. I..."

A man rushed from one of the other suites holding a Lugar pistol.

When the stranger took aim at Harry, the American realized that further protest was useless. He quickly turned and raced off.

A second later, the there was a loud explosion and a bullet buzzed past the American's ear, instantly lengthening Harry's stride.

***

"Where's Kalandarishvili?" Mikhail Shkarov asked, as Innokenti Rakhmelevich climbed behind the Peugeot's steering wheel.

"Dead."

"I told you..."

"The bastard tried to stab me."

"Stabbed? I heard a shot."

"Not my doing." Rakhmelevich closed the car door.

Shkarov held out his hand. "Give me the memory-stick."

"Kalandarishvili didn't have it."

"He must have it, you fool!"

"Kalandarishvili told me he'd slipped it to an American on the ferry."

"He was playing you."

Rakhmelevich wagged his head. "I don't think so."

"Couldn't you have disarmed Kalandarishvili?" Shkarov flared. "As it stands, he's dead and we've got nothing."

"Relax." The patch-eyed Chechnyan started the car's engine. "I know who the American is, and I know where he is. We'll have the memory stick within the hour."

"More of your empty promises, I don't need."

"I'm telling you the American is as good as in our hands."

"Who is this American?"

"A Jew by the name of Harry Bronstein."

Shkarov frowned in suspicious disbelief. "Kalandarishvili hated Jews."

"He must've taken a liking to this one."

"Where do we find Bronstein?"

"Alessandra Hotel." Rakhmelevich put the car into gear and it rumbled away from the curb, merging quickly into traffic. "I called and verified. Bronstein's got a suite there."

After lighting a cigarette Shkarov said, "I smell blood. Kalandarishvili's, or yours?"

"His."

"You killed him because you wanted to."

Rakhmelevich glanced over at his partner quickly and then put his eyes back on the pavement. "You'd have done the same, under the circumstances."

"Did you think to search him?" Shkarov spat out the side-window; his emotions rife with anger, and disgust.

"Of course I searched him. The hotel suite, as well. I had barely started when the telephone rang. I thought it might be you, so I answered. It was the reception clerk. He said that Schmidt had a visitor. I told him to send the guy back tomorrow morning. But, that must not have set well. I'd just finished when someone knocked on Kalandarishvili's door."

"Were you seen?"

"No. I slipped out onto the verandah and then crawled across to the adjoining suite. There, I jimmied the sliding door to get in. After that, I made my way to the hallway and down the back stairs to the lobby."

"Could it have been Bronstein wanting to see Kalandarishvili?"

"At this time of the morning?"

"Who else might pay Kalandarishvili a visit?" Shkarov smiled a small weary smile. "Does Bronstein know what is on the memory stick?"

"Kalandarishvili didn't say."

"I assume you gave him the opportunity to explain his relationship with the American?"

"I did what I had to do, Shkarov!"

"How often I have heard that tired wheeze cross your lips."

"It all happened so fast. I just reacted."

There was a moment or two of engine rumble. Then Mikhail Shkarov asked, "Was there cash in the room?"

"No. Why?"

"I was just considering possibilities."

"Like what?"

"Like the possibility that Kalandarishvili sold the stick when he left the hotel."

Rakhmelevich shook his head. "Kalandarishvili told me he bribed the American to bring the stick into France, to get it past the GRU. He said the American still had it."

"I wonder how Kalandarishvili knew the GRU were closing in?"

"He knew your tart was feeding them information."

"Nonsense."

"He tried to kill her, didn't he? You heard how she wanted to watch Kalandarishvili die. She sure as hell didn't want him talking to you."

"Galina has her faults, I grant you. She's vindictive and greedy. Nevertheless, my beautiful blonde isn't stupid. Helping the GRU would've reaped her nothing but my revenge."

Rakhmelevich snorted, "She's made a fool of you."

There was a long moment of engine noise, car horns and tire whining. "Jew or not, I can see where Kalandarishvili might pay Bronstein to bring the stick into France," Shkarov said tightly. "With the GRU on his tail, he would've been worried about Calais. What troubles me is why he didn't drive to Bronstein's hotel to recover the stick?"

"Obviously, he and the American agreed to meet at that café Kalandarishvili holed up in on the way to Paris. It's the only explanation for the time he spent there."

"Only explanation?" Shkarov mocked. "I watched the man eat three bowls of soup and half a loaf of bread."

"He also made a telephone call."

"If they agreed to meet," mused Shkarov, "why didn't Bronstein show?"

"Maybe he got cold feet? Maybe he got lost? How would I know?"

Shkarov shook his head. "Something's not right about this."

"You worry too much."

"I think Schmidt tossed out a ferry passenger's name hoping to save his own hide. He'd learned where Bronstein would be staying. He hoped you'd take the bait, and leave." Shkarov stopped, his upper teeth biting into his lower lips. Then he murmured, "Or, was there more than survival behind Kalandarishvili's cooperation?"

"He couldn't have been lying." The patch-eyed Chechnyan swallowed thickly. "He couldn't have been."

"And Santa Claus can't be a myth, eh?"

"Where else could the stick be but with Bronstein?"

"Kalandarishvili's suite comes to mind."

"It wasn't. I'm telling you, I tore the place apart."

Shkarov's made a derisive noise, deep in his throat. "For the GRU to catch up with Kalandarishvili, they must have been following him the entire time."

"So what?"

"So why did they wait until Calais to make a move?"

"You know how they are. GRU Field Operatives don't do shit unless Moscow Central authorizes it."

For several more minutes, the Peugeot rumbled through Paris traffic. Then Shkarov said, "Why didn't Galina know about Bronstein?"

"I say she did. I say she kept quiet about it."

"How would silence profit her?"

"You think every woman falls for you. You think they're all eager to do your bidding. Get it through your head, Shkarov, that's not the way it is. They hook up with you to get what they can from your wallet."

"As I said, how would keeping quiet about Bronstein profit my greedy blonde?"

"She could've been promised money."

"She could've been. Galina is no fool. She knows better than to trust the GRU." There was another length of traffic noise before Shkarov resumed speaking. "Cheng will think the worst when he reads about Kalandarishvili."

"How will he know? Kalandarishvili registered at the hotel as Klaus Schmidt."

"Fingerprints don't lie. The French police will send Kalandarishvili's prints to Interpol. The story will hit the presses about a Russian criminal murdered in Paris." He studied his fingernails. "Your impulsive act might kill our deal with the Chinese."

Rakhmelevich glanced over at his companion frowning. "Why would Cheng care about Kalandarishvili?"

"When Cheng and I made the deal, he warned me about creating complications." Shkarov voice went tense with renewed irritation. "At the very least he'll use Kalandarishvili's death as justification to cut our price."

"Then we won't sell to him," Rakhmelevich said, negligently.

"If not to him, then who? As much as I boasted to Cheng about entertaining other offers, there are none."

"Maybe not now, but in time…"

Shkarov cut in with, "Are you certain Bronstein will be at his hotel when we arrive?"

"No. But, the clerk said Bronstein was expected — unless there was a God and Bronstein was struck dead."

"I take it he hates Bronstein?"

"That's how it sounded."

"Kalandarishvili doing business with a Jew." There was a hint of mockery in Shkarov's voice. "That is one for the books."

"He was in a tight situation. He made do, no different than you or me."

"Did you consider the possibility that Bronstein might be GRU?"

"A Jew in the GRU? Don't make me laugh."

"You idiot! Aliases are part and parcel to GRU operations, just like any other country's espionage."

"If Bronstein was GRU, why would Kalandarishvili give him the memory stick?"

"Your brain is one of a kind, Rakhmelevich," Shkarov chuckled.

"I may not have your smarts, but if Bronstein was GRU there'd have been no need for Anitchka to tail Kalandarishvili."

"She followed for a far more insidious reason."

A windshield-blurring downpour started. The patch-eyed Chechnyan turned on the wipers.

"Is Bronstein staying at the hotel alone?" Shkarov asked.

"I didn't ask."

Shkarov cocked an eyebrow at his partner. "We could be walking into a trap and you didn't ask?"

"Bronstein doesn't know we're onto him. How could there be a trap?"

"Anitchka and the Customs Agents detained Kalandarishvili for nearly an hour in Calais." Shkarov gave his head an exasperated shake. "That was plenty of time for her to convince our dead friend to make a deal."

"What kind of deal?"

"He told her about us, of course, to avoid a death sentence for espionage. She, then, informed her father about our unexpected resurrection. Pasha then sent his team to join forces with Bronstein." His face tightened sharply. "That's why Kalandarishvili gave you Bronstein's name. To send us right into Nabatov's sights."

"I don't believe it."

"That's the only way this mess works."

A quick jerky smile played across Rakhmelevich's face. "If that's the deal Kalandarishvili made, why did Anitchka hang around at the Montmartre?"

"To watch for us, of course. She knew we'd be looking for Kalandarishvili. She knew we'd track him down. Once Anitchka confirmed that we were alive, she contacted her father. I saw her using her cell-phone, didn't I? Pasha told her to follow us, and keep him informed." Shkarov twisted in the seat to look out the rear window, at the sea of headlights following. "Kalandarishvili told you just what she told him to say. She knew it would send us after Bronstein, just like it did.

Only when we reach the Alessandra, Bronstein won't be alone. Pasha and his gang will be there. They'll hold fire until Anitchka arrives. Then, you and I will be cut down in crossfire." He twisted back, nervously wetting his lips. "How can so much go so wrong in so little time?"

"You're paranoid."

"Am I?"

Rakhmelevich's big hands flexed upon the steering wheel. His voice was thin and brittle. "Do we go to the Alessandra, or not?"

"We don't have a choice." Shkarov let go a long sigh. "It will be good to see Pasha, again."

"I say we forget it. I say…"

"The state of our finances nullifies your quivering ideas," Shkarov cut in, bitterly. Then he pointed at the windshield. "Next right is the Alessandra Hotel." He pulled his pistol from its shoulder holster and checked for a round in the chamber. "Tonight is as good a night to die as any." Then he looked over at his partner, and grinned. "You are willing to die for the cause, aren't you, Rakhmelevich?"

"The Chechnyan cause, yes. Our business with Cheng? I'm not so sure."

Shkarov laughed. "Rakhmelevich with nerves of steel, and a buckling spine."

Chapter 6

Twenty minutes after leaving the Montmartre Hotel, Harry Bronstein was still driving aimlessly. Heavy rain kept the windshield wipers on the Range Rover thumping. He sat tilted over the steering wheel; his eyes glazed upon the road ahead, his thoughts running wild.

"Shit, shit, shit!" As Harry saw it, he would face arrest on a charge of murder before the sun came up. "Why in hell did I go to the Montmartre?"

Harry knew that an American arrested in France had few legal options. Unlike English-speaking countries, which use Common Law, also known as an adversarial system, France supported Civil Law, sometimes referred to as an inquisitorial system. In the case of murder, France's *Cour d'Assises* would take charge. Unlike a Judge in his own country, whose role was more or less to act as an umpire, an *Assises Magistrate* would take an active role in determining the truth. This meant that Harry's trial would be far from impartial. Further undermining the American's confidence were two other judicial tidbits. First, as an American, he would be a flight risk. Therefore, Harry would sit behind bars until his trial, a period of incarceration that might extend over several years. Second, should Harry's legal efforts fail, France would hand him a life-sentence in La Santé Prison; a citadel constructed in 1867 with the reputation of being the worst prison in the world.

Harry ran trembling fingers through his hair. His dark mop was soaked at the temples. The hairs were so wet, that little rivulets of nervous perspiration trickled down in front of his ears. He could not face a lifelong stay in La Santé. Somehow, he had to avoid arrest. To do that, he would have to catch a plane back to the States. Once there, he would have a good chance at thwarting efforts to extradite him. Unfortunately, to board a plane Harry would need his passport. Harry inhaled deeply through his open mouth. He would have to risk arrest by returning to the Alessandra Hotel.

An oncoming car splashed past, offering up a hiss of rain-spray. As the wipers cleared the windshield, Harry's thoughts drifted a thousand miles away and twenty years back. When he was fifteen, he had been in another criminal circumstance. Grand Theft Auto. It had not been Harry's doing. However, the evidence had spoken volumes to the contrary. A friend of his, Calvin Pickering, had picked Harry up in a car, a nice, shiny red Oldsmobile convertible. The vehicle had been fitted to the nine's with black leather, stereo and lots of glinting chrome. Not having seen Pickering driving the vehicle, before, Harry had asked about it.

"My Old Man's new wheels," Calvin had explained.

Unfortunately for Harry, that had not been the truth. Minutes after Harry had climbed into the stolen car, the police arrested the two youths.

At trial, Harry's attorney had urged him to tell the truth. Naturally, the idea of fingering his friend for the theft had been repellent. What teenager would have felt any different? However, as his mother had frequently pointed out: *"A halber emes iz a gantser lign."* *A half-truth is a whole lie.* Reluctantly, Harry had agreed.

Unfortunately, for Harry's defense, Calvin Pickering's attorney had also urged candid testimony. So, with tears flooding his eyes, and his voice fraught with emotion, Pickering had taken the stand as a prosecution witness against Harry. Not only did Calvin blame Harry for the theft, but gave a detail description of how Harry had forced him into the stolen vehicle. In the end, Harry had no chance at acquittal. What group of *Goys* would have taken the word of a Jew? In less than ten minutes, the empanelled *shiksas* and *shkotzim* had returned their verdict. Harry received probation. Not surprisingly, Calvin Pickering had gotten off Scott-free.

A horn blared from behind, jerking Harry back from his thoughts.

He looked into the rearview mirror and saw a set of flashing headlights. A moment later, the Range Rover passed through a well-lit intersection. To Harry's horror, the tailing vehicle was a police cruiser.

"Shit, shit, shit!"

The blue lights mounted to the roof of the shadowing car, flashed on.

Harry's stomach rolled, as he swung the Rover to the side of the road. However, instead of pulling in behind the American, the police cruiser roared past.

He swallowed several times, trying to regain control of his cramping bowels. Surely, the police had taken the reception clerk's statement. So, why hadn't they stopped to arrest him?

Perhaps his luck had changed. He was long overdue for something good. He caught a glimpse of his own face in the mirror. His pallor looked greenish in the light reflected from the dashboard. His tongue moved like a red sidewinder across his lower lip. It left no moisture behind.

Harry swung the rental back into the flow of traffic as his thoughts turned to Maggie, his ex-wife. What would she think of his desperate situation? Would she laugh? Would she taunt? Would she cry? Maggie, he was certain, wouldn't cry. Not over Harry's misery. She was far too vindictive.

"What do you do want from me, Harry?"

Those had been Maggie's favorite words to him, during the latter part of their marriage.

"To hell with you!"

That had become his favorite statement to her, shortly before they divorced.

It had not always been that way. Initially, Harry and Maggie had enjoyed the usual lifestyle of a newly married couple: Lots of shopping, sex, cooking, more sex, dancing, and even more sex. Then, after about a year, their relationship chilled. Maggie, the woman who initially had taken delight in providing Harry with any pleasure he desired, began to cringe beneath his touch. He had tried to discover the reason. She had refused to discuss it.

"God will get you for marrying that *zoyne*, Harry."

His mother's words to him over breakfast, on his wedding day.

"I'm going to piss on your mother's grave, Harry."

Maggie's words to Harry after the wedding reception.

When Harry reached the Alessandra Hotel, he drove past the parking lot; his eyes straining against the darkness for any sign of a police presence. After several turns around the block, without seeing hide not hair of a gendarme, Harry pulled into the lot and found a shadowy parking spot.

Harry climbed out of the Range Rover and gave the darkness another visual search. Still not seeing the police, he hurried to the hotel's rear entrance. The light above the door reminded Harry of Schmidt's tragic end. The dead man's blood still coated the American's hands. Instantly, he began to retch.

Several guests passed the American on their way out of the hotel. They gave Harry catcalls for overindulging.

He paid no attention to their misdirected mockery being far too busy with his present problem. He had to find a place to wash his hands before entering the hotel. Otherwise, the less than amiable Sidoine Benoît would ask questions. Questions Harry could not answer without further incriminating himself in Schmidt's murder. And, he had to manage this in a big hurry.

He started back to the Range Rover intending to look for an all-night spot where he could wash. Before he reached the car, Harry heard the sound of flowing water. He focused his hearing, turning his head back and forth until he caught the direction of the sound. Then Harry hurried toward it.

A few steps later, he was alone in the hotel's rear courtyard in front of a small fountain. Quickly, Harry lowered his hands into the water and scrubbed at the dried blood. It floated away, bit-by-bit giving the water a murky surface.

When he was satisfied that his hands were clean, Harry hurried into the hotel.

"You found your friend, M. Bronstein?" Sidoine Benoît asked, as Harry reached the reception desk.

The American rubbed the side of his face with a damp, clenched knuckle. "What friend?"

"M. Schmidt, of course."

"Ah, him." Harry gave the clerk a long-suffering look. "One might say that Klaus Schmidt was just about dead when I got there."

"Considering the timing of your arrival, I'm not surprised. Still, you managed to return his property?"

Harry blinked in bewilderment. "Property?"

"That which had been mismanaged on the Calais ferry."

"Oh, that." The American nodded, grinning crookedly. "You've got quite a memory."

"It is an essential part of my profession, Monsieur." Benoît cocked an eyebrow. "And, M. Schmidt's property?"

"I think I can say, without fear of contradiction, that Schmidt won't have anything mismanaged again."

"Excellent." Benoît narrowed his eyes and pressed his lips together. "You had no trouble finding the hotel?"

"None whatsoever. Surprising, considering the source of my directions. Were there any telephone calls for me, during my absence?"

"There were two. However, neither left a message."

Harry cleared his throat. "A man telephoned?"

"One caller was male. He sounded real eager to locate you."

"French?"

"A foreigner, I think."

"Any country in particular?"

"Russia, probably. His French was guttural."

Harry considered Benoît's information. Obviously, a gendarme wouldn't sound Russian. Could it have been Schmidt? No. Schmidt was dead. Or was he? Had the injury been less serious than it looked? Was it possible that Schmidt had merely fainted? Then upon recovering had telephoned Harry? Or had the telephone call been made before Schmidt's ordeal? Or worse, could the caller have been Schmidt's killer, Rakhmelevich?

"How long ago did the calls come in?" Harry asked

"About forty minutes ago, just a few minutes apart. The man telephoned first."

"The woman... Was she foreign?"

"French, I think." Benoît smiled expectantly. "Are foreigners pursuing you, M. Bronstein? Perhaps, with murderous intent? Or will my dreams not come true this night?"

"Could you get my bill ready?" Harry said. "I'd like to check out."

"Why?"

"I want to leave."

The clerk's face froze, as if Harry had suggested that French cooking was a gastronomical obscenity. "Don't you like your suite?"

"It's fine."

"Then, why do you want to leave?"

"I don't like you."

Benoît grimaced impatiently. "I must charge the full price for the room because..."

Harry cut in with, "Just charge the damn thing to my credit card, Okay? I'm in a hurry."

The clerk pointed at the splotch of blood on Harry's shirt from where Schmidt had grabbed it. "That looks like blood." His mouth tilted up at the corners to make a smiling-clown face. "Were you assaulted, M. Bronstein? Perhaps brutally? Resulting in injuries that are hideously painful and rampant with life-threatening possibilities?"

Harry Bronstein pulled his jacket closed to cover the stain, turned, and quickly headed for the elevators.

It was not until Harry was in the elevator and pressed the call-button for his floor that he remembered the memory-stick intended for Schmidt. He had to get rid of it. If the worst happened, and the police arrived before he left the hotel, the fact that Harry maliciously altered the stick would prove the animosity between him and Schmidt. Revenge, after all, was a very common motive for murder. The other memory stick, the unaltered one, Harry intended to keep. On its own it did not compromise his situation. Moreover, it might be useful in getting the CIA to locate Rakhmelevich and turn him over to French authorities, should extradition become an issue.

Across from the elevators, he spotted a trashcan. Quickly Harry abandoned the lift, went over to the bin, and deposited the stick. Then he got back on the elevator just before the doors closed.

On the screeching ride up to the third floor, Harry cursed his vengeful temperament. Why in hell hadn't he just let Schmidt come to him? Why in hell had he gone to Paris in the first place? Why in hell hadn't he listened to his mother and not married Maggie?

Harry was still engrossed in self-imputation when he stepped into his suite. For a moment, nothing registered. Then his eyes widened as Harry took in the disaster that lay before him. Someone had ransacked the place. With a cry of concern, Harry rushed forward looking for his computer. Then terror took hold as he considered another possibility. What if Schmidt's killer, Rakhmelevich, was responsible for this mess? What if…

The soft click of the lock, after the hotel room door closed, came to his ears. Harry stiffened. Then, he smelled lavender aftershave: a fragrance completely foreign to his toilette. Slowly, the American turned.

Standing in front of the only point of escape was a burly, patch-eyed man wearing a blue suit. He held a pistol affixed with a silencer.

"Slumming?" Harry's body shuddered inside his clothes, twitching like a naked nerve against a chunk of ice.

"You kidding," the other said in Russian, taking a step toward Harry.

"I have to tell you…," Harry said, in the same language. "I'm not the kidding type. Something about having bad timing, when it comes to jokes." He retreated several steps, his terror growing as he noted the blood on the other man's clothing. "My mother thinks I got it from my father. I'm not convinced. You see, she always referred to Daddy as a bad joke in need of a good punch line."

Another voice, behind Harry, said in Russian, "You are addressing Innokenti Rakhmelevich, Mr. Bronstein."

Harry whirled to face the speaker. This fellow's suit was dark gray. He, also, held a pistol affixed with a silencer. His eyes continually moved; the whites naked and glaring.

"I've heard of Rakhmelevich," Harry said. "Nothing good. Are you his keeper? Or the one who left his cage open?"

"My name is Mikhail Shkarov." The second intruder waggled his pistol; grim lines cratered his face. "You have something of mine. I want it."

"I don't know what you're talking about."

"The memory stick, Mr. Bronstein."

"Memory stick?" the American echoed, feigning ignorance.

"Don't attempt to deceive me, Mr. Bronstein. I know that Kalandarishvili gave it to you."

"Kalandarishvili?" Harry asked, in genuine bewilderment.

"You knew him as Klaus Schmidt."

"Ah, that Kalandarishvili. I should have guessed. Silly me for not seeing the connection."

Sirens sounded in the distance, as they approaching the hotel.

Harry smiled. Help, of a sort, might be on the way. If he could keep his visitors there until the police arrived, Harry's worries over Kalandarishvili, would be over — assuming the two guns pointed in his direction did not go off.

"You and your pal are Chechnyans." Harry rubbernecked between the two men, somewhat cocky at the prospect of being in on a killer's arrest. "On holiday? Or has Paris become a terrorist's retreat?"

"How did you deduce our nationality?" Shkarov squinted, splaying his legs as he appraised the American.

"I have an ear for dialects." In spite of the forced calm in the American's voice Harry could feel the pulse jumping in his throat. "I'm curious… What does your kind of spineless shit do for fun, when you run out of explosives?"

Shkarov gritted his teeth. "Where is it?"

"Your memory stick?" Harry spread out his arms for an instant as if preparing for crucifixion. "I don't have it."

"Do not try my patience, Mr. Bronstein."

"The police are nearly here. Shall we all go downstairs and meet them?" Harry struck an attitude with his left hand on his hip. With his right hand, he made a vague, albeit trembling, sweep through the air. "I think they'll have questions for Rakhmelevich. If not, I'll prompt them to ask about his bloody clothes."

Shkarov's eyes dipped, slightly, and focused upon the bloodstains on Harry's clothes. "What about yours?"

Harry drew his lips back and made a half-hearted attempt to lick them. "Mine are the result of your pal's efforts. Something a polygraph should prove."

"So you did visit Kalandarishvili?"

"I happened to be in the neighborhood."

"You left the memory stick there?"

"You know how dying people are. They want to take everything to the hereafter." Harry jabbed a thumb over one shoulder, at Rakhmelevich. "I don't think your patch-eyed friend will pass his polygraph."

Mikhail Shkarov raised the pistol and took aim at Harry's head. "If you left the memory stick in Kalandarishvili's suite, then the police have it," he said laboriously. "Which means you're no good to me."

"Wait!" the American shouted, suddenly realizing the tenuousness of his situation. "I didn't leave it in the suite. I panicked, after seeing Schmidt. I dropped it into one of the trash cans in the hotel lobby."

The sounds of the approaching sirens grew louder.

Shkarov's voice was strained and harsh. "I don't believe you."

"Look, you've searched the suite," Harry said. "Search me. Then, when you realize that I don't have the stick, I'll take you to it. What do you have to lose? You can always kill me."

"You stalling bastard!" The patch-eyed man rushed over to Harry and twisted him around.

With a desperation born from fear, Harry put all his weight behind a thrust with his right knee to Rakhmelevich's groin.

The patch-eyed man, buckled in agony.

Harry gave the whimpering antagonist a shove and rushed for the door.

As the American reached it, there was a popping sound. Instantly, wood splinters from the jamb flew in all directions. Harry stopped and raised his hands.

"One more step will be your last, Mr. Bronstein," Shkarov warned.

Harry turned to face the two Chechnyans, his hands still overhead.

Shkarov tilted his head toward Rakhmelevich, who was still trying to regain his feet. "Help him up."

"He's no friend of mine," Harry said, with boyish candor.

Shkarov kept the pistol on the American and extended his free hand. Rakhmelevich gripped the offered limb and managed to get back on this pins.

"I'm going to kill him." The patch-eyed Chechnyan took a staggering step toward Harry.

Mikhail Shkarov blocked his partner's path. "Don't be impulsive." Then Shkarov aimed his pistol at Harry. "Mr. Bronstein is going to take us to the memory stick."

From the loudness of the sirens, the police would be at the Alessandra in less than a minute. All Harry, had to do was continue to stall.

"What are friends for?" said Harry, grinning with genuine pleasure at Rakhmelevich's misery.

"He's lying!" Rakhmelevich screamed

***

In two strides, the patch-eyed Chechnyan was in front of the American. Quickly Rakhmelevich rummaged through Harry's pockets. Finding nothing, he let go a howl of rage and swung a heavy fist, knocking Harry to the floor; unconscious.

"You killed him!" shouted Shkarov.

"I didn't hit him hard enough."

"I don't see him breathing." Mikhail Shkarov quickly rushed forward and squatted next to the American. He pressed fingers against Harry's carotid artery. "Damn you, Rakhmelevich! I can't find a pulse." His breath went out in an angry surge. "Wait. There it is. Just barely."

"He's got the stick, I tell you."

"Hidden where neither of us could find it?"

"That memory stick's worth a million Euros. He's not about to throw it away." Rakhmelevich's voice was high and harsh. "We just haven't found it."

The sirens fell silent, outside the hotel. Mikhail Shkarov stood up and hurried over to the window. In the parking, below, lot he saw several police cars; their blue lights flashing.

"The time for searching is over. The police are here."

Rakhmelevich started for the door, but Shkarov called after him. "Did you forget something?"

"What?"

"We're taking Bronstein with."

"We can't! They'll see us."

"The police are not looking for us." Shkarov pointed to Harry. "I suspect they've come for Bronstein."

"Why?"

"Unlike yours, I'm certain his visit to Kalandarishvili did not go unnoticed."

Shkarov returned to Harry. As he knelt, Shkarov took a small leather case from inside his coat and unzipped it. After withdrawing a syringe and a small bottle of brown fluid from the case, he filled the syringe from the bottle. Quickly, he pulled the American's shirt collar down to expose the carotid artery. Then, the Chechnyan injected the American.

"That will keep Bronstein quiet for an hour, or so." Shkarov stood, returning the syringe and bottle to the leather case. "Pick him up. We'll take him down the hall."

"To what end?" the other Chechnyan demanded, his panic growing. "The police will be on this floor in less than a minute. They'll take both the steps and the elevator. We'll be trapped."

"Our destination is the linen room. You'll hide in there with Bronstein while I deal with the police. When they leave, we'll take Bronstein out through the rear exit."

"It isn't worth the risk, Shkarov!"

"I don't agree."

"You can't believe that story about tossing the stick."

"No. However, I do believe the American hid the memory stick, intending to sell it." Shkarov smiled. "I'll make him tells us where it is."

"What if the cops search the linen room?"

Shkarov closed his eyes. The lids twitched a little. He spoke with them closed, as if not being able to bear the sight of his companion. "You should have anticipated these difficulties when you killed Kalandarishvili." His eyes opened and Shkarov pointed at Harry. "Stop stalling and pick him up."

Rakhmelevich bent over and grabbed Harry by the arms. Then, with the assistance of Shkarov, he slung the American over one shoulder. Two strides later, the two Chechnyans were out in the hallway. From the opposite direction came the whine of elevators.

"Hurry, damn you!" Shkarov said.

When they reached the linen room, Shkarov took out a credit card and slipped it between the latch and the jamb, thus opening the locked door. Then, with unconscious Harry as baggage, they stepped inside and closed the door.

"Set him down," Shkarov said.

Rakhmelevich bent over, tumbling Harry onto the floor.

"Keep alert," said Shkarov. "I'll misdirect the police in the direction I want them to go." He placed his ear to the door and listened. After a few seconds, he pulled the door open a crack. "When you hear them leave, get ready to move Bronstein."

After his partner returned to the hallway, Rakhmelevich closed the door and then pressed his ear against it, listening intently. A few seconds later, he heard running feet approaching from two directions. Then Shkarov's voice came through the door.

"What's happened officers?"

"My name is Lt. Damien Fournier, *Police Nationale*. I'm looking for an American by the name of Harry Bronstein."

"As you and your men will discover, the American isn't in his rooms," Shkarov said. Glibly. "He left a few minutes ago."

"What direction did he take?"

"He literally ran toward the stairs."

"Get some men to the rail depot, the Metro and the airport," Fournier ordered, in French.

Rakhmelevich heard mumbled orders followed by hurried footfalls rushing off.

"Bronstein seemed like such a nice chap." Shkarov said. "What did he do?"

"We are investigating a murder, Monsieur."

"How terrible."

"May I see some identification?"

"I have my driving license."

Rakhmelevich heard the sound of rustling clothes. Then Shkarov said, "As you see, my name if Pierre du Pre and I live in Alsace. I have a vineyard, there. You should visit and taste my wine."

"You know M. Bronstein well?" Fournier asked.

"I don't know him intimately, you understand. What I mean is, we are not friends. We met on the ferry from Dover to Calais."

"What did you and Bronstein talk about, during the crossing?"

"Actually, he did most of the talking. Bronstein was very angry. Apparently, a man named Schmidt had cheated him. I don't know the details. However, I did hear Bronstein vow to kill Schmidt. At the time, I thought it was just foolish talk. You know how drunks get. Otherwise, I would have reported it."

"We will need a formal statement from you."

"Tonight?"

"Your cooperation would be appreciated, Monsieur."

"What about tomorrow morning?" Shkarov pleaded. "I'm expecting a guest; a young lady. She's flying in from Spain. The taxi will be here any moment."

"Very well. Tomorrow morning, then." There was a rustling of clothing. "My card. I will expect to see you at 11 rue des Saussaies no later than 10:00 am. Understood?"

"I promise to be on time, Lieutenant."

Rakhmelevich heard the sound of more footsteps, and then there were slow steady strides toward the linen room. A moment later, there was a soft knock on the door. Rakhmelevich cautiously opened it. Shkarov stepped inside.

"Well?" asked the patch-eyed Chechnyan.

"As you heard, they suspect Bronstein of killing Kalandarishvili. How very lucky for you." Shkarov pointed down at the unconscious American. "How is he?"

"Bronstein's snoring so loud I thought the police would hear." Rakhmelevich bent over, and with Shkarov's assistance, grabbed up the unconscious man and laid him across one shoulder. "We'll never get away with this."

"Relax. I'll go down the back stairs first, in case they've left someone to watch. If not, we'll drag him between us as if he were drunk. No one will take any notice."

"Are you seriously going to the police, tomorrow?"

"What better way to keep their investigation going in the direction I want?" Shkarov grinned. "With Bronstein under police scrutiny instead of you, Cheng will have less to complain about."

"But, we cannot allow Bronstein to live."

"What's your point?"

"If he's dead, the gendarmes cannot arrest him."

"We will leave his body where it will be found. The police, after examining him, will assume that Kalandarishvili's associates killed Bronstein." Shkarov chuckled, softly. "Which, coincidentally, will be the truth." Then his face became closed and dark. "We cannot afford any more mistakes, Rakhmelevich."

Chapter 7

"**W**here in hell is she?" Pasha Nabatov paced the front room of Ambrosii Golovkin's spacious, Paris apartment. The trouser legs of his gray suit whistled slightly as he moved. His blue shirt showed dark splotches of perspiration. His crimson necktie dangled loosely around his throat. "It's nearly two in the morning."

A French-style window in the apartment's north wall opened onto a second-story balcony, girdled by white ironwork. The balcony overlooked Rue De La Sebastopol. In the darkness below, a pulsing stream of vehicle headlamps passed by. An arch went through the apartment's west wall. Beyond it was a dimly-lit corridor punctuated by several closed doors. The south wall had another archway leading to a spacious kitchen. At the middle of the kitchen a half dozen wooden chairs encircled a large wooden table. Coffee mugs and a makeshift ashtray, consisting of the cut-down base of an M1937 howitzer-shell, occupied the tabletop. Across the kitchen, yet another arch accessed the hallway that led to the apartment's entrance. A maroon davenport backed against the windowless east wall, a matching armchair on either side. To the right of one chair was a huge roll top desk, its oak wood dusty from lack of use. On its writing surface sat an ivory cigarette box with gilt hinges. Oak parquet, set in a zigzag pattern, covered the floors throughout the dwelling.

"Maybe Kalandarishvili stopped to eat?" Kazimir Sokolof stood near the balcony, using a thumbnail to scrape at a food stain on his brown tie. His brown suit looked like he had slept in it. The collar of his white shirt was yellow with perspiration. "You know how Kalandarishvili can eat."

"Nearly as much as you." Nabatov eyed the bearded man with sharp impatience. "Try Anitchka's cell phone again."

Kazimir let go of his tie and took out a clumsy, gray satellite phone. He punched the recall button. After many seconds of ringing, he shut off the device.

"No answer, Pasha."

An interior door opened and closed. A moment later, Ambrosii Golovkin came into the room, his footfalls silent in leather sandals. He was a tall spindly man of the red-haired variety with milky, freckled skin. His face was gaunt; all nose with no chin. A down-turned, fuzzy moustache nearly covered his protruding upper lip. His Adam's apple jutted like a golf ball from his lean neck. A yellowish stain marred one knee of his tan slacks. His green sweater had holes in both elbows.

"Moscow wants Kalandarishvili alive," Golovkin announced.

"So Moscow can execute him?" Kazimir asked, his face widening with a grin.

"Only after a fair trial." Golovkin gave the bearded man a wink. Then he directed his attention to a pacing Pasha Nabatov. "What about Anitchka?"

The older man ground his teeth and shrugged, his heels clicking loudly on the floor.

"Can't reach her," Kazimir said.

Golovkin put his hands to his narrow hips. "I'm certain there's nothing to worry about, Pasha."

"Something's happened to her." Nabatov's His big hands flailed the air as he tramped about the rectangular space. "When I get my hands on Kalandarishvili, I'll return him to Moscow in a box."

Golovkin tossed a concerned look at Kazimir. The other let go an exasperated sigh. Anitchka would have contacted her father, if possible. Her failure to do so strongly suggested that something unexpected, and probably unpleasant, had happened to her. Neither was going to share their fears with their superior.

"Why doesn't she listen to me?" Pasha Nabatov stopped and made a pleading gesture at the other men. "Am I not a good father?"

"She's no longer your little girl, Pasha." Golovkin's eyes dipped and he addressed his feet with, "Anitchka's always been strong."

"I can vouch for that, Pasha," said Kazimir. "She yells at me — especially when I don't deserve it."

"You're not helping, Kazimir," Golovkin said, out of one side of his mouth.

"Even as a little girl, she disobeyed." Nabatov thrust a finger toward the high ceiling. "I blame her mother."

"But, your wife died in childbirth." Golovkin's long face showed confusion as he looked up and caught his superior's stare. "How can she be at fault?"

"For dying, is for how!"

"In order to intercept Kalandarishvili, Pasha, we had to cover all points of entry." Kazimir casually moved away from the balcony, both hands in his trouser pockets. "Without Anitchka, we could not have done it. You had no choice but to assign her as you did."

"I'm certain Anitchka followed your orders to the letter, Pasha," said Golovkin. "Which means there's nothing to worry about."

"Since when has my daughter ever followed my orders?" Pasha Nabatov's expression flashed from anger to despair. "I should have blocked her recruitment by the *spetsnaznacheniya*."

"If you had done that Anitchka, would never have infiltrated that Chechnyan outpost in Duba-Yurt," Kazimir said. "And you would never have popped your vest buttons when she received her medals for assassinating the leader of that terrorist group."

"You're pushing your luck, Kazimir," Golovkin said, under his breath.

Again, the white-haired Russian's hands became animated. "Why is she doing this to me?"

"Anitchka might've had car trouble," the spindly man said, in an encouraging way. "Peugeot's are always breaking down. It's what makes them the pride of France's rental fleet."

"You see, Pasha?" Kazimir said. "There could be a hundred reasons we don't hear from her — all French."

"A hundred reasons?" Nabatov looked at the bearded Russian sharply. "A hundred reasons her phone doesn't respond?"

"Béarnaise sauce is insidious," Kazimir said, almost absently.

"Are you telling me you tampered with Anitchka's phone?"

"I had nothing to do with it, Pasha," Kazimir said. "But, even if something did happen, it was an accident."

"I'll give you an accident, you…"

Golovkin cut in, soothingly, "Anitchka's a clever girl, Pasha. She'll be fine."

"Too damn clever." Nabatov pulled out an age-blackened briar pipe and started to fill it. "Even as a little girl, she outsmarted me."

"That was because you weren't strict enough."

"Let it go, Kazimir," Golovkin warned.

Pasha Nabatov shifted restlessly. "I should've have put her into a convent the day she was born."

"But, you're not Orthodox, Pasha," the bearded Russian pointed out.

"Shouldn't you be dialing her number?" Nabatov shouted, his eyes fixed upon Kazimir Sokolof.

A bell rang from another part of the apartment.

"That's probably her." Golovkin hurried off in response.

Kazimir Sokolof and Pasha Nabatov turned to face the kitchen, expectantly.

"I think you should give Anitchka a good scolding for making us worry," said Kazimir. "She's always faulting me and I never do nothing wrong — mostly."

"Nothing wrong? You, you... For two kopecks I would send you back to Moscow with Kalandarishvili's corpse!"

Kazimir smiled proudly. "As a special escort, Pasha?"

"No! As his coffin's cohabitant."

"What did I tell you?" Golovkin called, as he led Anitchka into the kitchen. "She's safe and sound."

Pasha Nabatov pushed Kazimir out of the way and rushed into the other room to confront his daughter. "Where in hell have you been?"

"Doing my job, Poppa."

"Then why in hell didn't you keep me informed?"

She took a cellular phone from the pocket of her jacket. It was a clone of the bulky unit Kazimir carried. "Because this damned GRU shit quit working!"

"The *Glavnoye Razvedyvatel'noye Upravleniye* does not issue shit," rebuked Kazimir, as he entered the kitchen. "Sure, sometimes you don't get the right number. But, Boris Belskaia, in GRU purchasing, got those at a big discount from..."

"It's never worked right," Anitchka cut in. Then she shook an accusing finger at Kazimir. "You took delivery of these phones. What in hell did you do to mine?"

"Nothing."

"Nothing? It reeks of vinegar and rancid butter."

"Belskaia says these are the best cell-phones in the world." Kazimir retorted. "They even work under water."

"There. You see, Anitchka?" said Pasha Nabatov. "It even works under..." Abruptly her father stopped and scowled at Kazimir. "What in hell good is it under water?"

Kazimir shrugged. "That's what Belskaia told me."

"Belskaia is so crooked a fair wind would screw him into the Siberian turf," Anitchka complained. She tossed the useless phone onto the kitchen table. "He collects kickbacks, and we get shit." Then she pointed at the cellular phone, her eyes once more glaring at Kazimir Sokolof. "Did you dunk this in water?"

Kazimir hesitated, his frantic thoughts twisting his face into a worried grimace. "It has not been near water — more or less."

Golovkin gave out a dry cackle. "My nose tells me it kept company with freshly cut tarragon."

"Never mind the phone." Pasha waggled a finger in front of his daughter's face. "What about Kalandarishvili?"

Anitchka went over to the stove. She picked up the coffee pot from a burner and filled one of the mugs sitting on the adjacent counter. Then she took the mug over to the kitchen table.

"Kalandarishvili is dead," she said, and sat down.

"Dead," echoed Kazimir, in surprise. Then his eyes narrowed at her. "Why in hell did you kill him?"

Her eyes closed for a second, and then her lids rolled back like a doll.

"Of course she didn't kill him." Golovkin took a bottle of peach brandy from one of the cupboards. He brought it to the table and poured some into Anitchka's mug. "How can you even suggest such a thing, Kazimir?" The spindly Russian settled into the chair next to Anitchka and gave the young woman a coaxing smile. "You didn't kill Kalandarishvili, did you?"

"Of course I didn't!"

"Then what happened to him?" Nabatov flopped into the chair across the table from his daughter.

"From the beginning." Kazimir sat down next to Golovkin and picked up the brandy bottle. "There is nothing like a little refreshment to help a good story with a very bad ending." He grabbed one of the mugs from the table and poured several ounces of liquor into it.

"When Kalandarishvili arrived in Calais, he didn't have the memory stick," she said, taking a sip of her mug's potent brew. "In fact, he didn't have anything suspicious on him or in his luggage or in his car. He did, however, have a face full of scratches."

"Ah," said Kazimir authoritatively, "he cut himself shaving."

"The kind of marks left by an angry woman's fingernails." She tossed the bearded man a scathing look.

Her father leaned closer, interested in Anitchka's story. "Did you ask about the woman?"

"Of course, Poppa. But, Kalandarishvili claimed the injuries resulted from a fall."

"No doubt, while he was shaving."

"Stop interrupting, Kazimir," Nabatov warned.

"It was obvious he was lying," she said. "So, I made the Customs Officers perform a very thorough search of his person."

Golovkin laughed. "Every orifice probed, eh?"

"Stop making it sound like fun, Ambrosii." Kazimir winced. "They put their whole hand up there."

The sound of steel meeting flint rasped across the table. Then a yellow flame formed on the wick of Pasha Nabatov's aging lighter. A moment later, the white-haired man held the miniature torch just above his pipe's bowl, setting the tobacco afire. As he puffed, a spiral of bluish smoke coiled above his head and then snaked toward the ceiling.

"I hid a transmitter on Kalandarishvili's car," Anitchka said. "After that, I had customs release him. Then I used the receiver, in my car, to follow Kalandarishvili at a safe distance. He drove aimlessly, for several hours. He stopped and went inside an all-night café. A few minutes later, I was able to observe him from my car using binoculars. Kalandarishvili ate several bowls of food. While doing so, he kept checking his watch. I assumed he was expecting someone. After about an hour, without making contact, Kalandarishvili made a telephone call. He spoke to someone for about a minute. Then he left the café, headed for Paris. The route he took was roundabout, as if he was concerned about a tail. Eventually, he stopped at the Montmartre Hotel.

"When I reached the Montmartre, I tried to phone you. As I explained, my cell-phone did not work. I went inside the hotel. I showed the reception clerk my DSGE identification and described Kalandarishvili. The clerk told me that Kalandarishvili registered under the name of Klaus Schmidt. He had suite 204. I asked if Kalandarishvili was in his suite. The clerk told me that Kalandarishvili had gone out right after putting his luggage in his rooms. Since I had not seen Kalandarishvili leave the hotel, he must have slipped out the hotel's rear exit. Because I had seen Kalandarishvili eat, I assumed his exit resulted in a meeting with whomever he had spoken with during the telephone conversation. I went back to my car, again tried to reach you, failed, and waited.

"After about half an hour, without catching sight of Kalandarishvili, I went back into the hotel. The reception-clerk told me that Kalandarishvili had returned. I went back to my car and tried to call you, again." Anitchka gave the cell phone she had discarded a frustrated shove. "I don't know how many times I tried to reach you, after that. It was at least a dozen. Every time I dialed I connected with a nightclub on the Moulin Rouge offering discount tickets for private lap-dances."

"That nightclub's number comes automatic with the phone," Kazimir said, over the rim of his mug.

"Lap dances?" Nabatov interrupted, offering the bearded man a confused look.

Kazimir took a pack of Gauloises Blue cigarettes an antique Döbereiner Lamp lighter from his suit. "Lap dancing is very therapeutic, Pasha."

"It's disgusting," Anitchka said.

"It has its moments." Golovkin withed at Nabatov.

Kazimir sloughed up one of the cigarettes, caught it between is lips and tossed the pack onto the table. "You cannot imagine how a couple of those can improve the circulation, particularly in the lower…"

Anitchka cut in with, "I left my car and went looking for a *cabine téléphonique*. I thought it would be more secure than using the hotel's call boxes. The nearest one was two blocks away. Too far, I thought. Kalandarishvili might skip out before I returned. I felt I had no choice but to risk telephoning you from the hotel."

"But, I never got your call," her father said.

"Because I never completed it. When I got back inside the hotel, the reception clerk was no longer at his post. Several new guests had arrived. I heard one of them mention how they had been waiting for ten minutes, while the clerk tended an errand on one of the upper floors." She took another draw on her mug. "Not thinking anything was wrong, I headed for the stand of pay telephones at the rear of the lobby. I was just dialing, when I saw a ghost."

"I'm in no mood for jokes, Anitchka," her father scolded.

"It's no joke, Poppa. I saw Innokenti Rakhmelevich."

"Innokenti Rakhmelevich is dead," Kazimir said. A moment later, he had the Döbereiner Lamp alive, touching the flame to the cigarette. "Three years ago, he and Shkarov were killed. Isn't that so, Ambrosii?"

"Kazimir and I made the identifications of both bodies," Golovkin said.

"I can't speak for Shkarov," Anitchka said. "But, for a dead man Rakhmelevich was moving pretty good down the stairs."

"There must be some mistake," Golovkin insisted.

Pasha Nabatov took the pipe out of his mouth. "Let her finish speaking."

"There was no mistake." Anitchka gave her head a determined shake. "Rakhmelevich had fresh blood on his coat-sleeve, and a large splotch of wet blood on the front of his shirt. There was also a shiny blood smear on one of his shoes. When he neared the bottom of the steps, he buttoned his coat to conceal the stain."

"Pasha, I swear we could not be mistaken," Golovkin said.

"I'm telling all of you, I saw Rakhmelevich!"

"Anitchka? Is it possible he saw you?" her father asked.

"I don't think so." She worried her lower lip with her teeth for a moment. "I got distracted by another man. I caught just a glimpse of him as the elevator doors closed."

"Who?"

She gave an embarrassed shrug. "I think he was the American."

"Why would Rakhmelevich kill Kalandarishvili?" Kazimir asked, tipsily. "Dead or not, what's the Chechnyan's motive?"

"Innokenti Rakhmelevich doesn't need a reason,." Golovkin made a disgusted face. "*If* it was Rakhmelevich."

"What American?" her father asked.

"I'm coming to that," she said. "When I saw Rakhmelevich, because of the blood on his clothing, I assumed he'd done bad business on one of the upper floors. I set down the phone and headed for the elevator, intending to investigate. When I got into the lift, I pressed the call buttons for all the upper floors. When the doors opened on the second floor, the reception-clerk was running out of one of the suites screaming murder. I exited the car and hurried toward him. A few strides later, I saw a young American man race out of that same suite. He was chasing the clerk. The American was yelling denials, in perfect French, regarding the murder of Klaus Schmidt. However, to his discredit he had fresh blood on his shirt, knees and hands. Not only that, but in one hand he was actually carrying a bloody letter opener."

"You're certain you saw an American?" Golovkin asked. He picked up Kazimir's pack of cigarettes and lit one.

"Not just any American," she said. "I think he was the one from the elevator, I'm certain he was the one I saw leave the Calais ferry, and he looked like the one from the Berlin photo."

"The CIA operative who met with Kalandarishvili?" her father asked, in surprise.

She nodded. "Same build, same coloring, same hair and he was dressed the same."

"Did you speak with this American?"

"No. At that point, all hell broke loose. Some lunatic came out of another suite with a Lugar. The reception clerk pointed at the American and told the gun-carrier to shoot. The American ran. The gun went off. Fortunately for the American, the shot missed its mark. In the resulting confusion, I slipped into suite from which I had seen the American and the reception clerk leave; Kalandarishvili's suite.

"I found Kalandarishvili in the bathroom. He had been stabbed, his clothing searched. Items from his pockets were on the floor. I checked the other rooms. The entire suite was a shambles, furniture overturned, and drawers dumped out. If Kalandarishvili had the memory stick, I'm certain it left with his killer."

"How do you know that fellow was an American if he was speaking French?" Kazimir asked, flicking the ash from his cigarette into the makeshift ashtray.

"His build, clothing, and body-movements convinced me," Anitchka returned.

Pasha Nabatov stood and began to pace, puffing on his pipe. "If Innokenti Rakhmelevich *is* alive…"

"Poppa, I'm not mistaken."

"…then it follows," her father said, "that Mikhail Shkarov is also alive." He looked over at the other men suspiciously. "How could both of you mistakenly identify two corpses?"

The lanky Russian rose to his feet making a pleading gesture, his face the color of wet clay. "Pasha, we did our best."

"The bodies were burned beyond recognition, Pasha," chimed Kazimir, in a slurred voice. "We found bits of scorched ID on the corpses. But, without faces and fingerprints, that left only dentures for identification."

"We gave the dentures to Popovitch," said Golovkin, tilting across the table toward his superior. "He contacted our forensic dentists. It was their conclusions that led to the identification."

The apartment door opening and closing, rattled into the kitchen. Everyone jumped up, alarmed. Kazimir and Golovkin drew their pistols and started down the hall toward the sound.

"It is only Popovitch, Golovkin," called a familiar voice.

With a combined sigh of relief, the four GRU operatives resumed their seats at the table. A moment later, Dr. Dmitri Popovitch entered the kitchen.

"I was in the neighborhood so I thought I'd drop off Golovkin's allergy meds." The stooped physician took a prescription bottle from his pocket and set it on the table. "I'm sorry for interrupting."

"Golovkin," said Nabatov, getting to his feet. "Get on the horn to Moscow Center. Tell them what's happened — be sure they understand about Rakhmelevich and Shkarov."

"What about the Chechnyans?" Popovitch looked from face to face in astonishment.

"They are alive." Kazimir poured more brandy into his mug.

"Impossible," said the physician. "You and Golovkin identified their remains." He smiled proudly. "I received dental confirmation from our forensics lab."

"There is no mistake, Doctor," Anitchka said. Then she spoke to Golovkin. "There is more you should know before you contact Moscow." Her eyes returned to her father, her voice calm with certainty. "I found a notepad by the telephone in Kalandarishvili's suite. There was indented writing on the top page, so I used a pencil to raise a scrawl by rubbing the side of the lead over the dimples and groves. This disclosed a Paris telephone number. Using the telephone in the suite, I dialed that number. The reception desk at the Alessandra Hotel answered.

"After ringing off, I wiped my fingerprints from the telephone, left Kalandarishvili's suite and went down to the main floor. The reception clerk was back at his post. The poor man was still agitated. The tourists who had been waiting to register stared at him, aghast. He was on the telephone reporting Kalandarishvili's murder to the police. I heard him identify the killer as an American by the name of Harry Bronstein." Her dark eyes glinted with enthusiasm. "I returned to the pay telephones and again dialed the number on the slip of paper. This time when the Alessandra Hotel answered, I asked for Harry Bronstein. The reception clerk admitted that Bronstein was a guest at the Alessandra, but said he was out."

"Every murder turns on a floodlight," said Pasha Nabatov, grimly. His mouth turned down at the corners. "Everyone will stand naked before it. Not the least of which will be us, those who survive only in shadows." Then he spoke to his daughter. "How can you be certain the American didn't kill Kalandarishvili? You saw the blood on him. You saw the letter opener in his hand. You heard the reception clerk's accusation."

"I cannot be certain, Poppa. But, based upon what we know about Rakhmelevich, the blood I saw on his clothes, and that fact that Kalandarishvili had a long working relationship with the Chechnyans, I think it is very unlikely that Harry Bronstein was the killer."

"Then how did the American get blood on him? Why was he holding the letter opener?"

She shrugged. "That, I cannot rationalize."

"But, if the American did not kill Kalandarishvili, why was he there?" Kazimir asked, his speech thick with alcohol.

"Bronstein couldn't be CIA," Golovkin said.

"What do you mean?" Nabatov asked.

"A CIA operative wouldn't have tried to dissuade the clerk. If Bronstein was CIA, he would have left the scene as quickly as possible."

"Anitchka, could Kalandarishvili have met someone at the café before you arrived?" her father asked.

"I admit that's a possibility, Poppa. I was about seven minutes behind him."

"Perhaps Kalandarishvili expected to meet the American at the café?" The spindly Russian's narrow shoulders rose and fell, as he spoke. "Perhaps the American was late, so Kalandarishvili telephoned him? That is when they agreed to meet at the Montmartre Hotel."

"Possibly," said Anitchka. "I know Kalandarishvili did not have the stick with him when he arrived in Calais. I know the memory stick was not in his suite after he died. So I suspect the American brought the memory stick into France and attempted to deliver the stick to Kalandarishvili — but did not leave it."

"What memory stick?" Dr. Popovitch interrupted.

"It contains the locations of our missile installations in the Irkutsk region." Kazimir snuffed out his cigarette in the shell-case. "Which tossed the shit into the fan at Ulitsa Bolshaya Lubyanka, Two."

"Moscow Center knows about this?" Popovitch gasped.

"Why would Bronstein bring the memory stick into France?" Nabatov asked.

"Kalandarishvili knew we were after him," she said. "The stick was the only evidence against him. What better way to protect himself than to have someone else bring the stick across the border?"

"So, the American accepted a bribe?"

"Why not?"

Nabatov gave an agreeing nod. "So, Kalandarishvili passed the stick to Bronstein on the ferry."

"I believe so," she said. "I saw Bronstein drive through the Calais checkpoint after leaving the ferry."

"How could you recall Bronstein among the hundreds who were there?"

Anitchka flushed. "Harry Bronstein is very handsome."

Kazimir slurped at the rim of his cup, noisily. "So where does that leave us, besides not knowing the location of that damn memory stick?"

"I don't like the idea of an amateur being involved," said her father. "It will complicate matters." He resumed his seat at the table, hitched-up one trouser knee and put that leg across the other. "But, I agree that

Bronstein helped Kalandarishvili. That being said, how could Kalandarishvili know he would be searched at Calais?"

"Perhaps a touch of paranoia on Kalandarishvili's part," Popovitch suggested.

"Or maybe this is how Kalandarishvili worked border crossings?" Golovkin said.

"Both of those ideas make sense." Kazimir sounded drunk. "A thief usually follows the same path to perdition."

Golovkin squinted at the bearded Russian. "What is perdition?"

"It's someplace near St. Petersburg."

"I've never heard of it."

"Neither had I until I heard an American tourist, in Moscow, say it was the next stop on his tour."

Anitchka suddenly looked at the others, one by one. "Was anything unusual reported on the news regarding that ferry crossing?"

"Like what?" Popovitch asked.

"A murder," she replied.

"Nothing was on the news," said Golovkin. Then he frowned. "Who would've been murdered?"

"The woman who tried to take the memory stick from Kalandarishvili," she said.

Kazimir squinted dubiously at her. "How could you possibly think such an event took place?"

"The scratches on Kalandarishvili's face."

"You've lost me, Anitchka," her father said.

"We know Kalandarishvili got involved with a woman named Galina Vishnevskaya in the Irkutsk region," she said. "Both disappeared about the same time. It follows that she participated in his efforts to get the memory stick to Paris. Since she was not with him at the Montmartre, something must've happened to her. What if she tried to take the memory stick from him on the ferry?"

"Why?" asked Popovitch.

"A disagreement over profit sharing. Or, maybe she intended to sell the information, herself."

"We'd better get to the Alessandra Hotel," Pasha Nabatov said. He put his pipe down and leaned forward, his forearms upon the tabletop. "The American must still have the memory-stick."

"It's too late for that, Poppa," she said.

Her father rolled his eyes. "What do you mean?"

"After leaving the Montmartre, I drove to the Alessandra Hotel. As I arrived I saw Innokenti Rakhmelevich and another man dumping a third man into a car. The second man looked very much like Shkarov. He had the same build. However, it was too dark to see his face. From the way the clothing worn by the third man, I'm certain he was Harry Bronstein."

"If it was dark, how do you know who was who?" Kazimir asked.

"Because of body styles and movements." Anitchka resumed speaking to her father. "Rakhmelevich got behind the steering wheel. The second man got into the car on the passenger side. Then the three of them drove off. I followed. They headed…"

"Why in hell can't you ever do what I tell you?" Nabatov interrupted, slamming a fist down on the tabletop. "Didn't you realize how dangerous it would be to follow those animals?"

"Don't get your blood pressure up, Pasha," warned Popovitch. "Your daughter is safe. That is all that matters."

"Poppa, let me finish. I trailed them to what looked like an old repair shop. It was on Cité Bienaymé near the outskirts of Paris. They stopped and carried the third man inside." She opened her hands and then put them back into the table. "At that point I drove here."

Kazimir Sokolof crinkled his eyes, adding more brandy to his mug. "All this and we still don't got a memory stuck up the ass."

The white-haired man sighed wearily, reached across the table, and took the cup away from Kazimir. "Obviously, the Chechnyans went to the Alessandra Hotel to retrieve the memory stick from the American. Equally obvious, they did not get it. Therefore, they intend to extract the stick's location from Bronstein. So, what would Bronstein have done with it?"

Kazimir slurred, "Those Chechnyan bastards will put Bronstein's feet to the fire. He'll have smoking toes and they'll have memory stick before sunrise."

"They'll kill the American when they finish," said Golovkin.

"Bronstein is incidental," said Nabatov. "Our goal is to get the memory stick. On the other hand, one should not work blindly." Nabatov looked over at Golovkin. "When you finish your report to Moscow, ask them to develop a dossier on Harry Bronstein. I'm still not comfortable with his involvement. The clerk at the Alessandra hotel should be able to provide basic information on the American. Have one of your agents go there and question him."

Golovkin hurried out of the kitchen.

"Why was Kalandarishvili killed at this time?" Pasha Nabatov mused. "We know he spent several years working for the Chechnyans. So why would Shkarov order Rakhmelevich to terminate that arrangement? Was it because Kalandarishvili tried to cut a deal with the Americans? Very likely. But could there be more to it?"

"Maybe Shkarov has the hots for the face-scratcher?" suggested Kazimir. "We all know what a womanizer he's."

"The pot calling the kettle black, Kazimir?" Nabatov knitted his fingers and looked directly at his daughter. "Why kill Kalandarishvili before laying hands on the memory stick? How would the Chechnyans know about Bronstein?" He splayed his hands. "You see the problem?"

Kazimir spoke, drunkenly. "You took my brandy."

Nabatov made a disgusted sound, tossing a glare at the bearded Russian.

"I think Rakhmelevich lost his temper with Kalandarishvili," she said. "I think Kalandarishvili, in an effort to save his own skin, told Rakhmelevich about Bronstein."

"That fits." Her father scowled. "Is it possible Bronstein knows the memory stick's value?"

"That might explain why he did not hand it to them at his hotel," she said.

"He knows." Kazimir's voice slurred. "The bastard has a million Euros up his ass."

"I'm still having a hard time believing Shkarov and Rakhmelevich are alive," Popovitch cut in. "The identification we made was absolute."

"Dentures are not a proper identification, Doctor," Nabatov said. "What goes in one mouth can fit into another."

Golovkin returned to the room, wagging his head. "There is nothing on file for Bronstein. I have people on their way to the Alessandra. We will have something on the American by tomorrow night." He hesitated as if reluctant to continue. "Pasha, Moscow wants independent confirmation on the Chechnyans. If they are alive, Moscow does not want them terminated. Their capture and return is to be our top priority."

"That won't be easy," said Kazimir. "Those assholes are not about to be taken alive. Not with death sentences hanging over their heads."

"How many men can you muster, Ambrosii?" Pasha Nabatov asked.

"I can provide only three mercenaries."

"But..."

"Pasha, you and I and Kazimir know far too well the risks of going up against those Chechnyans. It is more or less a death-sentence.

Consequently, none of our French agents are eager." Golovkin held up a slip of paper. His eyes became opaque. "Moscow wants you to make contact on the encrypted line as soon as possible."

Nabatov took the note, glanced at it, and stuffed it into his pocket. Then he reflected for many seconds. He had faced Shkarov and Rakhmelevich before, with tragic results. The chattering machinegun fire, from that terrible night, was still a vivid memory. Eight out of the ten men in his charge found graves because of that horrific interaction. Only he, Kazimir and Golovkin had survived. Admittedly, that incident was in war-torn Chechnya, rather than bland Paris. Moreover, Shkarov had been leading a platoon of battle hardened rebels, rather than just Rakhmelevich and, possibly, a collection of local goons. Nevertheless, the level of risk was greater than Nabatov liked. The Chechnyans trained their terrorists well. Each was ready to die rather than surrender.

"When can you get your men together?" Nabatov asked. "Our best chance to capture Shkarov and Rakhmelevich is while they're occupied with the American."

"They will be ready when you are." Golovkin's face tensed. "Will you need more than your side-arms?"

Nabatov dipped his chin. "We will take three *PP-19 Bizons* from your armory."

"How many extra clips?"

"The standard 53 round rotaries will do. Direct your people to meet us on the road outside the repair shop as soon as possible. Anitchka, you go with Golovkin and draw a map to that location. He can scan it and then transmit the digital image to his people. When you finish, you, Kazimir, and I will head out there."

"If there's nothing else I can do…," Popovitch said, glancing at his watch.

"You might want to remain on standby for the next four hours — just in case we require medical attention. I will notify you when the mission is complete."

After Popovitch left, Kazimir tapped a finger on the table to focus his superior's attention. "I don't trust mercenaries. I say we wait for Moscow to send our own people."

"Worried about facing the Chechnyans, Kazimir?" Anitchka taunted."

"You damn right I'm worried. You would be too, if you had any sense."

"Anitchka," her father scolded.

Without another word, she got to her feet and strode off after Golovkin.

Kazimir leaned across the table toward his boss. "I think your daughter wants me dead."

"You're drunk."

"I'm serious, Pasha. Anitchka told me she'd blow my balls off if she caught me peeking up Anais's skirt, again." He thumped his own chest. "And me, your best friend."

"You and your women worry me, Kazimir."

"I know what you mean. Some days they worry me, too."

Chapter 8

Harry Bronstein's brown eyes flickered open. He had been dreaming. The groggy, memory of it still cradled him. In his sleep-fantasy, Harry had been rock-climbing with two strangers. One of the men had been above him, on the cliff-face, the other below. Both had tried to dislodge him from the rope that spanned between them. The reason for their antagonism had not been clear. Nevertheless, the other climber's persistence: during the nightmare, had been chilling.

Slowly, his vision came into focus. A few yards in front of Harry stood the two men who had been in his hotel room, the same two from his nightmare: Mikhail and Innokenti. They huddled together, talking completely unaware of the American's interest.

"Did you reach Yu-tung Cheng?" Shkarov asked his partner.

Rakhmelevich shook his head. "The phone lines to Sao Paolo are tied up because of a hurricane. I rang his home in Port-Bou, hoping his servant could arrange for a radio message. But the radio operator is with Cheng. They're supposed to be back in Port-Bou next week."

Harry looked upward to assess why his aching arms stretched overhead. The answer was clear and to the point. A rope lashed his wrists together, the cord extending upward many feet into murky darkness.

Several yards to his right an oval light fixture dangled on a thick cable. It created a dim circle of yellow light on what looked to be an oil-stained, concrete floor.

To his left was a set of double doors, the type used on machinery sheds. He twisted on the rope looking as far behind as his neck could swivel. All he saw was blackness.

Harry stretched his legs, attempting to touch the floor in order to ease the strain on his arms. His shoes dangled several inches above the dirty concrete floor.

"Why so soon?"

"Cheng decided to cut his visit short."

Shkarov fumbled with his lower lip, thinking. "Is the memory stick preying upon his mind? Or is he concerned about Kalandarishvili?"

"There's nothing linking me to Kalandarishvili."

"Nothing you know about."

The two men seemed oblivious to Harry.

"You'll have to try reaching Cheng, again," said Shkarov. "It's essential that he understand our change in circumstance."

"Bronstein has the memory stick, I tell you. Why worry Cheng with this?"

"A million Euros is a strong silencer. The American might die rather than give up the memory stick. Cheng needs to know there could be a delay."

"I'll get it out of Bronstein."

"Like you got it out of Kalandarishvili?" Shkarov gave his head a weary wag. "Bronstein is our only hope of recovering the memory stick." He took a ragged breath. "If the American proves to be a dry well, you and I will have to return to Irkutsk."

"What for?"

"To start again."

"But, Moskalenko was arrested."

"The *Raketnye voyska strategicheskogo naznacheniya Rossiyskoy Federatsii* is rampant with underpaid and overworked traitors. We will find another. The time delay is the issue." Mikhail Shkarov paused to light a cigarette. "On reflection, when you speak with Cheng's servant, tell him there will be a slight delay while we correlate the material."

"Going back to Irkutsk will mean more than a *slight* delay."

"I'll deal with that issue when the time comes."

As Rakhmelevich moved off, Mikhail Shkarov walked over to Harry Bronstein.

"I see you're once more with us, Mr. Bronstein." There was a ghastly cheerfulness in the Chechnyan's voice. Casually, he made a sweeping gesture. "As you must have observed, this place is not as pleasant as your hotel suite. But, it serves my purposes." He took a drag on the cigarette and blew smoke toward Harry's face. "Shall we begin?"

"I have to tell you..." Harry said, "You've completely outfoxed me."

"I'm glad we understand each other." The voice ended on a sharp, ragged note. "How is it that you were selected by Alexi Kalandarishvili?"

"Initially, he mistook me for someone else. Later, it seemed like I was his last hope. How 'bout cutting me down? I talk more freely when my hands can move."

"You will talk quite freely, Mr. Bronstein, I assure you."

"Silly me for not realizing that."

"You must have had some previous history with Kalandarishvili, or he wouldn't have used you."

"Not so much as a handshake." Harry glanced around, worrying about Rakhmelevich's location. This caused his body to twist back and forth on the rope. "What was his arrangement with you? Perhaps we can work the same deal? Excluding Rakhmelevich's unpleasant activities, of course."

Shkarov dropped the cigarette butt to the floor and crushed it underfoot. "You seem to find your circumstances amusing."

"Who am I to mock when I'm dangling at the end of my rope?"

"Since bringing you here, we investigated the possibility of the memory stick being in your car."

"You must have been disappointed."

A grin slowly spread across the Chechnyan's face. "Where is it, Mr. Bronstein?"

"The memory stick? Cut me down, and I'll take you to it."

"That's not possible."

"Must be frustrating for you. All that money on the come and no way to collect — unless I help."

"You'll help."

"Not unless there's something in it for me." Harry glanced up at his aching hands; the blood circulation completely cut off by the ropes had turned them blue. "Why did your pal, Rakhmelevich, kill Kalandarishvili? Did he do it accidentally? Or is Rakhmelevich as evil as he looks?"

"Evil is in each of us, Mr. Bronstein. This, of course, makes the world a very dangerous place. Not because of evil, itself. But, because there are so many amateurs playing at it." Then he jabbed a thumb in the direction his companion had taken. "Rakhmelevich is a professional in every respect."

"Your boy hasn't got the brains God gave baby geese."

"Where is the memory stick?"

"What's in it for me?"

"Don't be foolish, Mr. Bronstein. Your situation is untenable."

"But, I'm the only one who knows where the stick is. You kill me, and you'll get *bupkis*."

Shkarov frowned with confusion. "Bupkis?"

"Less than nothing. Now, if you were to cut me down, and offer a substantial remuneration for my services, we could do business."

"That's not going to happen."

"Then we both lose."

"I never lose, Mr. Bronstein."

Harry sighed, "Would you like to make a side-wager?"

Rakhmelevich stepped into the light, slipping on a pair of thick, lead-lined leather gloves. Harry felt his face tighten with fear.

"I got through to Cheng," the patch-eyed Chechnyan told Shkarov, eyeing the American. "He wasn't concerned." Then his right hand balled into a massive fist. "Has our friend talked?"

"Not yet," said Shkarov.

"I'm, however, open to bribes," Harry said. "Cash preferred; diamonds acceptable."

Mikhail Shkarov stepped back into the shadows.

Rakhmelevich moved back and forth in front of Harry for many seconds, tapping his right fist into his left palm. Then with cry of rage, he lunged forward. The blow struck Harry in the rubs, spinning the American's body until the twisting rope absorbed the impact. Then it spun Harry back like an unfurling flag. The American groaned.

"Where is the memory-stick, Mr. Bronstein?" Shkarov asked.

"I hate to admit it, Rakhmelevich," Harry said, his words choked. "But, you're a lot better at this than I thought possible. I think you cracked a couple of ribs." Harry coughed and his mouth filled with blood. He lolled the salty liquid around with his tongue, for a few seconds. Then he spat it into the patch-eyed Chechnyan's face. "You deserve a doggy-treat."

Rakhmelevich wiped away the blood and cocked his arm to strike again.

Shkarov interceded by stepping between Harry and the other Chechnyan.

"Don't be foolish, Mr. Bronstein," Shkarov said. "Tell me what I want to know and the pain will end."

"Not for my ribs," said Harry, with a gasp. "Those puppies will be complaining until I'm dead."

"Your dying won't do either of us any good."

"Sure it will. The pain stops. There's no more frustration. No more failing. No more smelling Rakhmelevich. Frankly, it's worth dying on the last count alone."

"The Jew needs more convincing, Rakhmelevich," Shkarov said in a low growl,

The patch-eyed Chechnyan swung at Harry, putting all his weight behind the blow. Rakhmelevich's huge fist struck the American in the face.

Again the rope spun. Again it spun back. However, this time it required many seconds before Harry Bronstein's world settled down.

When it did, he was staring at his antagonists through his right eye. The swollen tissue around the left one had closed it, tightly. Blood dribbled from the corner of Harry's mouth, and from his nostrils.

"I'm going to enjoy beating you to death, American," said Rakhmelevich.

"Let me give you a word of advice," Harry said, his words coming thick and slow. "When you want cooperation from a Jew you hold out a carrot, not an axe."

"The 'axe' as you put it does not necessarily have to fall, Mr. Bronstein," Shkarov said, stepping forward. "There is no need for all this."

"I'd like to believe you," Harry said. "Unfortunately, Rakhmelevich has already given your game away. I'm dead no matter how this turns out."

Shkarov backed out of the way, and Rakhmelevich waded in. This time his rapid blows landed on Harry's midsection.

"Surely a quick and painless demise would be preferred to this, Mr. Bronstein," Shkarov said, when the other Chechnyan stopped to rest.

Harry stared at his adversaries in fascinated horror. "I'm looking forward to it."

"Where is the memory-stick?" Shkarov asked.

Harry's good eye rolled back into his head as he fought to remain conscious. "I don't have it with me. But, if you'll…"

Once more Rakhmelevich pummeled Harry. This time the beating went on for several minutes.

"Now look what you've done, Mr. Bronstein," Shkarov said, as Rakhmelevich backed away, wheezing. "Poor Rakhmelevich is nearly exhausted by your ordeal."

"My heart is breaking — along with pretty much everything else." Harry spat out another stream of blood. "But, no matter how badly your pal is suffering, I'm not about to point you in the direction of the one thing that can save my skin."

Again, Rakhmelevich hit Harry. This time his fist split the helpless man's upper lip.

"That's enough, Rakhmelevich," Shkarov said, stepping forward. "We need him alive."

"Only just," Rakhmelevich said. Still, he backed away.

"Where?" Shkarov asked.

"Cut me down," Harry groaned. "I'll take you to it."

Shkarov threw his hands to his hips, impatiently. "We are beyond the point of negotiations."

Harry spat out another stream of blood, this one striking Shkarov's shoes. "In that case, let's not delay your long-suffering associate."

Rakhmelevich rushed forward and hit Harry so hard on the side of the head; the hapless man simply drooped, falling silent.

"You idiot, you killed him." Shkarov rushed forward; the fingers of one hand touching Harry's neck, trying to find a pulse.

"He was stalling."

"Dead men can't talk, you fool!"

"He couldn't be dead," Rakhmelevich said, his voice suddenly worried. "I didn't hit him hard enough. I know I didn't."

"I can't find a pulse. Wait. I feel a tremor."

"Look, he's still breathing."

Shkarov angrily twisted toward his companion. "How many times have I warned you about losing your temper?"

"He'll be fine. He'll talk. You'll see."

"He damn well better talk, for your sake." Shkarov grabbed Harry by the hair and jerked his head up with one hand, while tapping the unconscious man's temple with the fingers of the other. "Mr. Bronstein? Can you hear me, Mr. Bronstein?"

With a groan, Harry opened his good eye.

"The pain will only get worse," Shkarov said. "End it now. Tell me what I want to know."

There was a pause as if the American was trying to gather his thoughts. Then he said, "I threw it in the trash."

"What trash?"

"There's a can by the elevators at the Alessandra." Harry's eye rolled back in his head as he drifted back into unconsciousness.

Shkarov backed away. "Go to the hotel."

"You don't believe him?"

"Go and check, damn you! Call me either way."

As Rakhmelevich hurried off, Harry choked out another mouthful of blood. Then his good eye opened and he smiled at Shkarov. "Happy, are we?"

"You see how easy it was?" The Chechnyan lit a cigarette.

Harry laughed. "You poor sap."

"You're the one spitting blood, and I'm the sap?"

"Six, two and even you never see your pal Rakhmelevich again."

"I have every confidence he'll be back."

"Who's Yu-tung Cheng?"

Shkarov blinked in surprise.

"I overheard you talking," Harry said.

"He's a business associate."

"Is he buying the Russian defense information?"

"Ah, so you examined the memory stick."

"I must admit. I was a very naughty boy. Those happy-snaps of the old couple made a good beard. Not as good as you might have created using a computer program to hide the important images. But, good help is hard to find."

"One must make do, Mr. Bronstein."

"You should have hired me. I could have made it all invisible, except when you wanted it seen."

"Unfortunately, I was not aware of your valuable talents."

"You could hire me, now."

"Unfortunately, there are no openings on my team."

"It's not been my day, has it? First, I'm accused of murder. Then, I'm nearly beaten to death. Now, I blow a job interview."

"I must admit, it would seem that your luck has run out."

"Would it help if I mentioned how much you're going to need me?"

"I'm afraid not."

"Then you have someone who can correct the misinformation on the memory stick?"

Shkarov's face suddenly twisted with concern. "What are you saying?"

"You're going to love this," Harry said, with a chuckle. "I was so pissed at Kalandarishvili for slipping that damn memory-stick into my pocket, that I erased the damn thing."

The Chechnyan threw his cigarette to the floor, glaring. "You did what?"

Harry Bronstein laughed, creating flecks of foamy blood at his nostrils. "That scared you, Shkarov. Good. I can go to my grave, happy."

"I don't believe you. Kalandarishvili would have examined the memory-stick before paying you."

"But, he didn't pay me."

"I'll spend a week killing you."

"I'm afraid I can't give you the time." The American paused for a beat, enjoying the worry on his tormentor's face. "Now, if we can come to terms I could recover those missing files." Then Harry's eye flickered and closed.

"Bronstein? Bronstein!"

For the next thirty minutes, Shkarov smoked and tried to revive Harry Bronstein. However, the American remained in his injury-driven stupor. Then Shkarov's cellular phone rang.

The Chechnyan strode several yards away before answering it. After speaking with someone on the other end of the connection, he rang off. Then he dropped the cell-phone into his pocket, and once more grinned with confidence.

Harry opened his good eye and looked over at the Chechnyan. "From your body language I'd say my bluff didn't work."

"Rakhmelevich examined the data on the memory stick using his camera viewing screen. Everything is as it should be."

"Is it? Or did I alter some of the files?"

Shkarov pulled a pistol from his pocket. His eyes were aflame. "A man should accept when he's beaten, Mr. Bronstein."

Harry heard the click-click of the hammer going back. Then he saw the Chechnyan take aim and squeeze the trigger. After that, there was nothing but blackness.

Chapter 9

Moving clouds split the pre-dawn sky giving the curl of moon some vent for its bluish light. The latter glowed through the heavy mist among the high branches of a twisted oak growing along the edge of Cité Bienaymée. The air smelled of fuel oil and cow dung. Pasha Nabatov, Anitchka, Kazimir, and the three mercenaries huddled next to the Russians' black Peugeot.

"Are you certain this is the place, Anitchka?" Her father squinted at the darkened repair shop. The stone structure was flat-roofed and one story high. "I don't see lights or vehicles."

"I'm positive," she said.

"Their cars may be parked behind it," said Kazimir. "Or, maybe they left."

Nabatov grunted. He had no doubt about his daughter's information. This was where she had followed Shkarov and Rakhmelevich. However, the darkened building suggested they had long since departed.

"Let's synchronize our watches." The white-haired Russian raised one arm and studied the illuminated dial in his Vostok timepiece. "I have twenty seven minutes and thirteen seconds after the hour." He pointed to the three mercenaries. "I will give you five minutes to secure the perimeter." His focus shifted to the bearded Russian. "Kazimir, you will go with them. If there's a rear entrance, take up a position there. I want you to wait until thirty-five minutes after the hour to enter. I will go to the front and time my entrance to match yours. Should Shkarov and Rakhmelevich be in there, try to take them alive."

Kazimir's face puckered like a prune. "I don't like taking alive, Pasha. It usually means somebody else gets dead."

Nabatov gave his dark eyes a weary roll. "If they resist shoot the bastards, okay?"

"What about me, Poppa?" Anitchka asked, as Kazimir and the mercenaries hurried off through the darkness.

"You stay with the car."

"Shkarov may have a dozen or more men inside."

"There's nobody in there." Nabatov gave the repair shop another squinting look. "But, in case there is, I want you in the car with the engine running — so we can get the hell out of here should things turn badly."

Anitchka Nabatov made a frustrated gesture. "I'm not a child you have to protect."

"Then, as an adult, you should understand the importance of taking orders from your superior." With a snort, her father turned and hurried through the darkness toward the repair shop.

Seconds later, a momentary flash of light silhouetted the shop in an orange fan of flames. Instantaneously, there was a deafening roar. Pasha Nabatov dropped to the ground, his ears perked, his eyes straining to see through the darkness. When he heard running feet approaching from the direction of the road, he squirmed on the grass to take aim with his Bison submachine gun. He caught himself as Anitchka rushed into view.

"What in hell happened?" she whispered, crouching down next to her father.

"Something very unpleasant." He said got to his feet.

"The Mole?"

"I'm certain he was the precipitator of Rakhmelevich's workmanship."

"Kazimir must've set off the booby-trap."

"You go back to the car, while I check on him."

"Not likely, Poppa," she said. "If he's in pieces, I want to see it." Then, she hurried off, around the side of the building.

When they reached the rear of the building, Nabatov spotted Kazimir staggering about in a daze. The bearded Russian was about ten yards from the smoldering structure. His clothing was in shreds. His face and hands were as white as cold lard. His machine gun was on the ground, not far from the shop. What had been the building's rear entrance, locked in place by blocks of stone, was now a smoke-filled hole that was several feet wide.

Nabatov rushed over to the wounded man. "Are you okay, Kazimir?"

The bearded man blinked in confusion for several seconds. Then he nodded. "There is a ringing in my ears and parts of me have gone numb."

"What happened?"

"I got the mercenaries positioned. Then I headed toward the back of the shop. I had not gone very far when I chased up a rabbit. It hopped off, ahead of me. When it reached the rear door a bomb went off. It scared the hell out of me." He took a rattling breath. "I don't think it did the rabbit much good."

"Can you make it back to the Peugeot?" Nabatov asked.

Kazimir walked over and picked up his machine gun. "If I don't die first."

"Tell the mercenaries to head back to Golovkin's for debriefing. Then go back to the car and wait."

"What if there's more trouble?"

"You can barely stand, Kazimir. If there's more trouble you will more hindrance than help." Nabatov looked around, but Anitchka was nowhere in sight. "Where in hell is she?"

"She went inside the shop. The lights are on in there, now."

"Why can't that girl follow orders?"

"Because she's a constant pain in the ass; especially mine."

Pasha Nabatov hurried past Kazimir over to the smoky opening in the repair shop wall, and looked within. From where he crouched, a light dangling from the ceiling illuminated a male figure suspended from a rope. Anitchka was approaching the man from the opposite direction, her PP-19 Bizon draped casually over one shoulder.

"What in hell were you thinking, coming in here alone?" her father shouted as he stepped into the repair shop. "You turn on the lights and walk around like this is your apartment?"

"The building is secure, Poppa."

His eyes quickly darted around the interior for a second time. The warehouse was completely empty, expect for the man hanging from the rope.

Nabatov was not worried about Shkarov or Rakhmelevich. The terrorists were miles away. What bothered him was the lack of concern his daughter had started exhibiting. Years of living in a safe haven, like Paris, had lulled her into a false sense of security. That was often a fatal mistake in their line of business. Take nothing for granted. Always assume the worst. Be forever vigilant.

"Did you stop to think that Shkarov might have rigged a bomb on the other door? Did you consider the possibility there might be one near the dead man?"

"Yes, Poppa, I considered both possibilities."

Her father carefully went inside the repair shop, still uneasy, again looking around. "Well?"

"There is a bomb affixed to the front entrance. It is set to go off when the door is moved." She pointed at Harry Bronstein. "Help me cut him down."

"Leave his body as it is, for the police."

"Bronstein is not dead."

"Close enough for counting." Nabatov moved toward her, rubbernecking as he went. "Did the Chechnyans leave anything that might lead us to them?"

"No."

"You're certain this is the same man you saw at the Montmartre."

"I'm certain he's Harry Bronstein."

Her father stopped. "Let's go."

"I want to take Bronstein back to Golovkin's."

"What in hell for?"

"If he lives long enough to talk, he could help us locate Shkarov and Rakhmelevich."

"They are not going to confide in him, Anitchka."

"People talk. People overhear. In our business that's how we get most of our leads."

"Agreed. But, most of those leads go nowhere." Nabatov went over to the American, reached out, and touched Harry' throat. There was a slight pulse. "He won't survive the ride to Golovkin's."

"Give me your knife, Poppa."

"I don't want a body to get rid of." Nabatov's mouth twitched. "I don't want to hang around here, either. That explosion will not have gone unnoticed."

She held out her hand. "Give me your knife."

Reluctantly, her father slung his PP-19 Bizon over one shoulder. Then he took a large, folding knife from his pocket. After opening it, he handed the razor-sharp instrument to his daughter.

"We'll both regret this, Anitchka," he said.

"How is Kazimir?" she asked, putting the blade against the rope suspending Harry.

Her father squatted down and grabbed the American below the buttocks while she put the steel blade to work. "I don't think he'll be chasing Anais, for a while."

"She'll be glad to hear that."

As the Harry's body dropped, Nabatov moved forward.

The American flopped across the Russian's broad back. With a loud grunt, Pasha Nabatov straightened up holding Harry like a sack of wheat.

"What about the other booby-trap?" she asked, as her father staggered under Bronstein's weight on their way out of the repair shop.

"What will it take to disarm it?" he asked.

"I can't chance defusing it. The Chechnyans build their charges with a tampering switch. A burst from the Bizon will probably do it."

"I'll deal with that after getting this one to the car." Nabatov patted Harry's backside. "Is he still breathing? I don't want to carry a dead man."

She fell a step behind, grabbed Harry by his hair and lifted his head. Then she let go and caught up with her father. "He's breathing."

"He'd better be worth the effort, Anitchka."

"Do you want me to help carry him?"

"Don't worry about me," Nabatov snorted. "You worry about the police. They take a dim view of cadaver-dumping in the Seine; especially American corpses. It's bad for the tourist trade."

By the time they reached the car, Nabatov's legs were trembling from exhaustion. Kazimir forced himself out of the vehicle and staggered forward to help.

"Who is it?" the bearded Russian asked, as he and Anitchka dragged Harry Bronstein from her father's back.

"Harry Bronstein," the elder Russian wheezed, stumbling back a step.

"He looks dead," Kazimir said.

"Help me get him into the rear seat," Anitchka said.

"Are your sure he's alive?" Kazimir asked, as he helped place the American on the car seat.

"Of course, I'm sure."

"I'll take care of the other bomb." Nabatov unslung his Bizon.

"Let me do it, Poppa. Your legs are about to give out."

"I'm not ready for the knacker's yard yet, young lady."

"Close enough," she said, and set off for the repair shop.

"See?" said Kazimir. "Even you, she disrespects."

"Shut up."

"I think you should send her back to Moscow."

"How about I send *you* back to Moscow?"

Pasha Nabatov climbed into Peugeot on the passenger side, setting his machine gun on the floor. Then he closed the door.

"Why am I always the one in trouble?" Kazimir asked, as he crawled into the rear seat next to Harry.

"Because, you're always doing something stupid. Shut the door and shut up."

Kazimir did as instructed.

"I've got to find that bastard," the elder Russian muttered.

"Which bastard? Or, shouldn't I ask?"

"Is the American still breathing?"

Kazimir tilted toward the unconscious man and wagged is head. "I don't think so."

Nabatov cursed. "Why doesn't she ever listen to me?"

"I would tell you but you don't like to listen, either."

An explosion rattled the car doors.

"What in hell was that?" Kazimir demanded.

Nabatov twisted in the seat to look outside. Through the darkness, he saw Anitchka trotting toward the car. "Shkarov tries to cover all the bases."

Kazimir gave his head a shake. "I can't get the ringing in my ears to stop."

"Stop complaining. The ringing might act like an alarm to wake up your feeble brain."

Anitchka jerked open the rear door, next to the American. Then she leaned in, her ear over Harry's mouth. "I think he's doing better, Poppa."

"How can he be? He's dead."

"Nonsense. Bronstein's breathing much easier, now."

Nabatov glared over the seat at Kazimir. "You said he was dead."

"All I hear is ringing, Pasha," the bearded Russian said, in protest.

"Let's get out of here," Nabatov told his daughter. "After two explosions, somebody must've telephoned the police."

Anitchka shut the rear door, opened the front and quickly crawled behind the steering wheel. Then she set down her machine gun. Seconds later the car was roaring away.

"I don't like being set up," she said.

"No more than me," said her father.

"How could we be set up?" Kazimir asked. "Only the three of us knew we were coming out here."

"A Mole told them," said Nabatov.

"Mole?"

"Poppa!"

"There is a traitor among us, Kazimir."

"I don't believe it, Pasha."

"Moscow Center is convinced."

"You cannot believe Moscow." Kazimir batted the air with one hand. "They are always getting things wrong. Look how they keep investigating me?"

"Don't remind me."

"We need to set a trap for the traitor," Anitchka said.

Kazimir suddenly went google-eyed. "Does Moscow think it's me, Pasha?"

"Can you blame them?" A teasing smile crinkling the corners of Anitchka's mouth.

"Anitchka," her father scolded. "He's been through enough."

"What about Anais? What about what he has put her through?"

"They all hate me at Lubyanka Square," Kazimir whined.

"Stop acting paranoid, Kazimir, Anitchka is teasing you."

"She's not teasing, Pasha." The bearded man's body twitched as though he were being repeatedly jabbed with a pin. "She wants me dead, like everybody else."

Nabatov looked over the back of the front seat. "Kazimir, I'm convinced that you're not the Mole. If you were, you would have known about the bombs, and stayed well back."

"Thank you, Pasha."

"You must keep what we are discussing between us, Kazimir," Nabatov said, returning his attention to the road ahead. "Not even Golovkin is to know. Understood?"

"I swear it on my life, Pasha."

"Every day he swears on his life," she said.

Nabatov scratched one ear. "Anitchka, after we get the American into Golovkin's flat, I want you to request Popovitch's presence."

"I had planned to," she said.

"But, when you telephone him, only mention Kazimir. Don't say anything about Bronstein."

"I just realized something," Kazimir said, with a whimper.

"The light came on in the dark room?" Anitchka said, with a laugh.

"I'm totally numb from the waist down." Kazimir let go a choking sob. "I can't feel anything. No tingle, at all."

"Popovitch will check you out," Nabatov said.

"But, Pasha, a man should never be numb in my numbest part."

                                        ***

The Cafe L'Pulcinella, on rue Damrémont, in Paris, was an all-night eatery occupying the basement of a Rococo style building. The restaurant had no smiling maitres d'hotel to direct diners to tables, no background music from an orchestra, no conditioned air, or any other posh trappings. Instead, red-checked cloths graced each table. Wax-dripped wine bottles, each stuffed with a lighted candle, served up a mock Italian atmosphere. Brown walls painted with gladiatorial combat murals made a feeble attempt at replicating ancient Rome's glory. The place smelled of garlic, fish, tomatoes, and insecticide.

"What's eating you, Shkarov?" Innokenti Rakhmelevich asked.

Mikhail Shkarov leaned back in his chair, toying with his coffee cup. "Too many things have gone wrong."

The two Chechnyans sat at a table near the café's fire exit. Above their table, a ceiling fan stirred the obtrusive odors into a nauseating potpourri.

"We heard both explosions, didn't we?" Rakhmelevich said.

"Twenty minutes apart."

"What of it?"

"What happened in those twenty minutes?" Shkarov asked.

"Obviously, the first bomb did so much damage the walls collapsed, setting off the second charge."

"Twenty minutes later?"

"It happens."

"You live in hope, don't you?" Shkarov's breath made a soft hissing sound.

Rakhmelevich used his fork to spear several strands of linguini, coated in blood-red clam sauce. Then, pressing the trines against the bowl of the spoon in his other hand, the patch-eyed Chechnyan slowly spun the pasta into a tight, oozing ball.

"All right, what's you're theory?" Rakhmelevich asked, the forkful of dripping pasta hovering just inches from his mouth.

"Nabatov outsmarted us. He knew we expected them. It was he who detonated the charges when it suited him." Shkarov was staring at his companion, levelly. "Anitchka saw you on the stairs at the Montmartre…"

"So she says."

"We both know that woman wouldn't fabricate a story to her father. She said she saw you because she saw you."

"Stop belly-aching." With a satisfied grunt, Rakhmelevich shoved the ball of pasta into his mouth and chewed, lustily. "We got the memory stick, didn't we?"

Mikhail Shkarov looked around the big shabby cafe, his eyes abstracted. The frequent visits to L'Pulcinella did little to generate fond visions of Rome's Piazza Navone. Instead, the café brought back grim recollections of the Slums in the Zaryadye District of Moscow, where Shkarov grew up. However, Rakhmelevich had recently acquired a taste for Italian cuisine. And, this was his favorite fodder trough.

"In another week, give or take a day, we'll be handed a million Euros." The patch-eyed Chechnyan set down his eating utensils. Then, he tore a chunk of bread from one of the loaves in the basket between him and Shkarov. "Instead of moping, you should be celebrating."

"I don't want your mistake to come back and bite me in the ass."

"My mistake?"

Shkarov's large, manicured hands clenched on the table. "Have you forgotten Kalandarishvili?"

"Bronstein's been blamed for that." Rakhmelevich grinned. "He's dead, so who's to say different?"

"Bronstein's another thing that bothers me."

"Guilt? Over killing a Jew? What in hell's gotten into you?"

A faint smile came across Shkarov's lips, as he studied his companion. Rakhmelevich always grabbed for the obvious conclusion. It was one of the many predictable and weak facets to his impulsive personality.

"How closely did you look at the memory stick?" Shkarov asked.

"I checked half a dozen of the maps. Everything looked fine."

"What about the documents?" Shkarov crossed one ankle over the opposite knee.

"They wouldn't open with my camera. You don't still believe Bronstein's boast?"

"We can't afford another mistake."

The breeze from the ceiling fan fretted the wick of the candle, sending shadows darting across Rakhmelevich's stony face like chasing cats. "It's all past. Forget it." He put his knife down carefully on the edge of his plate. "We got what we wanted."

Three young couples entered the café, catching Shkarov's eye. They were party revelers, from their dress and intoxicated voices. He studied them with envy as they staggered toward the back of the café. It was only after the trio dragged three tables together and sat down, that his stare return to his companion.

"I want to go back to the repair shop," Shkarov said.

"What for?"

"Nabatov and his ilk are dead, remember?"

"The explosions will have brought the police."

"I want to go, anyway." He offered the other man a chilly smile. "You enjoy looking at corpses, don't you?"

Rakhmelevich tilted forward, the flickering flame from the candle on the table reflecting like molten amber, in his eye. "I don't like looking at police."

One of the young women let go a squealing laugh. Mikhail Shkarov glanced over to see her push her escort's hand from beneath her dress.

"Youth is wasted on the young." Shkarov rubbed the back of his left pinky finger along the edge of his chin. "They squander it."

"If you want to go back there, we'll go." Rakhmelevich eased back. "Seeing Nabatov in pieces will be like dessert."

Shkarov pushed his plate of untouched linguini off to one side, and settled himself facing the other man, with both feet on the floor. Then he smirked at his companion's analogy. Rakhmelevich could stomach the sight of anything, even the butchery of children, with his belly full of blood-colored clam sauce. He had no soul. He offered no pity. He operated strictly at gut level, unthinking, ruthless to the extreme.

"*If* he's in pieces," Shkarov said.

The patch-eye Chechnyan tore off another hunk of bread. Using it like a sponge, he ran it around his plate soaking up the remaining blood-colored sauce. "How much are you paying your tart?" He spoke without looking up.

"A hundred thousand."

"For what?"

"You underestimate Galina's value," Shkarov said, raising his eyebrows a little.

"What value?" The other man's mouth made a downward curve, as he glared at Shkarov. "She's nothing but a whore."

"She's a very clever woman."

"Clever or not, her cut comes out of your end."

"I think we should share that expense."

"Why? She doesn't share my bed."

"Without her we wouldn't have known about Kalandarishvili's plans to sell the memory stick to the Americans." Shkarov gave his head a determine nod. "My beautiful blonde *will* get her payment off the top."

"It would be cheaper to kill her."

Shkarov finished his coffee and looked at his watch. Then he stood up. "If your belly is full, I'd like to get going."

Rakhmelevich pulled a dappled thin cigar from inside his suit and placed it between the index and middle fingers of his left hand. "You don't think Nabatov is dead, do you?" He belched, getting to his feet.

The other man's dark eyes clouded. "With very good reason."

Chapter 10

"I've done all I can for him," said Dr. Dmitri Popovitch. It was after sunrise. The stopped man stared down at unconscious Harry Bronstein. "Frankly, I don't think he's going to make it." Popovitch took a weary breath. "This poor soul belongs in a hospital, Pasha."

The American lay on a bed in one of the back rooms within Ambrosii Golovkin's apartment. The room was bleak. Its furnishings consisted of an iron bedstead from which rumpled sheets dangled to a parquet floor; a bedside table; a straight-backed wooden chair and an unpainted armoire. French magazines littered the parquet. A painted wooden shelf below the space's small, boarded-up window held stacks of Garish American paperbacks. Everywhere was the stench of stale tobacco smoke.

"That's not possible, Doctor." Nabatov tilted his head, peering down at his *Nasha Marka* cigarette. "You said the bullet merely grazed Bronstein's skull."

"But this, undoubtedly, caused a concussion. Then there is the risk of internal injuries. He received a terrible beating. There are several fractured ribs. As for his left eye, I can only guess at the damage." Popovitch made a pleading gesture. "Pasha, we must consider what is best for the patient."

Anitchka, hovering over Harry from the side of the bed opposite Dr. Popovitch, tossed her father an impatient scowl. "Bronstein needs hospitalization, Poppa."

"We cannot protect him beyond these walls." Nabatov's voice was flat and final. "Not from the police. Not from Mikhail Shkarov. Until Bronstein tells us what we want to know, he must remain here."

"Surely Shkarov thinks he's dead," Popovitch said.

"Presumably, or he and Rakhmelevich wouldn't have left Bronstein. When the Chechnyans realize their mistake, they'll have good reason to finish the job they started."

"Why?"

"If you convinced the world you were dead to avoid execution, and one man is living proof that you're alive, wouldn't you look for him?"

"But, Anitchka saw Rakhmelevich. The Chechnyans must realize that Moscow knows they're alive."

"I don't think Rakhmelevich saw me," she said.

"Nevertheless," said her father, "there's a chance that Bronstein knows where those two terrorists are headed. That is what I intend to find out. Once I know what Bronstein knows…"

Popovitch cut in with, "Even so, Shkarov couldn't possibly find Bronstein."

"The Chechnyans have connections worldwide," Anitchka cut in. "In time, they'll know exactly where the American is."

"We must also consider the Parisian Police," said Nabatov. "The clerk at the Montmartre Hotel identified Bronstein as Kalandarishvili's killer. With no evidence to the contrary, the gendarmes will never stop searching for this man."

"I admit your reasoning makes sense, Pasha. But, Bronstein will tell you nothing if he dies." The physician's voice rose, urgently. "Why not hedge your bet? Get him the care he needs. I could arrange accommodations in a private hospital, under an alias. The police will never know."

"My decision is not negotiable, Doctor."

Dmitri Popovitch let go a resigned sigh. Then, he looked over at Anitchka Nabatov. "Assuming Mr. Bronstein survives the next few hours, he will need ongoing care for the week or so. The sutures in his head will dissolve by week's end. You must change the bandages on his head and face daily. I will leave you a tube of antibiotic."

"How soon will he awaken?" she asked.

"Frankly, the odds are against it." The GRU physician's hands gave a momentary flurry. "Without proper care, I'm giving this man a death sentence."

"I'm responsible for Mr. Bronstein, Doctor," enjoined Nabatov. "If he dies, it will be on my conscience, not yours."

Anitchka took a package of *Sobranie Black* cigarettes from her skirt's pocket, filched one out, stuck it between her lips, and lit it with a match. Through a cloud of smoke, her eyes drifted from the bloody pulp that once had been Harry Bronstein's handsome face, down to the tight bands of cloth encircling the American's muscular chest. Had Shkarov inflicted those horrific injuries during an orgy of preplanned physical abuse? Alternatively, had Bronstein foolishly stood his ground, refusing to speak? If so, why? He must have realized the futility of silence. Could he have been protecting someone? If so, who?

"What about his ribs, Doctor?" she asked.

"Leave the wrappings as they are," Popovitch said, in a matter-of-fact voice. "The less those are adjusted the better." He noticed the concern in her face. "Do not expect miracles, Anitchka. Bronstein is a man who should be dead." The physician glanced at Pasha Nabatov and raised his voice, slightly. "A man who will die before he can speak."

"Can you bring the American back to consciousness?" Nabatov asked.

"His breathing is irregular. His pulse is unstable. His blood pressure is nearly nonexistent." The physician's arms rose and fell with exasperation. "You should have left him where he was, Pasha. Bronstein would be out of misery, by now."

Nabatov frowned at his daughter. "Words along those lines were mentioned, Doctor, but they went unheeded."

"Right now, his best chance at survival is sleep." Popovitch picked up his Gladstone bag from the floor. "But, if you wish to tempt fate, I can inject him with…"

Anitchka cut in with, "That won't be necessary, Doctor."

Pasha Nabatov gave a noncommittal grunt.

Anitchka returned her eyes to Harry's swollen face. His dark brown hair formed a matted frame around the injured flesh. Despite the horrific beating, it was easy to imagine him with wide, expectant eyes, chiseled cheeks, a ruggedly carved nose and a squarish chin. She could not help but wonder about the beautiful wife and family who were expecting his return.

Popovitch set the Gladstone bag on the bed, and opened it. From within he removed a jar of antibiotic cream, a small bottle of clear fluid, several syringes wrapped in cellophane and half a dozen packets of sterile, alcohol swabs. He set these on the bedding. After giving Harry Bronstein a despairing look, the GRU physician withdrew a length of thin rubber tubing and added it to the other items.

"*Should* he awaken," Popovitch said, "Bronstein will be in a great deal of pain. Give him 10 milligrams of Morphine intravenously." The physician lifted his eyebrows in a questioning arch. "You know the routine, Anitchka?"

"Of course."

"If that doesn't calm him, give the American another ten — no more than twenty during a twenty-four hour period."

Nabatov interjected, "I don't want Bronstein given any medication until I speak with him."

The young woman casually picked up the items on the bed and put them into the table's drawer.

The doctor closed his bag. "I will plan to come back tomorrow, Pasha," he said stiffly, and then headed for the door. "But, if the American dies during the interim, please let me know. I do have other patients."

Nabatov moved aside to let the physician pass. "I will keep you informed, Doctor."

Popovitch swept out of the room, amidst a flurry of under-breath mutterings.

Almost immediately, the white-haired man hurried out into the hallway and called after him. "You might take a few minutes to examine Kazimir, Doctor. He is complaining of numbness."

"Numbness, where?" Popovitch asked, as he stopped and looked back.

"His lower extremities. In particular, the genital region."

"I should think a disability in that area would be a blessing, considering his history with women."

"To be frank, sexual rehabilitation need not be rushed." Pasha Nabatov lifted a hand resignedly. "My concern, however, that those symptoms might be indicative of something more serious."

"I will do what I can, Pasha."

Nabatov returned to the room and went over to the bed. "I meant what I said, Anitchka. If Bronstein regains consciousness, I want to talk to him. I do not care about his pain. I do not care about blood pressure or heartbeat. Once the Mole has informed Shkarov about Bronstein, this apartment will come under siege. We must find out what the American knows as quickly as possible. Understand?"

"What has Moscow discovered about Bronstein?" she asked.

"Based upon his credit information, obtained from a surprisingly cooperative clerk at the Alessandra Hotel, Bronstein is his real name."

She cocked an eyebrow. "Surprisingly cooperative?"

"Sidoine Benoît, according to Golovkin, was ready to give blood if it would help bring about Bronstein's ruination."

"Is the American CIA?"

"Not as far as Moscow can ascertain. He has a minor criminal record due to a car-theft conviction as a juvenile. His mother is deceased. She was a jeweler and ran a successful shop in Minneapolis, Minnesota. Upon her death, Bronstein sold the business for a handsome profit — which quickly disappeared."

"Gambling?"

"Divorce. His ex-wife took him to the cleaners."

"The poor man." A small, smile tugged at the corners of her mouth. "Children?"

"None. He has no siblings. Curiously, Moscow has a file on a Morris Bronstein. He's a weapons dealer living in Portugal. That particular Bronstein is quite popular among the South American drug cartels."

"A relation to Harry?"

"Possible his long missing father Morris Bronstein. Our American's father abandoned the family when Harry was about ten years of age."

"It sounds like good fortune is completely foreign to him."

"After graduating from the University of Minnesota, where Bronstein completed his Master's Degree in Computer Science, he did two tours in the United States Army as a decryption analyst for their Intelligence Division. That, I found, every interesting — considering his recent activities. He held the rank of Captain when discharged. He is a Jew. He speaks Russian, English, German and French — fluently. He has a developmental grasp of several other languages." Her father raised a finger for emphasis. "Be very careful about what is discussed in his presence. Since completing his military obligation, Bronstein has worked for a number software companies. For the last several years, he has done computer software consulting, on his own. He is thirty-six years of age."

"How long was he married?"

"Less than two years."

Anitchka's face changed slightly. A momentary brightness seemed to flash across it. "What a bitter disappointment for him."

Her father let out a very deep breath. "A short, bad marriage is better than a long beleaguered one."

"But, Bronstein and his wife barely got to know each other."

"Since when did you become sympathetic to marital woes?"

"Is there anything else on Bronstein?"

"He plays chess and cooks. His level of accomplishment in those areas is quite high. Bronstein has few friends. He likes women. He drinks occasionally. He lives beyond his means." The Russian waited many seconds to allow the significance of his last words to sink in. "That, too, I found interesting."

"Most Americans rely on credit."

"But, most Americans don't get involved with traitors like Kalandarishvili."

"Bronstein's financial limitations hardly damn him as an active participant in the theft of our intelligence data."

"You defend Bronstein without knowing him."

"You condemn him on the same lack of knowledge."

"I have a job to do, Anitchka."

"Poppa, my reluctance to label Bronstein a criminal is because he's unable to defend himself."

Her father's tongue darted to the edges of his mouth. "What other conclusion can we make, considering what we know?"

"The facts are open to interpretation," she said. "For example, Kalandarishvili hated Jews. So why would he collaborate with one? I think it is far more likely that Bronstein was duped into this mess."

"I don't agree." Nabatov went over to the ashtray on the windowsill, and snuffed out his cigarette. "Would you take a European vacation if nearly bankrupt?"

"No, but…"

"Neither would I. Unless, of course, that expedition promised to be a profit-making venture. Mark my words: Bronstein and Kalandarishvili met somewhere. Somehow, they came to a financial agreement and formed a partnership." Her father rubbed his chin with the knuckles of one hand, frowning. Then his voice became curious as he looked back down at the unconscious American. "That being said, what reason could there be for Bronstein taking such a beating rather than telling the Chechnyans what they wanted to know? Could he have been protecting someone?"

"I wondered the same thing."

"He was protecting a woman, perhaps?" The white-haired man put his hands to his hips, sucking his teeth. "Young men do foolish things when it comes to women."

She rolled her eyes. "Now, who is being sympathetic?"

"I merely made an observation."

"What about the memory-stick?"

"I think we can assume the Chechnyans have it."

"That should please Moscow."

"In my opinion, Moscow should be worried."

"Why? Shkarov will sell it. The information is misleading. Therefore, whoever buys the memory-stick will gain nothing of value. That was the crux of Moscow's deception."

"But, things have not gone as planned. The American threw a wrench between the gears."

"How?"

"His involvement with Kalandarishvili, whether planned or unplanned, could incite an investigation by the CIA. We don't need American spooks following in our shadows and possibly exposing our fraud."

"If Bronstein is not CIA, why would they take an interest?"

He stuck out his arm at random. "To undermine our efforts in Paris, of course. You may be amused at the Americans. But they are deadly foes."

"Poppa, are you listening to yourself? The Mole is making you paranoid." Then she returned her attention to the American. "Bronstein had been such a pretty man."

Pasha Nabatov fastened his sharp eyes upon his daughter. Anitchka always took the white-knight view of handsome, young men. Morality, or the lack thereof, was not based upon appearance. However, she frequently closed her eyes to that. It was her only fault. Nevertheless, Anitchka was a dedicated GRU soldier. He knew he could rely upon her to do what was necessary. She would kill Bronstein, if so instructed. Kill him without her pulse rate raising so much as a single beat.

"Pretty, huh?" Her father pointed his right forefinger down at Harry Bronstein. "And you complain about Kazimir's infatuation with Anais Duras."

Her face colored. "I meant it was a shame that Bronstein suffered so badly."

"First there was the shame of his short marriage. Then, you went to his defense claiming a misinterpretation of the facts. Now, you offer sympathy over the extent of his injuries." He shook a warning finger. "This isn't like you, Anitchka."

"Can't I express my feelings without hearing my father criticize?"

"Yes, well…" He let go a long, drawn out sigh. "My feet are killing me. It's these damn new shoes. I have to get off my feet." Pasha Nabatov turned and left the room, leaving Anitchka alone with the American.

She bent over Harry Bronstein and pulled the blanket up to his chin. In an absent-minded fashion, she stroked a lock of hair away from his face and kissed his forehead. Almost immediately, Harry's good eye opened.

"How's tricks?" Harry asked.

In spite of her astonishment, Anitchka Nabatov offered the American a well-trained smile, and stood erect. *"Comment allez-vous?"*

"Frankly, I feel like shit under a blowtorch." The American tried to turn his head to look around, but the pain quickly stopped his efforts. "Where am I?" Then he let go a groan, and clutched at his chest. "More importantly, where are my dance partners?"

"Dance partners?"

"The two Chechnyans who did the *Apache* number on me."

She blinked in bewilderment. "*Apache?*"

"A French dance with nasty overtones. Funny thing. Neither of them wore a striped cardigan."

"You were dancing when you were abducted?"

Again, he groaned. "Where am I?"

"Paris."

"I don't suppose you could get me a doctor?" Harry whimpered, curling onto his side in agony. "I think I'm going to die."

"The doctor left a few minutes ago."

"How long do I have?"

"According to him, you're already dead."

"Your quack must've missed a couple of diagnosis classes at Burdenko Clinic."

Her hands went to her hips. "How could possibly you know that Popovitch trained at…"

Harry cut her off with, "Just you and me in this dilapidated love nest?"

She held his face with her eyes for a few seconds, wondering how Popopvitch's diagnosis could have been so far off the mark. Bronstein was badly injured, that was obvious. Nevertheless, the American was far from being at death's door.

"My father would like to speak to you." She snuffed out her cigarette in the ashtray on the bedside table. "He's in the next room."

"Your English and French are excellent." He flattened out on his back, his good eye darted back and forth, taking in more of his surroundings. "But, you're Russian."

"I'll let my father know that you're *copus mentus*."

"Wait."

"Yes?"

"Did the doctor leave anything for pain?"

"I'll be right back."

"What's your name?"

"My name is Anitchka, Mr. Bronstein."

"How is it you know me?"

Her beautiful face widened into a sugary smile. "I make a point of knowing every man I put to bed."

"You undressed me?"

She shook her head. "Golovkin did it."

Harry offered up a crooked smile. "I don't suppose Golovkin looks a little like you?"

"No, *he* certainly does not."

"I can't tell you how disappointed I feel — not to mention violated."

"I suspect Golovkin shares that same view."

"What's a nice Georgian girl like you doing here watching me die?"

Anitchka crossed her arms, again surprised. "How is it you know where I was reared?"

"It's a dying gift." He raised one hand to his injured skull. "I saw Shkarov take aim and pull the trigger."

"Shkarov is alive, as well?" she asked, suddenly intrigued.

"As well?" he whimpered, his hands going to the wrappings on this ribs, because of the pain.

"As well as Rakhmelevich."

He paled. "Friends of yours, are they?"

"Where are the Chechnyans?"

"GRU?"

Anitchka turned and started for the door. "I'll be right back."

"You are Glavnoye Razvedyvatel'noye Upravleniye."

She stopped and looked back. "You're mistaken."

"Your father is going to kill me. Or, am I mistaken about that, too?"

She moved back to the bed. "Where are Shkarov and Rakhmelevich?"

"I don't know. Disappointed?"

"Frankly, yes."

"If it will get me some pain-killer, I have a fair idea where they'll be in about a week."

"Where?"

"What's in it for me?"

"I've given you your life, isn't that enough?"

He clenched his eyes shut, shuddering with pain. "Not even close, baby."

She hesitated. "I'll give you something. Then you must cooperate as I wish. Understood?"

"I have to tell you… If sex is on the menu, it may take a bit to get up to it."

"My interrogations would never be so brutal."

"Somehow, despite my misery, I feel rejected."

Anitchka Nabatov opened the drawer in the table and took out the rubber hose, a syringe, one of the alcohol wipes and the bottle of morphine.

"Are you married?" he asked.

"No."

The American uttered another agonizing groan. "I suppose you live with a cat?"

"I used to."

"A big one, I'll bet."

"A Siberian tiger cub. I bottle-fed him for a few months. His mother abandoned him."

"Orange or White on the Tiger front?"

"White." Carefully she removed the needled protector and inserted it through the hole in the rubber stopper that capped the bottle. "He is very handsome."

"He's not here, is he?"

"No. He is in the Moscow Zoo."

"That's a relief. Have you ever been married?"

"No."

"Engaged?"

"Once or twice."

"Twice, I'll bet."

Anitchka extracted a portion of the morphine into the syringe. Then she set the bottle and hypodermic aside.

"Normally, I'm not so nosey," Harry said. "But, I don't see a ring and you're a real fox."

"A description of beauty from a man who can see out of only one eye is always open to question." She quickly tied the rubber tubing around his arm, just above the elbow.

"What are you going to give me?"

"Ten units of Morphine."

"I've never tried that before."

"I'm certain you'll like it."

"As long as the pain goes away, I'm open to anything. How come the marriages fell through?"

"My fiancés died."

His eye focused upon the dripping syringe. "Did it have anything to do with Morphine?"

"Worried I might poison you?"

"You ask that of a Jew?"

While Anitchka waited for the veins to rise in the *ginglymus*, she tore open the alcohol wipe. Then she used it to cleanse that area of his skin.

"You're very good at this," he said.

"*Otkuda vy?*" she asked.

"I'm from Minneapolis, Minnesota."

"It's cold there, like Moscow."

"When it's not pissing-down rain." He cocked the brow above his good eye. "Have you been to the States?"

"Many times."

"Professionally?"

"This will sting." Anitchka grabbed the syringe, and carefully inserted its needle into the largest vein. "Stay still." A moment later, she released the rubber hose and slowly injected the fluid.

"You've done this gig before," he said, his voice starting to slur. "Are you a nurse, doctor or junkie?"

"Let's just agree that I get around."

"Holy shit!" His good eye suddenly widened with alarm. "I just got on a rocket."

"Relax," she said, removing the needle. "Don't panic. Everything will be okay." Anitchka folded his arm, pinching the alcohol wipe against the needle wound to stop the bleeding. "I'll give you a second injection after we talk."

He squirmed into a supine position, his words thickening further. "If one feels this good, why stop at two?"

"Tell me about you and Alexi Kalandarishvili?"

"Is this the same Kalandarishvili who I knew as Klaus Schmidt who Rakhmelevich killed while playing with a letter opener?"

Her dark eyebrows rose. "You saw the killing?"

"I saw the results." His shallow breathing made soft hissing sounds in the quiet room. "I heard Kalandarishvili identify Rakhmelevich as his killer. I saw that it wasn't a good way to die."

"*Is* there a good way?" She recapped the syringe and set it aside.

"Crashing and burning on the juice you just gave me holds promise."

"Did you know Kalandarishvili well?"

"We met on the ferry in the morning. By that night, he was dead. It was a brief but unpleasant association. I take it you and yours were after him, too?"

"You're certain you never saw Kalandarishvili before that day? In Berlin, perhaps?"

"I've never been to Berlin." Harry looked deeply into her eyes. "I have to tell you... I'm ready for all the sexual brutality your interrogations can dish out."

"Where is the memory-stick?"

He hesitated, licking his lips. "They got it."

"Who are they?"

"Shkarov and Rakhmelevich."

"How is it you're certain that's who they are?"

"Shkarov made introductions. For a sadist he was very polite."

"Sociopaths usually are," she said, looking at the floor. "What makes you certain they have the memory-stick?"

"Because I put it in the trash by the elevator in my hotel."

"And you think they found it?"

"Not think. I know. Shkarov sent Rakhmelevich to retrieve it. Rakhmelevich found it and phoned Shkarov. Shkarov, in order to express his appreciation for my cooperation, shot me." Harry smiled at her, again. "Have I mentioned my big feet?"

Her eyes returned to his. "Big feet?"

"Come closer and I'll demonstrate."

"Did you feel an obligation to Alexi Kalandarishvili? Were you partners? Is that why you held out so long before telling Shkarov where he could find the memory stick?"

"Partners? That bastard, Kalandarishvili, slipped the memory stick into my pocket without my knowing. Frankly, when I found out, I could've killed him." Harry paused a moment. "I'm sure most people think I did."

"How is the Morphine working?"

"I have to tell you... If Rakhmelevich hadn't broken every bone in my body, I'd have you right here, right now." He chuckled drunkenly. "I may try, anyway."

She smiled. "I shall be on my guard."

"Just don't let it stop you from slipping me another dose with the old syringe-a-roony." He suddenly reached out to her with one hand. "Hang onto my mitt, will you? I'm worried this is all a dream and you're going to disappear."

"I won't disappear." She sat down on the bed and grasped his hand. "Why did you go to Kalandarishvili's hotel?"

Harry raised his head slightly his eyes staring into the distance. "I can see through walls."

"It's just an illusion. There is nothing to worry about."

"Who's worried? There are three harem girls in the next room — all naked."

"You said you were angry with Kalandarishvili... Did you go to his hotel intending to kill him?"

"The rocket's slowing down. I think it's time to get off." Harry's head returned to the pillow. "Don't I have another ticket?"

"Concentrate, Mr. Bronstein. Did you intend to kill Kalandarishvili?"

"To tell you the truth, the guy scared me. I went there intending to hand over the memory stick."

"Kalandarishvili was expecting your visit?"

"He phoned me." Harry frowned. "I guess he wasn't such a bad guy." He frowned. "Have you ever noticed how good people become after their dead?"

"I saw you come out of Kalandarishvili's suite. You were carrying a letter opener."

"The poor, dying bastard begged me to take it out of his chest. As much blood as he'd lost, I knew it wouldn't make it any difference."

"How long were you in Irkutsk?"

"I've never been there."

"Who else was involved with Kalandarishvili?"

"A woman, I think." He squeezed her hand, hard. "Don't let go! I think my rocket's taking off, again."

"What was the woman's name?"

He blinked in confusion. "I haven't had a woman in six months."

"The woman involved with Kalandarishvili."

"I don't know her name. But she scratched the hell out of his face."

"You saw her?"

"I might've. All you have to do is look for a blonde broad with no panties and fingernails like meat hooks."

"Where did you see her?"

Harry squinted, thinking. "On the ferry. She had a bruised throat, bloody fingers and a beautiful bare ass." He grinned. "I'm the type of guy who notices that last little item."

"I thought you might be."

Harry's eyes widened suddenly. "I'm hitting the stratosphere!"

"Once Kalandarishvili put the memory-stick into your pocket, how could he be assured of getting it back?"

"He knew where I was staying in Paris."

Anitchka frowned, dubiously. "How could he possibly know that, if you were not associated?"

"Because he asked and like an idiot, I told him." Harry giggled, his high continuing to soar. "I have to tell you... This is better than sex."

"You said you knew where Shkarov and Rakhmelevich would be, in a week. Where?"

Harry suddenly gave her a serious look. "Pee?"

"Where is Pee?"

"Gdye tualyet?"

"The toilet is down the hall."

"I have to get there fast," Harry said, struggling to rise. "When your father starts beating me, I'd like to avoid a ruptured bladder. It's a terrible way to die."

"No one is going to hurt you, Mr. Bronstein."

"I have to tell you... I've heard that a lot, lately. But, so far, it's been lies." He tried to rise, again. "How about giving the dead American a little help? I don't think I can get out of bed on my own. Not without dropping my flaps."

"Flaps?"

"It's a guy thing."

Anitchka got up and hurried around to the other side of the bed. After several struggling tugs, she got Harry onto his feet.

"Don't move until you're sure of your legs," she said. "You're too heavy to carry."

"And I can't roll. I already tried lowering my wheels, but the lever didn't work. How far have I got to go?"

"About twenty paces.. Can you walk that far?"

"We'd better hurry. I've got to go so bad I can taste it."

Twenty-two whimpering steps later, they were in a tiny toilet. Harry had both hands on the papered wall, bracketing the pipe that fed the water-closet. He was trying to balance his bruised frame in an effort to align his penis with the commode.

"Stop waving it around," she complained, as his hips jerked and twitched.

"It's not my fault," he said. "One-Eyed Willie's never flown on morphine, before."

"If you don't stand still you'll piss all over the place."

"How about cutting me some slack, *duh-vahy*?"

Through the open window above the bathtub, came the rumble of Paris traffic.

"Why don't you sit down?" she suggested.

"Shit! I'm right up against the fucking moon." He shivered. "God, it's cold."

"It's cold because you've pushed your One-Eyed Willie against the porcelain water-tank." Anitchka reached out and grabbed his penis, pointing it toward the center of the toilet bowl. "Look... You try to stand still and I'll aim it while you..." Instantly, his member erected. "You're half-dead and you're thinking about sex?"

"I'm not thinking about anything except how I'm going to fly through Jupiter's rings."

"Then why did One-eyed Willie..."

"You were squeezing him."

"I was trying to get him going."

"You did, and we both thank you."

"Have you never heard of self-control?"

"I have. But, Willie's always been a free spirit."

She rolled her eyes. "Concentrate on getting the job done, please."

"I'm. But, with your hand on him, he's having trouble switching gears."

"I can't let go. If I do, he'll pop up and you'll piss all over the ceiling."

"You'll have to ride the clutch if you want any traction."

"What clutch?"

"Don't they teach you Russian girls anything?"

"If my father should walk in and see this..."

"Oh, God, you should see what I see."

"I have all I can handle right now, thank you."

"I'm passing Mars. It's full of naked, green women."

"I've got him aimed, Mr. Bronstein, why aren't you passing urine?"

"I can't seem to engage Willie's overdrive."

"You damn well better and I mean soon. I'm not doing this for the fun of it."

"That's not what Willie thinks."

"Damn it..."

"I'm trying to turn on the tap, but it takes time and concentration. Particularly, when he's received mixed signals — like your fondling."

She glanced up, sharply. "I wasn't fondling."

"Don't let go. He's almost ready." Then Harry let out a long sigh, and the urine stream started. "Ah, there it goes. Talk about relief. All it took was a little patience and perseverance. *Oj, spasibo!*"

"Yes, you're welcome."

He screwed up his good eye trying to focus down on her. "I've got to tell you… This gets better by the second. The peeing ain't bad, either."

After nearly a minute of watching a steady flow from him she asked, "How much do you hold?"

"This is nothing. In college, after a keg-party, I could pee for nearly three minutes. I hold the all-time-record at my Fraternity."

"You mean men in your country actually measure such things?"

"That's not all they measure. There's distance. Not to mention accuracy. Jack Bannister, at my Frat, held the distance record. Phil Jefferson could knock a fly off a wall at ten paces. Then there's size. Leigh Trosen had the record for that." Harry grinned down at her. "This is the first time I've ever done this."

"I truly doubt it, considering your informative college reminiscences."

"I mean peeing with a woman holding my schlong. *Vy prinimayetye kryeditnyye kartochki?*"

She frowned. "Accept credit cards for what?"

"Frankly, you could do this professionally."

There was a short pause, and then the urine stopped. "Can you reach the toilet paper?"

"What do I need that for?"

"Most people in my country use it to wipe."

"Guys never wipe the end, I don't care what country they're from. They just give it a shake."

Anitchka let go of him. "I think we'll risk a drip dry solution." Then she stood up and grabbed Harry by the shoulders. "Now, I'm going to turn you around. Are you ready?"

"Hold it a second. I'm coming up on Pluto."

"You'll have to stop leaning against the wall, Mr. Bronstein, or I can't turn you."

"If I let go, God knows where I'll end up. Have you never heard of black holes?"

"Mr. Bronstein, I'm running short on patience."

Harry gave her a crooked grin. "After what you, me and Willie have shared, I insist that you call me Harry."

Anitchka grabbed one of his wrists and pulled that hand from the wall. Then she twisted his body toward the bathroom door.

"There," she said. "Now walk. That's it. No. Don't grab the damn water pipe!"

"Are you sure you've got me?"

"Just put one arm around my shoulder to help balance. Then we'll... Get your hand off my butt!"

"Sorry. I had my eye shut and my hand didn't know where to grab."

"Well, open your damn eye and walk. That's it. Here we go. Quit banging One-Eyed Willie against my leg!"

Thirty meandering steps later, Anitchka eased Harry back onto the sheet. After covering him with the bedding, she refilled the syringe and then tightened the rubber tubing around his arm.

"You promised to tell me where Shkarov and Rakhmelevich are going to be in a week," she said.

"Port-Bou," Harry replied, giddily. "The name sort of slurps off my lips. Port-Bou. I like it."

The vein popped up and she cleaned the area, then gave Harry the second injection. "That's another ten units." Anitchka folded his arm tight. "Just relax and let it work."

"We both thank you."

She cocked one eye in amusement. "There are two of you, now?"

"Me, for the pain killer and One-Eyed Willie for..."

"Never mind One-Eyed Willie." She looked at him and her eyes softened. "You'll sleep, soon. When you wake up we'll talk, again."

"I've got to tell you... You and Morphine are the best time I've ever had. Not that Willie's complaining. You and he have definitely made a connection."

"Near enough, I noticed."

"Would you like to know a secret?"

"Not if it involves One-eyed Willie."

"I would die for you."

"Not soon, I hope."

"Want to know another secret?"

"Go to sleep."

"I know who's buying the memory stick from Shkarov."

Her dark eyes abruptly widened with renewed interest. "Who might that be, Mr. Bronstein?"

"Call me Harry."

"Okay, Harry, who is buying the memory stick?"

"It'll cost you a kiss."

Anitchka leaned down and gave Harry a light buss on his lips.

"That was the best kiss I've ever had," he said.

"I think the morphine helped. Now, to whom is Shkarov selling the memory-stick?"

"Who knew that morphine and kissing made such a great combination?"

"You promised to give me a name, Mr. Bronstein."

He smiled drunkenly into her eyes. "Call me Harry."

"All right, Harry," she said easily, "tell me who is buying the memory-stick?"

"A guy named Cheng. Can you believe it? He sounds like the bell on a Chinese cash register."

She frowned in disbelief. "Yu-tung Cheng is in Port Bou?"

"Nope." Harry glanced at her, then away as if not wanting to know the answer to his next question. "Do you know him well?"

"Cheng and I have had one or two unpleasant encounters."

He leered once more at her. "So there's nothing going on between you two?"

"Nothing worth mentioning."

"That means I still have a chance?"

"Mr. Bronstein, you're at the top of my list of potential lovers."

"Call me Harry?"

"Okay, Harry."

"I'll bet you'd like to know where Cheng is right now."

"Very much, Harry."

"It'll cost you another kiss."

Anitchka bent over and kissed him again. This time she took more time, making a point of giving and receiving pleasure from it.

"Mary, mother of God, that one knocked off my socks. If I had socks on, which I don't."

"Deliver on your promise, Harry."

"Cheng's in Sao Paolo. But, he'll be in Port-Bou in another week." Harry then closed his good eye. "You'll have to excuse me, now. It's been a long flight and I'm very tired."

"*Duh svee-dah-nee-uh.*" She kissed Harry on the cheek and then left his room.

When Anitchka reached the kitchen, her father, Kazimir and Golovkin gave her a questioning stare from their positions around the table. Piled on the table was Harry's clothing.

"He's not as seriously injured as Popovitch thought," she said.

Her father offered a dyspeptic grunt. "How can you be certain?"

"His One-eyed Willie popped to attention. I think it's a good sign."

"His one-eyed what?" squinted Kazimir.

She went over to the stove, her cheeks pinking. "It's too complicated to explain."

"Then Bronstein's awake?" Nabatov asked, getting to his feet.

"No, he's sleeping."

"But, if he…" her father began, gruffly.

"Poppa, I talked to him."

"But, I told you…"

"He was afraid you would beat him," she said. "He wasn't afraid of me. And he told me what we wanted to know, and more."

The elder Russian settled back into his chair, picking at his teeth with a toothpick. "Well?"

She poured a cup of coffee, joined the others, then relayed what Harry had disclosed.

Golovkin left his chair, at the end of her story. "What do I tell Moscow?"

"That I will be going to Port-Bou," replied Nabatov.

"But, we don't know if Bronstein is telling the truth."

"He wasn't lying, Ambrosii," Anitchka said.

Kazimir Sokolof gave her a teasing grin. "How do you know he wasn't lying? You didn't take advantage of his weakened condition, did you?"

"How is your numbness?" she said, in taunting return. "Still spreading, I hope?"

"You shouldn't mock me." The bearded Russian sank back in the chair looking desolate. "Dr. Popovitch says it'll get worse before it gets better."

"Anais will be happy to hear that."

"Anitchka," her father scolded. Then he addressed Golovkin, "Make sure Moscow understands that we have independent confirmation on Shkarov and Rakhmelevich."

As Golovkin hurried away, Nabatov turned his attention to Kazimir. "Go to the Alessandra hotel. Confirm that Rakhmelevich was there."

"What about my numbness, Pasha?"

"Dr. Popovitch said you're fit for duty, didn't he?"

"What does he know? He said the American was dying."

"Get going!"

After the bearded Russian left, Pasha took Harry's wallet from the American's jacket and gave it a thorough search. After returning each item to where it had been, Nabatov dropped the jacket back onto the table.

"For a man in financial distress, Bronstein has plenty of cash and credit cards." Then he looked over at his daughter. "You're certain the American is going to live?"

She gave her father a whimsical smile. "Harry's definitely a handful."

His brows shot up in surprise. "It's Harry, now?"

"He insisted."

"On what?"

"Now that Bronstein has told us what we want to know, what are we going to do with him?" Anitchka fiddled with her coffee mug. "Hand him over to the police?"

"Despite what he told you, I'm still not convinced he was a mere pawn in this."

She grinned into her coffee cup. "There is definitely more to Harry than you've seen."

"I'm equally convinced that he knows more about this affair than he told you." Her father shifted. "I think there's at least one more person involved. Someone he's protecting."

"The woman who scratched Kalandarishvili?"

"That would fit Bronstein's personality."

"What about helping Harry with the *Police Nationale*?"

Her father shrugged. "Bronstein's criminal predicament is not our problem."

"It's not fair to punish him for what Rakhmelevich did."

"We are not punishing him." He dropped his hands to his lap, turned them over and then looked at them. "It is up to France to mete out justice."

"When has France been just to Americans?"

"We only have your surmises and Bronstein's claims with respect to Kalandarishvili's death. Hardly sufficient justification for Moscow to intervene."

"We both know Rakhmelevich did the killing."

"We know nothing of the kind." He hesitated. "Although, if I were a gambling man I would wager on Rakhmelevich being the perpetrator."

"Why not reward Bronstein for helping us by helping him?"

"I'll think about it." Pasha Nabatov got to his feet. "Now, I must make arrangements to go to Port-Bou." He glanced at his watch. "I have just enough time to pack a suitcase and catch the next train. Tell Kazimir to ring me when he gets back." He paused, thinking. "If Cheng is involved, the importance of the memory-stick increases exponentially. It means the Chinese will be making future decisions based upon its information; decisions that could mean the difference between peace and war." Nabatov scratched the side of his nose. "Once I've established myself in Port-Bou, I will send for you." Then he shook a warning finger at his daughter. "Stick to business with the American. Moreover, keep a close watch on him. I don't want Bronstein poking into things, he shouldn't."

Anitchka's mouth turned up at the corners but she made no reply.

***

Walnut wainscoting created an ornamental band around the sitting room in Mikhail Shkarov's hotel suit. A band of grayish-pink baroque circled above the paneling. The high ceiling was high inset with copper panels imprinted with flying cherubs. The air smelled of brandy and coffee.

Shkarov rang off from a telephone conversation, looking furious.

"What's the matter?" Innokenti Rakhmelevich asked.

"Bronstein's alive."

"And you complain about my mistakes." Snickering, the patch-eyed Chechnyan took out a cigarette and lit it. "I would've made sure he was dead before leaving."

"Like you did with Kalandarishvili? The reason we are in this mess?"

"Where is Bronstein?"

"According to our Mole, he's at Nabatov's safe-house; 13 Rue De La Sebastopol."

"Golovkin's flat? I'm not about to break in there."

"I don't think we have a choice."

The patch-eyed Chechnyan leaned back and blew smoke at the ceiling from one corner of his mouth. "Bronstein can't do us any harm."

"He knows about Cheng."

"Nonsense."

"He said as much."

"But, how could he?"

"Bronstein must've overheard us talking." Shkarov drew his thick black eyebrows close together and fingered the side of his nose, his eyes still on his partner. "See how nicely your screw-up twisted what should have been a simple but profitable enterprise into an absolute disaster?"

"If you hadn't mentioned our names to Bronstein…"

"Just like your inventive booby-traps decimated Nabatov's entire sector?"

Galina Vishnevskaya came out of the bedroom, pulling a pink robe across her naked body. "Don't you two ever stop arguing?"

"Breakfast is out on the balcony, my sweet," Shkarov told her.

"Some breakfast. All I ever get is cold coffee and day old rolls."

Shkarov ground his teeth in annoyance. "If you want something else, my sweet, then call room service."

Galina tossed him a glare and then swayed out onto the patio.

"We have to kill Bronstein," Shkarov told his partner.

"The risk isn't justified."

"I don't see that we have a choice."

"As far as I recall, our discussion concerning Cheng revolved around him being in Sao Paolo. Let the Russians look for him there."

"I'd forgotten that." Shkarov nodded, relaxing a little. "Maybe things are not as bad as first I thought."

"They never are."

"How closely did you examine the memory stick."

"The maps are all there."

"We need to examine the text documents."

Rakhmelevich dropped his cigarette into his coffee cup. "Why?"

"I don't want to take a chance with Cheng." Shkarov put his hands to his hips, white slashes forming at the corners of his mouth. "Go out and buy a laptop computer." He pulled the memory stick from his pocket and tossed it to his partner. "Make sure it has a slot to read this."

Chapter 11

For the next three days, Harry Bronstein's routine was the same. Dr. Dmitri Popovitch and Anitchka Nabatov entered his room early each morning. She would change the American's bandages while Popovitch assessed Harry's convalescence. Then Popovitch would leave and Anitchka would assist Harry as far as the door to the lavatory, him wearing one of several pairs of pajamas purchased by her for that purpose; white linen with colored stripes. There, Harry would complete his morning ablutions — more or less on his own. Whereupon, Anitchka would assist the American back to bed. Then Anitchka would leave and Kazimir Sokolof would arrive with Harry's breakfast — a bowl of oatmeal. While Harry ate, Kazimir would toss out questions. These centered on his prospects with American women, should he visit the United States. When the bearded Russian left, Ambrosii Golovkin would enter and request Harry's order for lunch. Harry's response was always the same — a cheeseburger. Golovkin's response was also the same — a bewildered shrug. After this, Anitchka would return. She and Harry would chat. Sometimes, when he coaxed her onto the bed with convincing lies as to his change in morality, they would play chess or cards. These games were generally short-lived bouts between Harry's feeble romantic passes and her unerring escapes.

When Kazimir delivered Harry's lunch, invariably a bowl of Zharkoye, Anitchka would depart and the two men would have another Women-of-America quiz-session. After lunch, Kazimir would take his leave and Golovkin would return to take Harry's request for supper — again, a cheeseburger. Golovkin would depart exhibiting his usual air of confusion and Anitchka would return for an afternoon of question and answer; the bed avoided at all costs.

After a supper, which usually involved a plate of Koulibiaca, the Russians left Harry to his own devices. The next morning, the round-robin would repeat itself.

By the fourth day, Harry was strong enough to sit on the edge of the bathtub for a sponging. Anitchka administered this after Golovkin and Kazimir adamantly refused. Her experiences with the American prompted the young woman to lay down restrictions for the event. Harry was to keep his hands to himself. Under no circumstances was he to stare down her blouse or up her skirt, accidentally or otherwise. Her duties were limited to scrubbing only the places he could not reach, and in particular avoiding One-Eyed Willie. Harry, of course, eagerly agreed. It quickly became apparent that Harry Bronstein had no inhibitions and felt that rules should stretch to the breaking point.

Day five did not include a sponge bath, much to Harry's and Willie's mutual disappointment.

On day six, Harry's injured eye opened. But after that, things changed dramatically…

"I have to tell you, Anitchka." Harry aimlessly toyed with a button on his pajama top. "I think you've fallen for me." The swelling around his left eye had diminished to the point where he could open it, slightly.

"We're just friends, Harry." She sat on the bed across from him holding a fan of playing cards. There was the scent of sandalwood, about her.

"I don't agree."

She laughed, a telling flush spread along the slope of her throat. "Forever the optimist?"

"All week long you've looked after me like I was the most precious thing in your life." He let his eyes drift from her blue blouse, down to her short white skirt, to her shapely legs, to her feet; the latter encased in expensive-looking black pumps. "You wouldn't have done that for just any guy."

"I might have."

"Now, that's not to say that I haven't fallen for you."

"Lucky me."

"The fact is, I find you irresistible."

"Three stars for today's diary entry."

"As for One-eyed Willie, you've been tops with him since day one."

"Don't remind me about Willie." Her eyes glittered when she smiled at him.

"The point is you and I should get better acquainted."

"Harry, I've seen you from all angles. Getting better acquainted is impossible." Anitchka's nostrils flared as she breathed. "You've never said anything about your father."

"What's to tell? Pop walked out." He scratched the back of his neck. "I guess he couldn't stand the sight of me."

"I'm sure that wasn't the case."

"You didn't know my father."

"No, I didn't." Anitchka looked at him carefully. "Your mother had a jewelry store."

"She inherited it from her parents."

"Did your father work for her?"

For a moment, Harry looked puzzled. Then, he smiled. "Why is my father of interest to you?"

"You can't blame us for taking an interest in your background."

"I don't. Nobody trusts a Jew, except another Jew — and then, only if the two of them are related." His brown eyes gave her a level look. "If you've been digging, then you know I sold my mother's shop. You also know that my ex-wife took the proceeds as part of our divorce settlement." He took a ragged breath. "I've never had much luck."

"Did your father work at anything?"

"Just trouble. You see, my old man was one of those people who stayed out of step with everyone. Even when he was at his best, there wasn't much good to say. He was always running a game — usually on friends or family." Harry hesitated, reflecting. "I'm not being fair. My dad was a tailor. Not a great one. He wasn't likely to set the design-world on its ear, but he could stitch a straight seam and fit a suit when he had to. He learned the trade from his father. In fact, the men of the Bronstein line have always been tailors — me being the exception. Rumor has it Herod the Great recognized my forbearers as clothiers."

"Impressive."

"Not really. That same rumor has it my people got the job through bribery and blackmail."

Her smile was tentative. "Did your father have any hobbies?"

"When he was flush, he gambled. Not very well, I might add." Harry shrugged. "Who does?"

"Did he drink?"

"I don't remember ever seeing the old man drunk. That's not to say he didn't drink. Marriage to my mother would have turned even the most devout teetotaler into a raving drunk. What about your father? Is Pasha a devout family man?"

Her shiny eyes stopped their inquisition. "Poppa was gone most of the time when I was growing up. Sometimes it was a year or more between his leaving and my seeing him, again." She studied her cards, shuffling one over the other, through a pause. "That's a long time, when you're a kid."

"It must've been hard on your mother."

"My mother never knew me, or I her." Her eyes whitened. Then they darkened as her lids lowered. "She died giving me life. Perhaps I would have turned out differently if I'd known her."

"You've got criminal tendencies?"

"That depends on who's assessing my credentials." She smiled at him. "When was the last time you saw your father?"

"About twenty-five years ago." Harry sat straight up in bed. "He's probably dead, the poor bastard."

"Do you recall what he looked like?"

"Sure. Pop was short, thin, and always well dressed. He had a long, pale, narrow face. He was clean-shaven. His nose was a match for mine — before my Chechnyan interlude. He wore glasses. Gold rimmed. He used to take them off and study the ceiling when my mother wailed about his endless inadequacies." Harry's chin dipped in affirmation. "I think he was praying."

"Your father sought forgiveness for his sins?"

"I suspect he was praying for God to strike her dead." Harry laughed, grimly.

"Do you recall anything else about him?"

"Pop had three gold caps, two of these on his front upper teeth. The last time I saw him, his black wool overcoat dangled on the arm of his favorite charcoal suit. Black suede gloves graced his hands and a bowler perched on his bald head, jauntily cocked to one side. As my father passed me on the way out of the house, I asked about his plans. He merely checked the time on his phony Rolex, as if I did not exist, and headed for his car." The American made a clucking noise with his tongue. "His other arm kept cadence with his steps. In that hand, he carried a black, leather briefcase. I suppose it contained his lunch."

"Was your father a violent man?"

"I can't speak for my mother. With me he was very tolerant. He had to be. I was the one who filched the cash from my mother's purse when he needed it."

"Have you ever been to Lisbon?"

"What's in Lisbon?"

She wrinkled her forehead. "Have you been there?"

"No." Harry tilted toward her smiling. "I'm getting to you, aren't I?"

When Anitchka did not withdraw, he reached out and pulled her forward so their lips were nearly touching.

"Have you ever made love with an American?" he asked.

Anitchka's hand came up and gripped his neck, pulling his mouth to hers. At first, his lips trembled in surprise. Then passion took control and their bodies crushed together. A moment later, the weight of his form pressed her against the bedding. Her arms wrapped tightly around his back; her fingernails digging sharply into the pajama top. Harry slid his free hand to her left breast and held it, feeling the nipple harden under his touch. Then he moved that hand down across her flat stomach. She moaned softly. For a moment, her legs drifted apart. Then, as if some inner mechanism suddenly took control, Anitchka gave a frantic push and squirmed from beneath him, quickly rising from the bed.

"What's wrong?" Harry's eyes bulged with sexual frustration.

"This cannot happen, Harry." Her words came huskily, her cheeks and ears a deep red.

"Of course it can." He reached out for her. "Feel free to fake it."

Her head wagged as she stepped backwards. "Sex is out of the question."

"Don't say that. The prospect of sex with you is what's kept me alive."

"I'm sorry about what happened, Harry. I didn't intend to lead you on."

"The leading I didn't mind. It's the stopping that frustrates me." The American slumped back against the pillows.

"It's not you."

"I have to tell you... I hear that a lot."

"You caught me at a weak moment."

"Do those moments happen often? The weak ones?" A broad smile made funny lines and bumps in his slightly swollen face. "And could you schedule another very soon?"

She smiled. "I do like you, Harry."

He squirmed onto his side facing her, one hand propping his head as his elbow dug into the pillow. "Just not quite enough for a little shared passion?"

"I have to do what's best for both of us."

"Trust me, when I tell you, sex is definitely in my best interest."

"You're still healing from your ordeal."

Harry winked. "Parts of me heal faster than others."

"There are other considerations."

"Like what?"

"The rules I must live by: rules that exclude any chance of our having a relationship."

"I'm willing to bend the rules."

"So I've noticed."

"What do you mean?"

"Your sponge bath."

"Ah, that. My hand going up your skirt was an accident."

"Like when that same hand went down my blouse?"

"You've got me all wrong, Anitchka, if you think I'm only interested in a long term tumble involving complicated emotional ties. I want to build a future with you based, more or less, upon empty passion."

Her face became grim. "You're making fun of me."

"No. I'm trying to ease my disappointment by making light of a painfully testicular situation." The American made a vague movement with one hand. "Are we, at least, friends?"

"I'd like that." She took a perch on the edge of the bed.

After several seconds of silence, he asked, "What about you?"

"What about me?"

"Would you help a friend in need?"

"I would, if possible."

"Then what about helping me — one friend to another?"

"Giving consideration to your rule-breaking habits, how am I to do that?"

"Simple," he said. "Help me get my life back."

"It's not my province to change your history, Harry. Or create your future."

"I was thinking more along the lines of you getting your government to make a public declaration that exonerated me in regard to Kalandarishvili."

"Why would Moscow do such a thing?"

"I have been some help, haven't I?"

She nodded her head. "But, it won't happen, Harry. There is…"

He cut in with, "It wouldn't have to be anything dramatic. Perhaps something like Moscow's investigation proves that I was not Kalandarishvili's killer. The pure simplicity of the declaration would enthrall the French."

"Even if I could arrange such a thing, it wouldn't work. Moscow has no power here. France would continue its own investigation. And, frankly, the evidence is not in your favor."

Harry fell silent for nearly a minute, staring down at his hands. If he could not woo her into assisting, perhaps he could extort her cooperation. His eyes rose back up to hers, his stare cool and calculating.

"Okay, forget friendship. Let's move to plan 'B'," he said. "Has your father gone to Port-Bou?"

"How do you know about my father's activities?" Suspicion crowded the question.

"My time in the military gave me a good understanding of GRU tactics. Once I told you where the Chechnyans would be, your organization would have sent someone." He pursed his making a raspberry sound. "Since I have yet to meet Pasha Nabatov, it follows that he made the trip."

"What is being done is not your concern."

"All right. Let's have a chat about someone else."

"Who did you have in mind?"

"Yu-tung Cheng? Or are his activities on the do-not-discuss list?"

Her eyes narrowed, her expression cold. "He's an operative for the Chinese government."

"That's it?"

"What's your interest in him, Harry?"

Harry's smile was as thin as the gilt on a Buddha. "The Chechnyans are selling your secrets and that's all you know about Cheng?"

"He's an opium addict and a criminal."

"In what way is he criminal?"

"He smuggles drugs. He manufactures illegal documents. He runs a string of agents throughout Europe. They gather espionage. Cheng passes that data onto his government, and sells it to any other countries willing to buy. Now, answer my question."

"I'd like to meet him."

Her dark head shook sharply. "That's not possible, Harry."

"The police won't get wise if you drive me to Port-Bou. You'll be going there at some point. Why not make the trip sooner than later?"

"I cannot do that."

"All right. What about dropping me at the train depot?"

She curled her lip slightly, her head slowly shaking. "Harry, you can't leave here."

The American clamored from the bed his face white with worry. He had assumed that his relationship with the Russians was one of information supplier in exchange for protection. It had never occurred to Harry that he was their prisoner.

"What's your game, Anitchka?"

She stood up, pulled a pack of cigarettes from one of the pockets in her skirt and shook one loose. "My father suspects you of being in league with Kalandarishvili."

"That is ridiculous! I told you how I got involved."

"My father didn't believe it."

"Do you believe me?"

"Yes, I do." As she grabbed the cigarette with her lips, her free hand came out of another pocket with a lighter. Anitchka put flame to the cigarette and stuffed pack and lighter back into their hiding places. Then she regarded Harry through a cloud of smoke. "But, I don't make the decisions."

"What's the plan? Your father has me dragged back to Moscow for a quickie trial followed by an even quicker execution?"

"It won't come to that."

"I'm not so sure." His tongue darted dryly over his lips. "You said you liked me."

"Harry, Yu-tung Cheng won't do anything unless there's a profit in it." She squinted sideways at the American. "You have nothing that would be of interest."

"Has Shkarov contacted Cheng, yet?"

Anitchka squirmed, slightly, reluctant to continue their conversation. "Cheng is still in South America."

"Can you get a message to him?"

She blew a silky-gray smoke ring. It floated upward like a twisting halo until it tore apart in fragile wisps. "What message?" Her voice had become indifferent.

"Tell Cheng he's getting the dirty end of the stick from Shkarov. Tell him the memory-stick is a phony."

Her face suddenly congested. "What are you talking about?"

"The data on the memory-stick is contrived."

"How could you know that?"

"Because I changed it."

"Harry, no!"

"Tell Cheng to examine the modified-date on the files when he gets the stick from Shkarov. The date on some of the files is several weeks after the date on others. He'll get the idea. Tell him I have a second memory stick. Tell him that one is pristine. Tell him I'll trade it in exchange for clearing my name with the Paris police."

She took a step toward the American, her voice sharp. "Where's the other memory stick, Harry?"

"Alternatively…" He made an airy gesture. "I can give it to you — in exchange for Moscow resolving the Kalandarishvili issue."

"Where is it, Harry?"

"Do we deal?"

"Hear me carefully, Harry. What Shkarov and Rakhmelevich did to you is nothing compared to we'll do, unless you hand over the stick."

Anitchka's words shook Harry. He had pushed her too far. Unfortunately, there was no going back. He was not about to spend the rest of his life in a French prison for a murder he had not committed.

"Do your worst," he told her.

Dr. Popovitch entered the room and gave Anitchka a nod. "How is our patient?"

"He's about to experience things from his nightmares," she flared, and stormed away.

"What happened?" Popovitch asked. He looked at Harry with slow, inquiring eyes.

"I got a little impulsive."

"I'm glad to hear that you're feeling good enough to be impulsive." There was a thoughtful pause as Popovitch scratched his thin, blond hair. "Being so with that young woman, however, takes a man with guts and a great deal of stupidity."

"I'll buy the last bit." Harry took a deep, quivering breath.

"What, exactly, did you do?"

"I changed some data on a memory-stick. Then I made the mistake of mentioning there was a duplicate. Neither tidbit sat well with her."

"I see."

"It's worse than it sounds. I think she's out there right now making arrangements to kill me." Harry gave the doctor a confused look. "You are one of them aren't you? I mean I'd hate to think you're a Russian expatriate who's going to send me a bill for all this personal medical treatment when I'm about to be murdered."

"Tell me more about these memory-sticks?" Popovitch enveloped him in an entreating smile. "Maybe once I understand what's happened I can salvage the situation."

When Anitchka reached the kitchen, Kazimir noticed her agitated state. He sat at the table holding a cup of coffee. There was a chessboard in front of him. The pieces stood on it as if in the middle of a game. Golovkin was at the stove making coffee.

"Is Bronstein worse?" Kazimir asked, over the rim of his mug.

"Idiot!" she shouted.

The bearded Russian jumped up from the table bleating, "What have I done, now?"

She crossed her arms. "I was talking about Harry."

Kazimir grinned, with relief; his thick, black eyebrows bobbing up and down. "Trouble in paradise?"

"Leave her be," Golovkin warned the other man. "You'll only make it worse."

Ignoring Golovkin, Kazimir offered Anitchka a teasing finger-wag. "You've taken quite a shine to Bronstein."

"I was doing my job."

The bearded man's eyes glinted. "How is the American in the romance department?"

"You're disgusting," she said.

"Me disgusting or him disgusting?" Kazimir asked, frowning.

"Shut up!" she growled.

"There. You see, Ambrosii? I try to be nice and she kicks me like a dog."

"Did I or did I not, tell you to keep your mouth shut?" Golovkin asked him. The spindly Russian turned from the stove and gave Anitchka a scolding stare. "There's no point in taking your frustrations out on Kazimir. All of us, including your father, noticed your personal interest in Bronstein."

Kazimir made a pleading gesture. "I'm sorry, Anitchka."

She murmured. "Bastard!"

"I'm not a bastard," Kazimir shouted. "My mother and father were married in St. Petersburg."

"I was talking about Harry."

"What's the American done?" Golovkin asked, coming over to her.

After a few seconds hesitation, Anitchka Nabatov relayed what Harry had said about the memory-sticks.

"But, that solves our problem," Kazimir said, when she finished talking. He leaned back in his chair, crossing one leg over the other. "Shkarov ended up with useless information. Therefore, there's no need to push this thing further."

"There's still Shkarov and Rakhmelevich to bring down," Golovkin said.

"We shoot them and tell Moscow they refused to surrender. No trouble."

"Poppa was right," she said, more to herself than to her companions. "The American did throw a wrench between the gears."

"Of course he didn't," said Kazimir. "In fact, Bronstein's improved things."

"How?" Golovkin asked.

The bearded man put a cigarette in his mouth and lit it with his ancient lighter. "Shkarov will sell the altered stick to the Chinese, right?"

"Right."

"Cheng'll figure that out and shoot those terrorist bastards." He stood up. "Stay put, while I get the other memory stick from Bronstein."

"You don't understand…" she blurted, and then caught herself. "We don't know what Shkarov will be selling Cheng."

"Bronstein will tell us."

"How can he possibly remember each and every change?"

"Anitchka is making a good point, Kazimir," Golovkin said. "Bronstein won't remember. And because of that, he may have severely compromised our position with the Chinese."

"In what way?"

"If they think we are less prepared than we are, at Irkutsk, the Chinese may test our resolve."

"They'd have to be insane to invade Irkutsk," Kazimir said. "It's nothing but a shit hole."

"Yes, Kazimir," Golovkin returned, "but it's *our* shit hole."

Kazimir's eyes brightened. "We still don't have worries. After I get the memory stick from Bronstein, we'll get somebody to deliver it to Shkarov. We'll send along a message. It'll tell him the one he has is shit. He'll think Christmas came early. After he delivers it to Cheng, we'll shoot the bastards." He splayed his hands. "Am I brilliant?"

"Send a message to my father, Ambrosii," she instructed. "Tell him what I've just learned from our guest. Tell him that I'm on my way to Port-Bou." Then she glared over at Kazimir; looking sharply into the bearded Russian's dark eyes. "Don't do anything to Bronstein while I'm gone, understand?" With that, she stalked out of the apartment.

"Have you noticed that no matter what happens, I'm always in the wrong?" said Kazimir, as he and Golovkin watched her leave.

Golovkin smiled noncommittally. Something was wrong. However, for a change, it had nothing to do with Kazimir Sokolof. Anitchka was far too upset over too small an incident. Yes, Bronstein's manipulation of the data was cause for concern. Yes, the fact that he had a second memory stick meant getting it from him. However, the resolution of those matters was easily done. So why had she acted as if the world was about to end?

"When Anitchka marries," Kazimir said, "her husband will endure a short, miserable life filled with unimaginable pain and suffering." Then he turned to Golovkin and asked, "Should I warn the American?"

"Why spoil the surprise?"

Dr. Popovitch appeared at the kitchen door, with his bag. "I've removed the wrappings from Mr. Bronstein's ribs. I think he is well enough to get around on his own." The physician made a face at the thick brew in Kazimir's mug. "But, he's not to do anything strenuous for another week."

"Would you like some coffee, Doctor?" Golovkin asked.

"Not if you put a gun to my head, Ambrosii, and whistled up my ass."

Kazimir blinked in confusion. "What in hell does that mean?"

"I'm not entirely sure." Popovitch headed down the hallway to the apartment door. "It's something Bronstein said when I offered to reset his broken nose."

An hour or so after the doctor left, Golovkin brought Harry a change of clothing, the American's jacket, and Harry's personal property. The Russian dropped the items on the bed and told him to get dressed.

"Are we going somewhere?" Harry asked, with no small amount of alarm.

"Not you."

"Where's Anitchka?"

"Gone," said the Russian, and left the room.

Harry quickly checked the hiding place in the jacket's quilted lining. The memory stick was still there. However, it being where he had left it did nothing to resolve the immediate problem. Anitchka's warning had been no idle threat. Moreover, the only way to avoid her wrath was to get free of this place and somehow make his way to Port-Bou.

The American pulled on the clothing: underwear, a short-sleeve blue shirt, white worsted trousers, blue socks and a pair of black leather loafers. After fitting his wallet and cash into the slacks, Harry slipped on the jacket and followed the smell of strong coffee to the apartment's kitchen.

He entered a large and airy room. In the middle, six wooden chairs encircled a big wooden table. On two sides of the room's perimeter lines of upper and lower cabinets were broken up by a large refrigerator and a massive gas stove. Surprisingly, the atmosphere was cooler than in the bedroom. The Venetian blinds covering two, large windows threw alternating bars of light and shadow across the gray tile floor. In the background, the coffee pot gasped out the end of its latest percolating ordeal.

"*Dobb-ruh-eh oo-truh*," Kazimir said, in greeting.

"It's not a good morning for me," Harry said.

"Why not? Your injured eye open, your lip healed." Kazimir squinted. "Can see with it?"

"Not with my lip, but the eye works good."

Harry held the top of one of the chairs, wondering where the apartment door was and how he was going to get past Kazimir and Golovkin, plus any others who might be in the apartment, to make his escape. Bulling his way out was not feasible. A newborn lamb with a touch of determination could knock him flat.

Kazimir tapped the chessboard. "You play?"

Harry nodded and sat down in the chair. "What happened to Anitchka? All I got from Golovkin was that she had gone. Gone where?"

"Not your concern." The Russian's voice was flat and colorless.

"When will she be back?"

"Better you forget her, Harry." Kazimir rose and went to the stove.

"Anitchka's already got somebody on the dangle?"

"What 'on dangle'?" Kazimir asked, glancing over at the American.

"She's stringing somebody along. Fiancé, if you like. Boyfriend, if that's too intimate."

A smile flickered across the Russian's mouth. "Possibly, yes. Possibly, no."

"She didn't mention anyone?"

"Why Anitchka tell 'bout private life?"

"What about your partner in crime?" Harry asked.

"I don't have crime partner."

"Golovkin."

"Ambrosii go market." The Russian returned to the table with a steaming mug of coffee. He set it in front of Harry. "You still got headache?"

"Like Golovkin's coffee, I'm getting used to it."

Kazimir went over to one of the windows, raised the blinds, and then pushed opened the pane. Satisfied with the influx of fresh air, he returned to the table and settled back into his chair.

"What wrong coffee?" the Russian asked.

"I've always been partial to the kind I chew." Harry took a slurp from the mug and grimaced as the gritty fluid rolled across his palate. "Your pal has outdone himself today. My cup contains the extra crunchy variety."

"That good for you."

"A daily dose of this, and I can certainly forget about tartar buildup." Then he looked toward the hall. "That the way out?"

Kazimir nodded.

"I don't suppose you and I could take a walk around the block?" Harry said. "I'd like to stretch my legs."

"Too dangerous."

As Harry moved the chessboard to the center of the table, and reset the pieces to their starting points, his eyes darted about for routes of escape. He had two choices. Leap out one of the windows, or bolt down the hallway to what he hoped would be an unlocked door.

"How dangerous could it be if you were with me?"

"Police everywhere."

Harry set down his mug and gave the other man an engaging smile. "Have you ever been to Port-Bou?"

"Many times."

"According to the directions I got from the clerk at my hotel, I'd have to board the Metro and then take it to *Gare du Nord* Station. From there, I would purchase a ticket to Port-Bou."

Kazimir shook his dark head. "He told wrong. Take the Metro to *Gare Montparnasse*. Then buy ticket."

"How long does the train take to reach the Spanish border?"

"About eleven hours. I get sleeper compartment."

"Pasha Nabatov went to Port-Bou, didn't he? To locate a guy named Yu-tung Cheng."

"Who says?"

"I'll bet Cheng's got a fancy apartment in a high-rise. Guy's like him always live high and wide."

"Yu-tung Cheng live on beach in big villa."

"A fancy, red tile roof I'll bet."

"You'd lose. Roof on villa blue."

Harry said, "You're from the Ukraine."

"How you come that?"

"Golovkin is a Chechnyan. That would make him an odd duck, in your group."

"Golovkin is proud Siberian."

Harry pointed to the chessboard. "Do you want White or Black?"

"Black."

"How did you get into this line of work?" The American moved a white pawn to e4.

"What line work?" Kazimir asked, moving a black pawn to e5.

"You're Glavnoye Razvedyvatel'noye Upravleniye."

For a moment, there was silence in the room except for the whispered crackling of Kazimir's burning cigarette. Then the Russian said, "Anitchka tell you?"

Harry moved a knight to f3. "It's the only way it figures."

"I'm women's clothing importer."

"A clothing importer who hangs out at a safe-house keeping an eye on an American who's wanted by the Paris police, for murder?" Harry took another pull on the coffee. "What did you do before the GRU vetted you?"

Kazimir moved a pawn to d6. Then he looked over at Harry. His usually bland dark eyes had become hard. His words were obstinate.

"I deny everything."

"Okay," said Harry, "let's just pretend you're not part of Moscow Center's infamous GRU." He moved a pawn to d4. "But, if you were, how would you have gotten into that business?"

Kazimir hesitated, and then said in a voice that was coldly polite, "Probably I recruited while in military."

"You were a foot-soldier?"

"Gunner in tank battalion. But, I'm still pretending."

"A T-90 Tank?"

The Russian nodded, grinning proudly. "You ever in one?"

Harry moved a bishop to g4. "No. But, I've heard they're damn tough."

"Damn right, they're tough." Kazimir hesitated, taking a deep draw on his cigarette. "You were Army intelligence; yes?"

"I worked in the code-room, decrypting and translating intercepted Russian transmissions." Harry smiled thinly. "I've probably handled one or two from you."

"I deny it." Kazimir flicked the ash from his cigarette into the shell-casing ashtray on the table. Then he tilted toward Harry and spoke confidentially. "You didn't decrypt any to a girl by the name of Ilinca in Romania, did you?"

"Did you sign them, 'The Big Kahuna'?"

"Are you saying she double timed me?"

Harry laughed. "Just joking."

The Russian grunted not amused. "Anitchka say you come Paris because of ex-wife."

"It was due to unbridled insanity."

"You crazy from asylum?"

"You know... I hear that a lot. But, so far I've never been committed."

"Your wife drove you crazy?"

"No, to bankruptcy."

"Ah, I hear about alimony. In Russia, no such thing. No child-support, either. In divorce, man walks with pockets untouched."

"The dollars that concerned me related to non-refundable plane tickets. You see Maggie — my ex-wife -- belongs to this very odd group of revelers. They're called the *American Association of Murder Historians*."

"She murder people?"

"No. But, there have been several near-misses during the annual barbeque."

"What they do?"

"Each year those kooks take a trip to visit historical murder locations."

"Why?"

"To relive the event — in their slightly demented way. Personally, I could never figure out the draw for it. The whole idea of killing is repellent to me. However, I have to tell you..." Harry shifted in his chair, leaning back. "Those old murders were a real turn on for Maggie. Mostly, I think it had to do with the prospect of spotting a hint of blood still remaining from the horrific incident."

"You wife sound like Anitchka."

"Anitchka has a blood fetish?"

"Don't know 'bout fetish, but she kill fiancés."

"She murdered them?"

"Only first one. Had help with second."

"You expect me to believe she actually murdered her own fiancé?"

The Russian nodded. "She put gun to his forehead and pull trigger. Got him twice before he hit ground, and he ballet instructor — you know how springy those guys are."

"Dear God!"

Kazimir let go a roar of laughter. "No. I'm just showing that Russian make joke, too."

"So she didn't kill him?"

"No, she kill him. But, shot only once."

"Is Anitchka planning to shoot me?"

"I wouldn't put on tutu."

"You said she had help killing her second fiancé?" Harry cocked his head, listening.

"Second one she meet Sunday. They engage Wednesday. He dead Friday."

"You're joking, again?"

"No. Her Siberian tiger ate him."

Harry made a disgusted face. "Ah, she did mention feeding a tiger. But, I never realized her fiancé was the main course."

"Sad thing."

"Was it an accident, or did she send the tiger after him?"

"Anitchka go out buy coffee. She left fiancé to feed the tiger." Kazimir shrugged. "He did."

"I suppose she shot the tiger?"

"Anitchka? Never! She love animal. She gave him Moscow Zoo." Kazimir paused to smile thoughtfully. "He most beautiful tiger I ever see. White with black stripes. Twelve feet long, nose to tippy-tip of tail. He love people."

"Sounds like it."

"Whenever I visit zoo, I see him. He curled up enclosure, looking at people watching him — licking chops." The Russian's smile faded. "You come see murder places with blood spots?"

"No. But, rather than dump a thousand Euros down the toilet, I decided to join the tour so I could use the flights abroad and back. Once I got to England, I went my own way." Harry brooded a moment. "I wish to God I'd never married that woman."

"Ah, I hear you religious man."

"That might be an overstatement. Let's agree that I'm a Jew."

Kazimir gave Harry a dazed look.

"It means I follow a certain way of life. In my case, the path I've taken is skewed — much to the complaint of family and friends," said Harry. "To them, I'm the Bronstein version of Baruch Spinoza."

"Ah, I think I buy car from him."

"Spinoza was a 17th century philosopher. He was one of the few members of the Jewish Community to face *Cherem.*"

"What that?"

"It's the Jewish form of ex-communication." Harry paused. "But, I have to tell you… during these last few days there has been a major rebirth of my beliefs."

"Karl Max say, 'Religion is opium of masses.' I think he right."

"Sometimes the masses need a little pain-killer." Harry gingerly touched his left side. "I can certainly recommend morphine."

"But, how God exist? A God watch over and at same time let everything turn shit?"

"You are not alone in seeking that answer, Kazimir."

The Russian made a noise in his throat. "If ask, God like bad joke."

"Or maybe our problems relate to God being a man."

"What else he be?"

"If God was a woman, the world would be entirely different. There'd be no wars. Men would be neutered after providing the required one-point-three children. And there'd be only one religion."

Kazimir leaned back in his chair, again looking confused. "Which religion?"

"The only religion that believes in action through inaction: Taoism."

"If there God, cannot be woman."

"Why not?"

"Women pain in ass." The Russian lit another cigarette. "No more woman for Kazimir."

"Ah, yes, Anitchka mentioned your numbness."

"She laugh?"

"No so much laughed, as felt there had to be a God or you would not be in such a limp state. Has there been any improvement?"

"*Nyet.*" The Russian's eyes winced. "It disheartening. My favorite part jump once and then droop."

A teasing grin tugged at the corners of Harry's mouth. "Have you tried putting a drop of hot sauce on the head?"

"Hot sauce?"

"It's a foolproof treatment for impotence. One dose, and within twenty-four hours your schlong will be pointing out the planets."

"Don't care planets; want fixed." Kazimir stood up and went over to the sink with his coffee cup. Suddenly he laughed. "Ah, I get 'bout planet pointer." Then he set the cup down for washing, and returned the table. "What brand hot sauce?"

"You have to make it."

"How?"

"Easy. Take a quarter teaspoon of ground red pepper and a quarter teaspoon of olive oil. Mix them into a paste and spread it across the head of your penis."

"Under foreskin?"

"That would be my recommendation."

"What nothing happens?"

"Trust me, Kazimir. When it starts to work, you'll know."

There was a buzzing sound from another part of the apartment. Kazimir got to his feet saying, "I deal with. You wait. I be not long."

Harry held up both thumbs. "Give Moscow my regards."

"I will." Then the bearded man hurried away.

As soon as the Russian was out of sight, Harry jumped up and rushed down the hallway. At the door, he spotted a dusty brown fedora dangling from a hook. It would not be much of a disguise but if he kept the jacket's collar up and the fedora pulled low, it might be enough to fool the police. Then another thought came to mind: why would the Russians be so careless? First, they failed to find the memory stick. Now, it was like they wanted him to escape. With a suspicious backward glance, Harry opened the door and slipped out of the apartment.

Moments later, Kazimir Sokolof crept back into the kitchen, his cellular phone to one ear. "Bronstein made big break for it like you say, Pasha." Kazimir went over to one of the windows and looked out. "He's heading for the Metro. Of course, he never suspected anything. Don't worry. Golovkin's outside tailing him. Of course, I telephoned Popovitch with the plan. He will be waiting to pick up trail of the American at the Metro Station. Pasha, stop worrying. We all understand your plan. Golovkin and Popovitch track Bronstein's movements until he gets on the train. I take that same train to Port-Bou, to keep eye on American. Yes, yes. Everybody understands. No interference when Shkarov and Rakhmelevich make a move on the American." There was a pause as Kazimir's sharp eyes spotted a young blonde woman climb out of a beige Jaguar. Sitting behind the vehicle's steering wheel was none other than Innokenti Rakhmelevich. "You were right about the Chechnyans, Pasha. They're already on the case. Rakhmelevich just dropped off a young blonde. Yes, a woman. She's got tits the size of Mount Elbrus. Pasha, I'm not watching her tits, I'm watching Bronstein. He's cutting through an alley, and she's following. What does it matter which of them kills the American as long as they get the memory stick? Pasha, I'm just saying, it ain't over 'til the naked snake charmer bangs the gong." Kazimir made a vague movement with his free hand. "I don't know what it means. It's something Bronstein told me."

***

"I don't like it." Innokenti Rakhmelevich he drove the sleek, beige Jaguar at a snail's pace along Boulevard Bonne Nouvelle. "I should be dealing with Bronstein."

"Your brilliant talents got us into this mess," Mikhail Shkarov said, impatiently.

Ahead, Galina Vishnevskaya walked briskly along the sidewalk. Beyond her, apparently unaware of the young woman's presence, limped Harry Bronstein.

"How could your Mole know when Bronstein would make a break for it?"

"The GRU arranged for the American's escape. Since Bronstein is without personal transportation, and we know his intended destination is Port-Bou, logic dictates that he will head for the nearest Metro Station. Ergo, our search for the Jew along this tree strewn boulevard."

"I don't like your tart being our only link to the Jew."

Shkarov closed his eyes with exasperation. "Consider this, Rakhmelevich: You expended a great deal of energy beating the truth out of the Jew. When you finished your efforts, I demonstrated my appreciation for his cooperation by shooting him. So given Bronstein's experiences, in Paris, who is he more likely to trust? You and I, or a beautiful woman he's never met?"

"How do we know there is a second memory stick? Bronstein didn't have it on him. We searched his hotel and car. So where is it?"

"That is what my lovely Galina will find out."

"What if she gets the stick and does her own deal with Cheng?"

Shkarov opened his eyes very slowly, as though sticky hinges controlled the lids. "Where was all this concern when you were killing Kalandarishvili?"

"Your tart knows Cheng. And, he's got the hots for her. It wouldn't take much—"

"You keep underestimating people, Rakhmelevich." Shkarov lifted his eyebrows as if it took a great deal of effort. The movement furrowed his entire forehead. "Once Galina offers Bronstein a lift to Port-Bou, he'll think she's a gift from his God." The Chechnyan's brows drooped, leaving the skin above etched with reddish lines. "On the way, they'll stop to retrieve the memory stick. And by the time you and I reach Port-Bou, my lovely will have it and Bronstein will be dead."

"You and your women…" Then Rakhmelevich frowned. "Give him a lift how?"

"Wherever she corners Bronstein, we'll leave the Jaguar."

Rakhmelevich tossed his partner a confused stare. "What are you and me supposed to do on foot?"

"The two of us will catch a taxi to the train depot. Weren't you listening when I explained all this to my lovely?"

"I've got better things to do than earwig over you two."

Chapter 12

After leaving Golovkin's apartment, Harry Bronstein darted down an alley and crossed several streets. Then he continued his limping flight on the sidewalk alongside a busy thoroughfare. He had no idea where he was or where his panic-driven strides were taking him. Instinct told Harry that safety meant putting distance between himself and the Russians, as quickly as possible.

At a street corner, he stopped to catch his breath. As he bent over to rest his hands on his knees, his eyes darted around looking for pursuers. The only person in sight was a young blonde. Her huge breasts rose and fell like floating melons beneath a tight pink sweater. Her very short gray skirt flitted upward and then fell back into place with each of her bouncing strides in his direction.

Harry smiled with satisfaction. In that outfit, she was not part of Pasha Nabatov's collection of spies and killers. In fact, in that outfit she was risking arrest for indecent exposure. He stood erect and eyed the street traffic in both directions. There was not a police cruiser in sight. At last, his luck had taken a change for the better. Not only was he free, but he had made a clean getaway. Harry turned, and continued his limping journey.

Several minutes later, he caught sight of an encouraging sign. According to the bold white print on a red background, a *Le Métro Parisien* station was merely a block away. He slowed his pace to a walk, shoving his hands into his jacket's pockets. There was no need to hurry, now. Once aboard the subway he would become invisible among the hundreds of other passengers. Then it was just a matter of waiting until the metro reached a stop within walking distance of *Gare Montparnasse station*. Once there he would purchase passage to Port Bou. After that, it would be a simple matter of locating Yu-tung Cheng's beach house with its unique, blue tile roof. Of course, he would still have to convince the Chinese crook that his offer, Harry's, was too good to turn down. However, that would be a mere matter formality.

A police cruiser turned the corner just ahead. Instantly, Harry's heart sank. The vehicle moved very slowly in his direction.

Had Kazimir telephoned the authorities to warn them about Harry being in the area? It was unlikely. Losing an American hostage to police custody wouldn't endear Kazimir to the rest of the Nabatov gang. On the other hand, a jail cell was a good place for the GRU to perform an assassination. With the deaths of Anitchka's fiancés in the forefront of his thoughts, Harry rubbernecked for a place of concealment.

Sixty feet ahead, on the same side of the street, Harry spotted *la Poussette Café*. The restaurant occupied a section of the ground floor in a Haussmannian-style apartment building. The gray, stone, four-story structure was far enough back from the street to provide vehicle parking and outdoor tables.

Harry tugged the fedora lower to better conceal his face and then lengthened his stride. All he had to do was get inside the restaurant before the police got close enough to recognize him.

Fifty feet to go.

As he moved, Harry tilted his head up slightly. Just enough to watch the approaching cruiser, below the fedora's drooping brim. The vehicle continued its slow, purposeful approach. However, there was no indication the officers within had taken an interest in him.

Forty feet to go.

Harry wanted to run. His legs begged him to run. It took all of his willpower to continue a steady, pace.

Thirty feet to go.

The police car was now less than fifteen yards away. Harry could see the officer's faces, clearly. They were staring at him.

Twenty feet to go.

The cruiser abruptly pulled to the curb on the opposite side of the street. From the corner of his left eye, Harry watched the parked vehicle. The officers were definitely studying him.

Ten feet to go.

The cruiser's engine fell silent. Then the car doors opened. Harry's heart clawed its way into his throat. Two officers climbed out, both of them still showing an interest in him.

At the café's entrance.

Harry's hand shook as he gripped the knob. A trembling twist of his wrist and two steps later, he stood inside the café. He took a deep, calming breath. Then with forced casualness, Harry closed door behind him. As long as the police stayed outside, he was safe.

The restaurant was a large cool space littered with small, round tables occupied by a chattering clientele. The air smelled of cigarette smoke, cinnamon and burnt sugar. All he needed was an out-of-the-way spot, where he could fade into the background. He let his eyes drift.

Unfortunately, *la Poussette Café's* clientele occupied every table; none of whom seemed to be in any hurry to leave.

Harry glanced back looking out through one of the door's glass panes. The two gendarmes talked in the middle of the street as cars raced past in both directions. Again, Harry's eyes scanned the cafe. Then, near the rear exit, he spotted an elderly couple abandoning a table for two. It was a shadowy spot not far from the kitchen and adjacent to the hallway that led to the toilets. Under normal circumstanced, that table would not be a preferred place of dining. In his present situation any seating was worth grabbing.

He hurried over to the table and sat facing the front entrance. His mouth tasted sour. Sweat poured out of his pores as if his body was on fire. His heart pounded and his stomach rolled from the steady influx of adrenaline.

Harry dragged his hands across his face and tried to calm down. If he did not get control of his emotions quickly, the police would not have to see Harry. The stench of his fear would grab them by the nose and lead them to him.

A plump, middle-aged waiter came over to take Harry's order. The short man had guilty eyes within a long, olive face. Harry choked out a request for a *Tranche Aux Fruit,* and coffee. The waiter gave a disinterested nod and waddled away.

The café's front door opened. Harry raised his hands to his face and peered between the fingers. Instead of the expected police officers, the blonde-haired woman he had noticed earlier came into view. She closed the door and looked around as if searching for someone. Then her eyes settled upon Harry. During happier times, her stare would have been flattering. In his current emotional state, her eyes felt like a pair of daggers jabbed against his throat.

What were the odds of her following him to the same cafe? As unlikely as it seemed, considering her appearance, could she be with the Paris police? Her tight sweater and revealing skirt would hardly qualify as a standard-issue ensemble, even for a rapist trap. Nevertheless, a trap might be the reason for her seductive garb.

With a toss of her head, the young woman strode directly over to Harry. He lowered his hands and smiled when she reached his table.

"How's tricks?" he greeted her.

"I thought you were an American," she said.

Her coppery blond hair had the look of bottled color. The coarse-grained strands clung tightly to her narrow head, held in ponytail fashion by a pink ribbon. Her thinly plucked eyebrows were several shades darker than her hair, almost a walnut color. Her nostrils flared when she breathed, going white at the edges. Her chiseled chin formed a sharp point. She wore a heavy patina of face powder. There was pink smear across her full mouth. Her eyes were cobalt blue with large irises. Her bare arms carried a light covering of downy hair. To Harry's eyes, she was beautiful in an exotic way.

"Hard to hide," Harry said.

"It looks like you're alone."

He lowered his chin, pretending to take an interest in the checkered tablecloth. "Hard to hide that, too."

"Busy place." She glanced around as if looking for an empty table. "May I join you?"

Harry raised his eyes and nodded. The blonde's curious Russian accent cancelled any possibility of her being a police officer. However, it revitalized his paranoia. How many Russian women, dressed like her, frequented Paris cafes on any given day? Not many. Of those, what were the odds against them being *Glavnoye Razvedyvatel'noye Upravleniye?* Beyond calculation, Harry decided.

"No problem," he said.

After she settled into the chair across from him the blonde set her purse on the floor, by her feet. "Wonderful day, yes?" She gave him a blazing smile.

His eyes darted from hers to the café entrance, and then back to hers. Despite not having seen her among the others, in Pasha Nabatov's employ, she looked vaguely familiar.

"I've had better," he said.

"I love sunshine." She let go a bray-like laugh.

Like a light coming on in his head, Harry suddenly remembered where he had seen her. She was the blonde from the ferry. His eyes drifted down to her throat. There, nearly hidden beneath a thick layer of makeup, were bruises.

"I hope I'm not intruding," she said.

"Depends upon your intentions."

"I'm thinking coffee and conversation." She swung a leg over the opposite knee. "Okay with you?"

"What's your name?"

"Galina Vishnevskaya." She looked down her pert nose at him. "What's yours?"

"Harry," he said, before thinking. Then the American lamely tried to remedy the mistake with, "Harry Smith."

"So many of you American's are named Smith." She frowned. "It is very curious."

"No really. Smith's come from a long line of passionate men and fertile women."

The waiter returned with his order, and Galina requested a coffee. After the man left, she leaned forward and stared at the *Tranche Aux Fruit.*

"That is the most beautiful thing I've ever seen," she said, hungrily.

"Help yourself." He slid the plate toward her. "It's too much for me."

With a cry of delight, the young woman picked up the tart and tore it in half, returning one portion to the plate. Then she immediately began to devour what was in her hand.

"I'm starving," she said, munching noisily.

What was she waiting for? Why play a game when her intentions must be to take him in tow back to Golovkin's? On the other hand, was she there to kill him?

"Nothing wrong with a good appetite."

From her lack of table grace, he assumed that she was not a high-ranking GRU operative. She had more of the fruit on her chin than in her mouth. Or, had he jumped to another wrong conclusion? Was she merely a tourist?

"I've seen you before," he said.

"I don't think so," she returned, swallowing. "I would've remembered."

He flushed and one hand instinctively went to his slightly swollen face. "I suppose my puss has changed for the worst."

The waiter returned with her beverage and Harry paid for both orders.

After the waiter left, Galina waggled the tooth-worn remains of her portion of the tart. "This is better than sex."

"Sounds like I should come here more often." He picked up his part of the pastry and took a bite. As he chewed, his eyes looked past her to the café's front door. "I thought I saw the police outside."

"There are two of them. When I came into the café they were checking the registration on a Citroën parked in the café's back lot." She smiled at him with a sudden glint in her eyes. "Stolen, probably."

"How can you be certain?"

"It happens a lot in Paris. The cost of living is outrageous and Citroën's are an easy target. Why pay when you can drive for free?"

A rush of sudden relief washed over Harry. Being able to forget the police after so much tension caused him to burst into chain of giggles.

"What's so funny?" she asked.

"I was thinking about an old movie. Two strangers see each other on a ship and then a week later they meet, by chance, in a small Paris café. Whereupon, they immediately fall in love."

"Do you think that's likely to happen?"

He shook his head. "I don't believe in coincidences."

"They happen." Her bright smile turned on again, like a flashbulb.

"Like you being here at my table?"

She blinked, her smile drooping. "I was driving past and noticed the café. You know how that is."

Harry stiffened at the sound of her lie. She had not arrived by automobile. He had seen her walking. No GRU operative would have made such a mistake. The lie, itself, meant her presence at Harry's table was not a coincidence. So if she was not a member of the *Glavnoye Razvedyvatel'noye Upravleniye*, and she had not arrived by chance, who might she be? Although, Galina's accent excluded a Chechnyan lineage, it did not rule out the possibility of her having an affiliation with the terrorists.

"Nice, your car?" he asked.

"It's my uncle's new Jag."

"You must have a rich uncle."

"Rich enough. Do you live near here?"

He wagged his head. "I just checked out of my digs."

"Digs?"

"Where I was staying."

"You Americans use many odd words." Galina coughed. Then she bent down and fumbled in her purse for a handkerchief. Finding it, she sat up and blew her nose. "Allergies."

"There are worse things."

She returned the white, lacy cloth to her handbag and then gave him a curious stare. "Where's your luggage?"

He hesitated. It had not occurred to Harry that a man without lodgings would have luggage. "I'm storing my bags."

"Where are you headed?"

"Headed?"

"You must be going somewhere, if you no longer have a place to stay."

"Port-Bou."

"What's in Port-Bou?"

Harry shrugged. "I heard the sea air was very therapeutic."

"I won't argue with that." Galina screwed up her pretty face. "Paris smells like a sewer, except when it rains. Then it stinks worse." She took another bite of the tart and chewed thoughtfully. "You know, on reflection, I *have* seen you before. I think it was on the ferry from Dover to Calais."

He raised his cup and took a sip of coffee, his eyes drifting back to the café entrance. "Memorable crossing."

"I'm going to Port-Bou."

He set down his cup, again looking at her. "Why am I not surprised?"

"We could drive together."

How often does a beautiful, young blonde offer a ride to a banged up stranger? It never happens. Not unless she had something other than being a Good Samaritan in mind.

"Thanks. But I'm taking the train," he returned.

Galina picked up her coffee and took a long draw on the brew. "Splitting the gas expense with me would be less than half the price of a train ticket."

"It's a very kind offer. But I'll pass."

She flexed her jaws, the muscles in her cheeks making hard lumps. "Don't trust me?"

"It's not you so much you as the company you keep."

Galina laughed harshly. "I'm a respectable woman."

"If so, your respectability came at a high price."

"What do you mean?" she snapped/

He pointed at the barely visible bruising. "Somebody did something nasty to your throat."

One of her hands darted to the makeup-caked injury, the long fingers lightly stroking it. "I had an accident."

"Accidents can be categorized under many names. Was yours Alexi Kalandarishvili?"

She blanched, unable to control her surprise.

"What, exactly, did you do to piss him off?" Harry asked.

Her reply choked, "I've never heard of him."

Six out of ten people would have asked him why he had linked her to someone they had not discussed. Galina had not. Instead, she chose to offer a simple denial in hopes the topic would go away.

"Where is Shkarov?" Harry asked.

She wet her lips and her eyes dropped away from Harry's suspicious stare. "Believe it or not, I'm here to help you — Mr. Bronstein."

He eased back, his heart suddenly thudding. "Into my grave?"

"That's up to you."

He stood up.

Galina clamored to her feet. "If you walk out of here without me, you're dead."

"The odds against Shkarov catching up with me will not improve in your company."

"There are the police to consider; the two outside, for starters." Galina hesitated, watching his face intently for a cooperative sign. "On the other hand, if you come with me you'll reach Port-Bou, and have your meeting with Yu-tung Cheng."

"You're well-informed."

"Mikhail Shkarov leaves little to chance."

"Including you?"

She reached down and picked up her purse. "Not if you and I come to terms."

"Over what?"

"The memory stick. Do you have it with you?"

The two *gendarmes* entered the café and looked around. Harry pulled the fedora low across his face.

"It's worth a million Euros to Cheng," she continued, glancing over at the two officers. "This is the deal: I'll get you to him. In return, I want half of what he pays you."

"That's a lot of money for a ride I don't need."

"Alternatively, I'll scream and those gendarmes will rush over, here. There's a reward offered for your capture."

The police officers split up and slowly wandered from table to table, scrutinizing the male occupants.

"On the other hand," Harry said, "I've always been partial to long rides with beautiful blondes in tight, pink sweaters."

Galina offered him a gloating smirk that formed sharp lines around her nose and mouth. "Then it's settled."

"I'll have to take a pause in the men's room. What color is the Jag? I'll meet you there."

"It's beige; plate number 074LTC." She tossed another look at the police officers. "Don't be long, Mr. Bronstein. I've got a good set of lungs."

"That was the first thing I noticed."

"If you're not by the Jaguar when I reach it, you'll be dead before the day is out."

Harry quickly headed down the café's back hallway. At the restrooms, he stopped and looked back. Galina was casually making her way toward the front door. The gendarmes were still checking faces at tables. Quickly, he ducked out the café's rear door and started down the alley. He had less than a minute to find another hiding place: one the police would not search.

Unfortunately, Harry had no sooner reached the trashcans than he spotted a police cruiser driving through the alley in his direction. He had no choice. It was take a chance with Galina and her magical Jaguar tour, or face arrest.

He skidded to a stop, spun around and raced around the café to the front parking lot. There, in the parking lot, left as if by some wizardry, was a beige Jaguar with the license plate number: 074LTC.

A moment later, he spotted Galina leaving the café. She was talking to someone on her cellular phone; Shkarov, presumably. The Chechnyan was probably giving her instructions in the fine art of murdering Americans. Once he was out of Paris, he would pick a spot to make his escape. Even in his weakened physical condition, Harry was certain he could easily overpower her. Unless, of course, Galina had a gun. Then things could get messy, what with the leakage potential of blazing bullets.

"Over there." She pointed to the Jaguar.

Harry trotted over to the vehicle.

"You're a popular guy," she said, upon reaching him. "The police were questioning everyone in the café about you."

"It's been a rough week." The words slipped past his teeth.

She unlocked the car with a remote control. Harry quickly climbed inside, relieved to be out of sight. Galina joined him, settling behind the steering wheel. Then she started the engine.

"The picture the police were showing was of you — before your accident — wearing that jacket. The hat and the bruises on your face make a good disguise. But, that jacket is a dead giveaway. You should've ditched it."

Harry slipped on his seat belt. "What did Shkarov have to say?"

Galina glanced into the rear view mirror. "Duck your head. The gendarmes are coming out."

Harry crouched as she eased the car away out of the parking lot and into the flow of traffic. After a block, she glanced into the rearview mirror and told him the coast was clear.

He straightened, but did not relax.

"What makes you think Shkarov won't kill you for helping me?" Harry asked, as they sped through Paris.

"He'll try, Mr. Bronstein." She quickly changed lanes heading for the A-75 highway. "But, half a million makes the risk worthwhile."

"How did you know where I was? For that matter, that I was alive?"

"Shkarov has a mole in Nabatov's organization." She tossed him a smile. "Clever, huh?"

He fell silent, eyeing the right hand mirror and the tailing police car captured within. "We've got company."

She looked into the rearview mirror. "Now's not the time for paranoia."

He traced his dry tongue across even dryer lips. "Paranoia is second nature to a Jew."

Harry had little confidence in his financial arrangement with Galina. Her cutting a deal with him most certainly was a death sentence for her. Nevertheless, until he was miles away from Paris, he had to pretend to be in league with her.

"The police are not interested in us," she said, returning her eyes to the road.

"Mole or not, how could you know that I would leave the safe-house?"

"We were warned that you would, and we were waiting. Since we knew where you were and where you were going, it was easy enough to keep watch until you appeared. Then I followed on foot."

"I saw you walking behind me. So, how did you miraculously end up with wheels?"

"Shkarov left it." She glanced over, grinning.

"Mole or not, he had no way of knowing I'd stop at that café."

"They were in the Jag following me. When I stopped, they left the car."

He cocked his head. "There was no guaranty I'd go with you."

"It was come with me, or I was to kill you." She blazed another smile. "You would not be my first."

"On that I have no doubts. Killing me wouldn't have gotten you the memory stick."

"Cheng is paying a million for whatever Shkarov hands him. As long as you didn't get to Port-Bou, Cheng would accept Shkarov's deal. Getting the stick you have is merely a bonus."

"Why didn't Shkarov and Rakhmelevich attempt to take me on the street?"

"Golovkin was following you. That made the risk unacceptable."

"I didn't see him."

"You weren't supposed to."

"What's Shkarov's plan for me?"

"He had two options. First, if you'd have made it to the Metro you would have been killed before you got on the Port-Bou train. I'm the second option."

"So at some point along the way, you're supposed to kill me?"

"That was the plan. But all that's changed since you and I came to terms."

Harry looked out the rear window. The police cruiser was no longer in sight. "That puts Shkarov and his patch-eyed helpmate at the train depot?"

"More or less." She bit her lip. "How is it you know Yu-tung Cheng?"

"I don't."

"Nabatov's people told you about him?"

"No. I overheard Shkarov and Rakhmelevich talking. They mentioned that Cheng was in Sao Paolo."

"He got back last night." She looked over at him. "You do have it with you, don't you? The memory stick."

"Not exactly."

She growled, "Don't jerk me around, Bronstein."

"I did have the memory-stick." Harry hesitated, thinking. Then he said, "But, I mailed it to Cheng."

Galina gave him a horrified double-take. "You what?"

"The memory-stick is password protected. It's no good to him without me. But, it being in his hands, along with an explanation as to why I sent it, makes what Shkarov's offering open to question."

There was another span of silence. Then she said, "If you overheard Shkarov and Rakhmelevich talking, how did you know Cheng's address? It's not like they would've mentioned it."

"I checked with directory assistance in Port-Bou. Telephone operators are paid to be helpful."

"But, you didn't leave the safe-house until today. I followed you. You never went anywhere near a mailbox. So, how could you mail a letter to Cheng?"

"Kazimir mailed it. He's not the brightest bulb on the Christmas tree. But, he likes me." Harry looked over at her suspicious face. "How would you like the entire million?"

"What's the gag?"

"No gag."

"What's the deal?"

"You tell the police that Rakhmelevich killed Kalandarishvili."

"What makes you think they'll believe me?"

"That's the wrinkle. The authorities have to believe you to get the entire bundle."

"That could be very risky. Shkarov has connections in the Paris police."

"Wouldn't a million make the risk doable?"

"I'm thinking."

Another round of silence fell between them. She drove. Harry studied the side mirror.

Then, Galina said, "Okay. We've got a deal as far as I'm concerned. But I don't think the police will buy my story any better than the one you're offering."

"You and Kalandarishvili had a personal or business arrangement?"

"Both. He was disgusting. I'm glad he's dead." She glanced over at Harry. "Don't cross me Harry."

"How much was Kalandarishvili being paid to deliver the memory-stick to Shkarov?"

"A hundred thousand Euros."

"Why didn't Shkarov get the plans himself?"

"Neither he nor Rakhmelevich could go back to Russia. Years ago, they faked their own deaths to avoid capture by the GRU. Unfortunately, Anitchka Nabatov saw Rakhmelevich at the Montmartre Hotel after he killed Kalandarishvili."

"That must've strained relationships."

"Not enough to put them at each other's throats, if that's what you're thinking. Whatever rift Rakhmelevich's carelessness caused was nullified by Shkarov's carelessness with you."

"How did Kalandarishvili get the memory stick?"

"From a Russian army officer by the name of Moskalenko."

"I only had a brief interlude with Kalandarishvili, but I would not have thought him capable of convincing anyone to turn traitor."

"He didn't. Moskalenko was married but had a mistress." She tossed Harry a smile. "A mistress can be very convincing."

"I take it, you were the mistress?"

"A girl has to get on in this world."

"Why would Kalandarishvili risk crossing Shkarov?"

"As I said, a mistress can be very convincing."

"To whom was Kalandarishvili planning to sell the memory stick? Cheng?"

"No. The Americans. All Kalandarishvili had to do was get the memory stick to Paris." She tossed him another look. "You're a dead ringer for the CIA op."

"What went wrong?"

"By the time Kalandarishvili and I reached Dover, I realized he had no intention of sharing with me. So, I contacted Shkarov. I told him what Kalandarishvili was planning to do. He told me to steal the memory stick."

"Thinking he would reward you, you stuck your neck out — no pun intended?"

One of her hands touched her throat. "Unfortunately, my efforts were not successful."

"I'm surprised he didn't kill you."

"He thought had." Then she gave him a frowning glance. "Kalandarishvili gave the stick to you. Why?"

"As you said, I'm a dead ringer for the CIA operative. Kalandarishvili approached me, thinking I was that man. When he realized his mistake, his mind did a quick analysis. I think he assumed that Shkarov prompted your efforts at theft. He also assumed that Shkarov would have a backup plan. What would be easier than to bribe one of the immigration officers at each entry point into France to stop and search Kalandarishvili? If he was going to sell the memory stick, he had no choice but to get someone else to bring it across the border.

"Why did you wait until Kalandarishvili was on the ferry before attempting to steal the memory-stick?"

"Kalandarishvili kept the stick in the safe of each hotel, wherever we stayed. Only on the ferry did he have it on his person for any length of time."

There were several minutes of quiet, while she drove and Harry watched the side mirror. A gray Citroën was following them, despite the fact that Galina was driving less than the speed limit. He could not see how many people were in the vehicle. However, his guarded instincts warned him to anticipate an end to Galina's allegiance.

***

Mikhail Shkarov put his cellular phone back into his pocket and looked around the train depot, grimly. A few yards away, he spotted Innokenti Rakhmelevich, returning from the ticket agent after purchasing their passage to Port-Bou. For a moment, he wished he were entirely alone. Free from everyone on the planet. No matter how he proceeded, of late, he kept taking wrong turns.

"Did your tart lose Bronstein?" Rakhmelevich asked, when he reached his partner.

"He took the bait as I expected," said Shkarov.

"Then what's bothering you?" The patch-eyed Chechnyan scratched his head. "Your face is as long as a hangman's rope."

The other man drew his lips back and licked the upper one. "Just a feeling that something is about to go wrong."

"I told you to let me deal with Bronstein."

Shkarov grimaced impatiently. "The last thing we need, right now, is more of your creativity." He reached out and took one of the tickets from his partner. "When does the train leave?"

"Thirty minutes."

"Our Mole has caught up with them."

"Isn't that risky?"

"When Galina stops to refuel, the Mole will assist Galina in getting the memory stick from Bronstein." His smile was as thin as the gold on a weekend wedding band. "And to dispose of the American's body."

"What about Nabatov?"

"Pasha Nabatov will have been informed of Bronstein's escape." Shkarov brooded at his partner a moment. "Nabatov will assume Bronstein is on the way to Port-Bou. Nabatov will assume he took the train and will try to intercept Bronstein. But, we will have already done so."

"Won't he see us arrive?"

"Probably. But, right now, he is more interested in laying his hands on the memory stick than killing us."

"I hope you're right," Rakhmelevich said, tightly. "Because if you're wrong, we're both dead — for real, this time."

Chapter 13

Six hours later, darkness was closing in on highway *A-75*. Rain thundered down. The drops slanted in front of the Jaguar's headlamps like a tangled curtain of glass beads. The passenger side-mirror kept a hypnotic hold on Harry Bronstein. Captured within were automobile headlights, the same since Paris.

"That car's still following," Harry said.

Hunched over the steering wheel like a blonde effigy, Galina Vishnevskaya kept her eyes on the rain-swept road ahead. The air smelled of her perfume; a heavy, cloying version of *Opium*.

"I hear that from you every turn of the hour." The blonde-haired woman ground her teeth. "Why don't you get a grip on your paranoia?"

"Paranoia is what keeps a Jew alive."

The windshield-wipers moved back and forth across the glass like frantic bird-wings, barely able to keep up with the downpour. The radio was playing an Edith Piaf tune: *Non, Je ne regrette rien.*

"Relax." Galina's eyes glinted in the darkness, reflecting the headlamps of oncoming traffic. "We made a deal. I'm keeping my end. All you have to worry about is keeping yours."

"If that's the case, why do I feel like a worm dangling from a hook?" he asked, looking over at her.

"Stop sweating it, Harry."

"I will, when we shed the guy in that car."

Galina beautiful face widened with a seraphic smile. "It's coming down in buckets." She glanced into the rearview mirror. "Some timid soul is following my taillights."

"As slow as you're driving, it's got to be more than the storm."

"Don't be ridiculous." Her eyes made another trip to the mirror. "It's probably an old woman with bad eyes."

"Pull over."

"Why?"

"To let the *old woman* with the bad eyes go by."

"If you don't trust me, Harry…"

Harry mocked with, "On such short acquaintance? Of course I trust you."

"There's petrol stop ahead. I'll pull in there. Happy, now?"

"Not much."

"You can say prayers while I buy fuel," she said dispassionately.

"How far are we from the Spanish border?" His eyes returned to the headlamps in the side mirror.

"About twenty kilometers."

"Then, how far to Port-Bou?"

"Seven kilometers." Galina darted a look at him, annoyance growing. "Stop shaking, Harry. Shkarov and Rakhmelevich are at least two hundred kilometers away."

"Planning something unpleasant, I'm sure." He examined the palms of his hands. They were wet with nervous sweat. "What did they tell you to do? Get me to some nice, dark, petting spot and shoot me?"

She made an exasperated face. "Get it through your head, Harry, I'm not going to kill you."

"Murder's an option for each of us, Galina. All it takes is the right situation."

Her head wagged. "Not me."

Harry fell silent, staring into the mirror. After about a minute, he returned his stare to her. "Who do you love most?"

"What's that to you?"

"I'm trying to prove a point. Who do you love most?"

Galina considered the question for a few seconds. "My niece, Katrina."

"How old is Katrina?"

"Ten. Why?"

"Let's assume, for the sake of my murder theory, that I have you and Katrina trapped in a not-so-nice basement in a building miles from everywhere. Due to the prior carelessness of a previous occupant, there are several shards of glass on the concrete floor; large pieces, as sharp and dangerous as butcher knives." He spoke in dull tones, once more eying the mirror. "Nobody knows where you are. Consequently, there's no chance of a rescue."

"We're playing the kidnapper game?" she mocked.

"It's far worse than that." Harry Bronstein tossed her a sidelong glance. Then his stare returned to the mirror. "In this nasty hideaway, there's only one door. It's locked. I, however, do have a key in my pocket. There are no windows."

"Clever you to find such a place."

"I, in my capacity as resident pervert, have raped you — repeatedly."

"Things to look forward to."

"I wasn't very discrete. Your niece was a captive audience."

Galina drew in a sudden breath. "You're being disgusting."

"I'm just getting warmed up." He made a throwaway gesture with one hand. His eyes remained on the mirror. "I've made it clear that I'm going to kill both of you. What's worse, I've been eying Katrina with lustful intent."

"Stop it."

"Do you protect Katrina? Or do you let me have my dirty way with the kid?" His mouth widened a fraction of an inch as he looked back over at her. "Remember, you'll both be dead if you do nothing."

"I'm not playing your sick game."

"In my fictional scenario, there are two things in your favor. First, the glass shards. One slash and I'll be dead. Second, I will be completely preoccupied with Katrina to concern myself with you. What are you going to do?"

She looked disagreeably at him. "I wouldn't kill you, if that's what you're trying to prove."

"You could and you would."

"Shuttup!"

"Once you saw me pawing your niece; once you heard her terrified pleas, you'd pick up a shard and make your move."

"You don't know anything about me."

"I know about people, Galina." He took a deep breath before continuing, "Maternal instinct would take control. You'd rush over like a lioness protecting her cub. You'd stab me until I was dead. Later, after you and the kid were safe, you might feel a twinge of remorse. Murder isn't everybody's idea of a good time. Nevertheless, under the same circumstances you'd do exactly the same thing."

She looked over at him, her face taut. "You're grating on my nerves, Mr. Bronstein."

"I have to tell you…" Harry laughed, softly. "I hear that a lot. Usually from people who don't like hearing the truth."

Galina Vishnevskaya flicked on the Jag's turn signal and took the off-ramp, leaving *A-75*. She drove on in silence until they reached the petrol station. In the side mirror, Harry noticed the same headlights in the reflection making the same change in course.

"Popular spot, this petrol station," he said. "That timid soul, the one who's been trying to kiss your ass for the past six hours, made the same detour."

"What do you think, Harry? Maybe he needs fuel, too?"

"He? What happened to the old woman?"

She slapped on palm on the steering wheel. "He, she, whoever! What in hell's wrong with you?"

"Mostly, it has to do with being persecuted for several thousand years. But, I have to tell you, this last week's been a contributing factor."

At the petrol station, white-walled, rectangular structure, Galina parked the Jaguar next to a fuel kiosk. The driver of the trailing car drove past the refueling stations and parked out of sight. Its driver's silhouette had been visible to Harry's stare; a man, hunched over the steering wheel, gripping it with both hands.

"What make of car does Shkarov and company drive — besides this one?" Harry asked.

"Rakhmelevich has a white Peugeot."

"The car with a passion for your taillights is a dark shade of Citroën." Harry scowled thoughtfully. "Since he drove past the pumps, he didn't need gas."

"Maybe his bladder's full?"

"Maybe."

"Well, mine is." The tone of Galina's voice made it clear that she was still annoyed. "So, after I get the petrol pumping, I'm going to the ladies' room. While I'm in there, I won't be building a bomb or loading a gun."

"What about knives and poison?"

"Drop dead, Harry."

He looked across the rain-choked fueling area in the direction the Citroën had gone. Neither the car nor its driver had reappeared. "Can you get in touch with Cheng?" His distrusting eyes returned to her. "I'd like to know whether he'll see us before your pals arrive."

"Dammit, Harry!" Her voice came across the car like a velvet snarl.

"Is that a yes or a no?"

"I'll telephone Cheng, okay?" Galina pulled the key from the ignition, opened the car door, and crawled out. "In the meantime, take a valium."

"Are you holding?"

She slammed the car door and then went over to the nearest fuel pump. After getting the gasoline flowing into the Jaguar's fuel tank, Galina strode into the petrol station.

Harry waited until she was out of sight. Then he crawled from the Jaguar. Something was dead wrong. Timid drivers do not make unnecessary lane changes or off-ramp usage during a storm unless they have no other option. They hang tight between the ditches hoping for the best. So if the Citroën's driver required neither fuel, nor bladder relief, why had he followed the Jaguar off the highway? And, more importantly, what was he doing now?

The American turned his jacket's collar up against the rain and trotted to the building through the downpour.

After relieving himself in the men's-room, Harry came out to the station's common area and looked around. From his point of observation, he could see wall to wall plus the pumps, outside. Galina was nowhere in sight.

He went to the women's toilet. Using his toe to push the door open, Harry peeked inside. There were no feet visible below the stalls. That meant Galina had gone outside, but not to the Jaguar. So where does a woman of questionable integrity go, during a rainstorm, if not back to her car? Logic dictated that she was paying a call on the Citroën.

Harry weighed his options. One, he could pretend all was well in his tiny, paranoid world — a sure-cure for breathing regularly. Two, he could take a twenty-seven kilometer hike in the rain. Or, three, he could steal the Jaguar.

The last idea held the most appeal. The only complication was getting the keys from Galina. Killing her offered a certain allure. She was used to strangulation, considering her relationship with Kalandarishvili, so there would be no surprises in methodology. Unfortunately, Harry did not have the stomach for cold-blooded murder. A more agreeable solution would be to leave her alive after getting the keys. However, that would risk arrest by French authorities, something Harry wanted to avoid. Of course, he could bring Galina along. Although driving through a rainstorm with a vindictive woman in the adjacent seat might mean disaster. Forcing her into the trunk would solve that complication. However, if the Spanish stopped him while doing a spot check at the border, they'd recognize his name from his driving license. He'd be arrested and held for the murder in Paris.

On reflection, Harry decided that option number two was his only chance to reach Port-Bou. He turned and hurried out the station's rear exit.

It was black as a bar mitzvah suit. It was also as cold as a dry-ice toilet. Harry started away from the building, heading back toward *A-75*, when the wind shifted. Carried on it, were the sounds of a man and a woman arguing.

Harry stopped and listened. He could not understand the verbal interaction. The female speaker was definitely Galina. Whoever the man was, he held a heatedly adverse viewpoint to hers.

Harry turned and returned to the building. Then he crept along its rear wall in the direction of the voices. When he reached the building's corner, Harry stuck his head out.

Galina stood beneath the shelter of an awning. In front of her was a stooped, man. She was protesting allegations of disloyalty. He was insisting that she pursue a vague course of cooperation. Their arms flailed the air. Their bodies tilted toward each other, both in stubborn noncompliance.

"I am following the plan," Galina shouted.

"Shkarov does not agree," the stooped man retorted. "That is why he sent me."

A flash of lightening crackled through the blackness. The resulting blaze, lit the arguing pair is if it was midday. Instantly, Harry recognized the man confronting Galina. It was none other than Dr. Dmitri Popovitch.

The presence of Popovitch confused Harry. However, a moment later, he remembered Galina's remark about Shkarov's mole. Then another worry darted through Harry's mind. Instantly, his body let go a shudder. Anitchka Nabatov had described Yu-tung Cheng as an operative for the Chinese government. However, she also described him as a drug-addict and a criminal. Such people were not immune from paying homage to multiple masters. What if Cheng also worked for Shkarov?

"If you don't inject Bronstein," Popovitch shouted. "I'll have no choice but to kill both of you." He extended one hand offering her an elongated, black box.

"I'll do it my own way," she screamed back. Her chin tilted up, in defiance. "Tell Shkarov I'll get the memory stick. Tell him that Bronstein will be dead before they arrive in Spain."

There was no need to listen further. Harry turned and hurried back the way he had come.

When he reached the other side of the petrol station, Harry hurried through the storm back to *A-75*. Then he moved parallel to the highway, in the direction of Port-Bou, keeping to the trees as much as possible.

After several minutes, Harry stopped and looked back. In the distance, he could just make out Galina standing by the Jaguar, rubbernecking. From his angle of view, Harry could also see the Citroën. However, he was too far away to tell if Popovitch was inside the vehicle.

As Harry watched, Galina climbed into the Jag and started it. With the headlamps on high beam, she raced out of the station, heading back toward highway *A-75*.

He crouched down in the cold rain behind a small shrub as the Jaguar roared past. Then Harry rose up and continued his shivering trek. There was nothing to worry about, now. He had merely twenty-seven kilometers to walk and all his worries would be over. With a little overdue luck, he should be able to do that in a few hours — assuming, of course, that pneumonia did not set in.

A branch snapped, behind him.

Instinctively, Harry crouched. His heart was in his throat as he stared through the downpour, back toward the sound.

At first, saw only rain-blurred brush. Then, about thirty yards away, Harry spotted a stooped shadow. From the figure's bent posture, it could only be Dmitri Popovitch. The traitorous doctor must have seen Harry leave the petrol station. It was a safe bet the unkindly physician was not pursuing Harry in order to assist in the American's plans to reach Port-Bou: at least not alive.

Harry raced off. However, seconds later, a bee going at the speed of light buzzed past his left ear. Realizing it was a bullet, presumably fired from Popovitch's gun, Harry dropped to the rain-drenched ground.

After hitting the grass, he rolled for several yards. Then Harry belly-crawled, like a frightened gecko, until he found a hiding place behind a large shrub. There he twisted on the ground to await his pursuer.

Less than a minute later, the physician rushed into view. The stooped man paused barely ten yards from Harry, his head turning back and forth, his eyes scanning the rain-swept darkness.

Not seeing what he expected, Popovitch cocked his head and listened. A split second later, a bolt of lightning crackled through the clouds. In the resulting flash, Harry noticed a pistol, fitted with a silencer, in the doctor's right hand.

"Bronstein?" the physician called. "I'm here to help you."

Harry fumbled along the ground until he found a small, fallen branch. He picked it up and tossed it to the right of the physician.

Popovitch twisted and fired the pistol several times in rapid succession; sending a popping stream of flames through the darkness.

If Harry harbored any doubts as to the not-so-good doctor's intentions, all was clear now. If Popovitch got Harry in his sights, the American would be no more.

"I think I can do without your assistance, Doctor," Harry taunted.

There was another series of pops and flashes. This time one of the rounds clipped off a branch on the bush just above Harry's head. The American hugged the ground, realizing that he had vastly underestimated the physician's firearm capabilities.

Popovitch moved forward, step by slow and careful step.

After what seemed like an eternity, the physician stopped next to the bush; his wet shoes just inches from the American's hands. The Russian's eyes jerked from side to side, under furrowed brows.

"Let's talk this over," Popovitch shouted. "I don't want to kill you, unless I have to. Give me the memory stick. I'll let you go. I'll tell the others you're dead. No one will come after you."

Harry could hear the stooped man's labored breathing, and smell his disinfectant-like cologne. One more step and the doctor would trip over Harry. At that point, there would be no talk. Or, for that matter, no chance of Harry's survival. The American had only once chance. He must turn retreat into attack.

With a desperate cry, Harry Bronstein scrambled to his feet and lurched forward, his shoes digging into the soggy turf as he reached for his antagonist.

Falling across the bush, Harry managed to grab the hand in which the doctor held the pistol.

The weapon discharged, the round burning Harry's thigh as it passed through his pants.

The American pushed down on the gun with all his weight.

Popovitch, in an effort to retain control of the weapon, jerked back. In so doing, he folded the pistol against his own body drawing Harry to within inches.

"You can't win, Bronstein!"

"I'm damn well going to try!"

As the two men struggled, there was another burst of flame. This time, the physician let go a groan as the fired round grazed his belly. Harry hooked one leg behind the Physician's and pushed. This tumbled both men to the ground.

They hit the grass, Harry and Popovitch still struggling to control the gun. The American heaved upward trying to free it from the Russian's grasp. A second later, there was another flash as the gun fired. This time the round grazed Harry's cheek, leaving a burning-wet trail past his ear.

With another desperate effort, Harry slid one hand onto the silencer. In spite of the metal's searing heat, he used that extra leverage to twist the gun into the physician's midriff. There was another pop. As the gun fired. Popovitch cried of agony. Instantly, the wounded doctor let go of the weapon.

Harry scrambled to his feet taking aim at Popovitch, with the pistol. "Don't move!"

Unintimidated, Popovitch climbed to his feet. "There's no escape if you keep the memory stick, Bronstein. You'll be hunted down no matter where you go." He offered an open hand. "Give it to me. It's your only chance."

"The stick is my only chance. And I'm taking it to Cheng."

With a roar, Popovitch lurched forward, knocking the American backward to the ground, the gun flying free.

Harry squirmed, trying to regain the weapon. Before he could break free, the doctor's icy fingers closed like a steel clamp around Harry's throat.

With a defeated whimper, Harry clawed at the other man's eyes.

Popovitch merely twisted his face away, his fingers clenching tighter and tighter.

Harry kicked and squirmed, finally managing to turn over onto his belly.

Instead of improving his prospects for survival, that move gave Popovitch the opportunity to coil one arm around Harry's throat while the other formed a lever at the back of the American's neck. An instant later, the pressure on Harry's esophagus increased, causing bright flashes of red to explode behind the American's eyes. Then shadows crumpled Harry's consciousness.

In a desperate effort to survive, the American rammed an elbow into Popovitch's side.

The physician let out a scream, and released his grip, rolling away. Harry struggled to his knees. Then, several frantic seconds of groping in the grass later, he had the pistol.

"Keep away or I'll shoot," Harry said, taking aim at the wounded man.

"You won't kill me," Popovitch sneered. He stared at the American with ugly eyes that were shaded no particular dark color by the lumps of flesh surrounding them. "You Americans are too soft."

Harry squeezed the pistol's trigger four times. In the flare of the gunfire, Harry saw Popovitch's face twist in agony. A moment later, a series of lightning flashes acted like a gigantic strobe. In the resulting stop-action, the physician collapsed to the ground.

In one sense, the struggle with Popovitch had cost Harry precious time. However, the favorable outcome, regardless of how morally repellent, provided Harry with an unexpected gain. Instead of walking to Port-Bou, he now had transportation — in the form of the physician's automobile.

Harry stuffed the pistol behind his belt and crouched down next to the dead man, fumbling through the physician's pockets until he found the Citroën's keys. He would have to ditch the car when he got to Port-Bou. There was no telling how long it might be before someone discovered Popovitch's body. Nevertheless, barring the unforeseen, he would get to Port-Bou hours sooner than the Chechnyans.

Chapter 14

Pasha Nabatov sat on the passenger side of a gray, rented Alhambra. He wore his usual dark suit and white shirt. The vehicle idled just beyond the parking area of the Port-Bou train depot. His eyes darted back and forth, peering through the rainy darkness, studying the passengers leaving the station. It was nearly midnight.

A moving female figure suddenly rushed from the crowd over to the car, climbed inside, and shut the door. "It's always pissing down rain, here," Anitchka complained, as she settled behind the steering wheel. She wore black slacks, a black blouse and black boots. "Whoever described Spain as warm and sunny should be arrested and shot for his lies."

Her father curved his lips. "What makes you think it was a man who fostered this country's weather falsehoods?"

"Only a man would describe this moldering pesthole in glowing terms."

The white haired Russian filched a cigarette from a pack and slipped it between his lips. "To lure gullible women, in all their naked glory, to the beaches?"

"What else?"

He made an amused grunt, striking an ancient lighter to life, and touching the yellow flame to the weed. "Shkarov and Rakhmelevich were on the train?"

"As you predicted."

"Did they see you?"

She shook her head.

"I hope they dumped Bronstein's corpse in France. I don't relish the idea of Spanish authorities making the rounds." He took a deep drag on the cigarette and blew smoke toward his feet. "Why isn't Kazimir with you?"

"He's hobbling about like a pregnant woman."

"What's happened to him?"

Anitchka pulled a lever near the clutch pedal and the trunk-lid popped open. "I didn't ask."

"Why not?"

"I didn't care."

Nabatov cracked the side window, and blew a plume of smoke outside. "He must not be fully healed from the explosion."

"It's more likely the train-food disagreed with him. You know how Kazimir feeds his face."

"Did you ask Kazimir about Bronstein?"

"He says it went like clockwork."

"Then there's nothing to worry about."

"There's plenty to worry about."

"Like what?"

"Harry wasn't stupid, Poppa." She clenched her lower lip between her teeth. "He'd have known we let him escape. And he'd have dumped the memory stick, his first chance."

"You give that American too much credit for brains."

"I give him the credit he deserved."

"You got emotionally involved with him, didn't you?"

Her voice choked. "I liked Harry."

"You knew it had to end this way. You should have known better."

"We could've handled him differently."

"He brought this on himself when he altered the memory stick."

"I don't agree." Anitchka hesitated. "I telephoned Anais this morning."

Her father winced. "From the sound of your voice, there's trouble."

"She's filed for divorce."

Her father flicked some ash off his dark suit, with a pinky finger. "I'm sorry to hear that."

"The entire situation is disgraceful."

"All divorces are shameful."

"I mean her being in love with Kazimir."

Nabatov gaped at his daughter, momentarily stunned. "I thought Anais hated him."

"Apparently her protestations were nothing but window dressing." Anitchka raised a hand, and then let it drop. "That woman thinks the sun rises and sets on Kazimir. When I told her he'd been injured, she broke down in tears."

"But I saw her hit him in the head with the phone."

"Anais didn't want Kazimir to think she was easy." Anitchka gave her tongue a scolding cluck. "She even admitted to knowing about the video camera under her desk. She said it was there a whole week before I spotted it."

"Then she was purposely letting him—"

Anitchka cut-in, "I don't know anything about purposes, Poppa. I'm just telling you what Anais told me."

He said with a ruminative grimace, "I don't understand young people."

"As far as I'm concerned, Kazimir should be sent back to Moscow."

He looked away from his daughter groaning, "Why, this time?"

"He's the root of her problem."

"How can you blame him for their divorce?"

"You know very well that if Kazimir had not been paying her so much attention, Anais wouldn't have ignored her husband and he wouldn't have gotten involved with that horrid pasty filler at the Nin bakery."

The cigarette jiggled in his mouth as Nabatov spoke. "I don't think the pastry filler is horrid. In fact, I find her to be a very sensitive and affectionate young woman."

She rolled her eyes, looking out the side window with embarrassment. "You've been involved with that creature!"

"Since when is it a crime to get lonely?"

"There's nothing wrong with being lonely." Anitchka spread the fingers of one hand. "But, there's a great deal to be said for curing the problem with someone you care for instead of a slut who makes jam-busters."

"You need to get married, Anitchka. You need to find a husband. Someone to worry about. Someone to nurture." Her father averted his eyes and cleared his throat. "Someone, besides me and Kazimir, to torment."

"You're one to talk about marriage. How long has it been since momma died?"

"With a man it's different."

"Since when?"

Nabatov squirmed in the seat, trying to get comfortable. "Anitchka, it's not healthy to be so involved with your work that you think of nothing else."

"Nothing in our business is healthy. That's why so many of us turn up dead."

"You give me such a headache!"

They fell silent. She let her eyes drift from face to face as she watched the passengers leave and enter the depot. He smoked the rest of his cigarette.

"You've never liked any of the men I've dated," she eventually said.

"Yes I did." Her father tossed the cigarette butt outside. "That ballet instructor was very nice." He rolled up the window. "What was-his-name? Boris something or other?"

Anitchka gave her father a disbelieving look. "You had me kill him."

"Only because he was a traitor." Nabatov waggled a forefinger in front of his nose. "But, that didn't mean I didn't like the man."

There was more silence. Then Anitchka murmured, "Harry made me laugh."

He looked at his daughter sharply. "Bronstein is dead. Stop thinking about him."

"I can't help it." She gave the steering wheel a slap. "I'm going to kill Rakhmelevich when I see him."

"He goes back to Moscow along with Shkarov -- those are my orders."

She snorted, "You are bursting with orders, aren't you?"

"Don't think you're too big for me to handle, young lady!" Pasha Nabatov pursed his lips and stared thoughtfully out the side window. "The important thing is that the Chechnyans now have the unaltered memory stick."

"I wouldn't bet my life on that."

"The American would have jumped on the train, the Chechnyans would've grabbed him, they'd have killed him and taken the stick. End of story."

"We could've helped Harry get it to Cheng. The end result would've been the same."

"Cheng would've not have trusted the American."

"Harry was a good talker. He'd have convinced Cheng."

"Just what did he talk you into?"

"Nothing, I'm sorry to say." Her voice choked. "Trapped on the train with Shkarov and Rakhmelevich, Harry would've stood out like a turd in a milk pail."

Nabatov frowned with confusion. "A what?"

"Something Harry told me." Anitchka heaved her shoulders. "I don't understand it either."

Pasha Nabatov thrashed around in the seat still trying to get comfortable. Then he said, "I should have found the memory stick when I first went through Bronstein's clothes."

"Golovkin said the hidden pocket in Harry's jacket was padded and the stick was small. It took him several searches to find it."

"Ambrosii's certain the data was just as we intended?"

She nodded. "Golovkin transmitted the stick's contents to Moscow for verification. It matched what Moskalenko gave Kalandarishvili, exactly."

A gleam pushed through her father's dark eyes. "Then we only have to wait for the Chinese to act on what they get from the Chechnyans."

There was a thump-thumping in the trunk. Then the lid slammed down. A moment later, Kazimir Sokolof crawled into the Alhambra's rear seat.

"The Chechnyans are right behind me." He pulled the door shut. Then Kazimir let go a shivering whimper.

"You didn't let them see you?" she snapped, to the bearded Russian.

"Of course not. Do you think I'm an idiot?"

"Do you have to ask?"

"What's the matter, Kazimir?" Nabatov asked, glancing into the rear seat. "You sound like you're in pain."

"Parts of me are on fire, Pasha," Kazimir said, clutching at his groin.

"What about Bronstein?"

"He didn't take the train."

Anitchka twisted to look over the seat. "You told me it went like clockwork!"

"It did — except he didn't get on the train."

"He had to!" said Nabatov.

The bearded Russian wagged his head. "Golovkin followed Bronstein to a café. In there, the American picked up a woman. Then the two of them got into her Jaguar and drove away. Golovkin was on foot so he could not follow. Fortunately, I was able to reach Popovitch. He was in his car not far from the Metro station. I passed on the Jag's description and plate number and Popovitch was able to catch up with them a couple of hours outside of Paris."

A cry of delight came from deep in her throat. "Harry's still alive!"

"Where's Bronstein, now?"

"My last contact with Popovitch was an hour ago. He said the woman and Bronstein had stopped for fuel just short of the Spanish border."

Anitchka scowled. "Harry knew this woman?"

"I doubt it. The description Golovkin gave me matched the blonde I saw getting out of Rakhmelevich's Jaguar — the same Jaguar she and Bronstein left in."

"How do you know it was the same car?"

"Because the plate number I saw on the Jag Rakhmelevich was driving matched the plate number Golovkin gave me from the Jag that Bronstein and the woman drive away in."

"Drive time to Port-Bou is shorter than train time," Nabatov said. "It follows, therefore, that Bronstein and that woman must be in Port-Bou."

"What did that woman look like, Kazimir?" she asked.

"She looked like tits on a stick, to me."

"Is sex all you think about?"

"Not since I went numb."

"She could be Galina Vishnevskaya," Nabatov mused.

The bearded Russian suddenly reached across the front seat and pointed at the windscreen. "That looks like the same Jag. And there's Shkarov and Rakhmelevich, putting luggage into the trunk."

Pasha Nabatov raised a pair of binoculars to his eyes. "That plate number is *074LTC*," he said. "And there's Galina standing beside the driver's door." After a few seconds, he put the viewing device on the seat between him and Anitchka. "I think we can assume that she killed Bronstein after getting him here."

"Poor Harry," Anitchka murmured. "He was probably staring at those huge boobs when she shot him."

Kazimir nodded. "I would have been."

"I'm sorry the American is dead, but it was imperative that we get our plan is back on track," Nabatov said, with smiling confidence. "Once Shkarov and Rakhmelevich deliver the stick to Cheng, we'll make our move on the Chechnyans."

"I'm going to shoot her, first," Anitchka gritted. "Then Rakhmelevich."

"We are taking them all back to Moscow!"

"The Jaguar is leaving, Pasha."

"Don't lose them." Her father looked all around carefully. "It will be good to see Red Square, again."

Anitchka put the Alhambra into gear.

"Keep the car in sight," Nabatov said. "But, vary your distance."

"Poppa, I do know this business."

Pasha Nabatov took out his cell phone and dialed. "It's Nabatov, Ambrosii. Do you have anyone on our payroll that Yu-tung Cheng trusts?" Using his free hand, the Russian dragged the fingers through his white hair. "No. I need to know the results of a pending exchange between Cheng and Shkarov. Yes. She will do, nicely. Call me back when you have something to report."

Anitchka pressed the accelerator and the Alhambra rolled forward.

Nabatov looked back at Kazimir, his forehead corrugated by confusion. "Why do you keep whimpering?"

"The hot sauce is killing me, Pasha."

"Ah, you're having indigestion." The white-haired Russian stuffed his cell-phone into his suit. "You'd better roll the window down, in case the distress gets out of control."

"It had better not get out of control." Anitchka tossed Kazimir a backward glare.

"I don't think opening a window is going to help, Pasha."

"After we deal with Shkarov and Rakhmelevich, we'll stop and get antacids for you."

"Did you and Golovkin rent another apartment, Kazimir?" Anitchka asked.

"Golovkin was to sign a lease this afternoon." Kazimir moaned. He raised a hand quickly. "I think I'm dying."

"How long before it will be operational?" Nabatov asked.

"It looks like they're headed directly for Cheng's." She shifted the Alhambra into high gear to shorten the gap on the Jaguar.

"Two days to set up the electronics," Kazimir said, gasping in agony. Tears dribbled from his eyes. "Then another day to build the armory. Pasha, I think I need a doctor."

Pasha Nabatov and his daughter exchanged glances.

"What in hell did you eat on the train?" she demanded, looking over one shoulder.

Nabatov twisted in the seat to take a closer look at Kazimir. "Is it food poisoning?"

Kazimir made another whimper, giving his groin fervent squeeze. "I'm on fire."

"They're turning onto the road fronting Cheng's villa," she said.

"Not so close." Her father returned his attention to the car ahead. "If they spot us, we will lose our advantage."

"It's like there's a blowtorch on it." Kazimir crossed his legs.

"For God's sake, roll down your window!" Anitchka said

"It's raining."

"I'd rather have the rain than a load of methane from your guts!"

Twenty minutes later, the Chechnyans' Jaguar pulled into the driveway of a huge villa, as massive as a fortress. The adobe-brick house was white in color, top-dressed by a heavy blue tile roof. A high, hurricane fence encircled the structure. A deep terrace ran along the villa's front. Cars on the drive's apron included a red Mercedes Benz, an ancient yellow Cadillac, and a silver Rolls-Royce. Tacked diagonally across one of the round porch's support posts were the numerals 7238. Rain still fell hard as the Jaguar's occupants climbed out.

"I want them alive unless we have no choice but to kill them," Pasha said, as he watched Mikhail Shkarov, Innokenti Rakhmelevich and Galina Vishnevskaya hurry into the huge house, through the binoculars.

"Only if you arrange for me to be their executioner in Moscow," his daughter said.

"I'll arrange it if that's what it's going to take to get them to Moscow." Nabatov lowered the glasses. "Now, find a spot to park. Someplace where we will not be observed from the villa, but close enough to take action as soon as the Chechnyans leave."

Anitchka eased the Alhambra forward until they reached the drooping braches of a tall pine about fifty yards from the villa. Then she stopped and put the vehicle into neutral, leaving the engine idling.

"I can't take it anymore!" Kazimir jumped out into the downpour.

"And you wonder why I wonder about him?" she said to her father.

Nabatov took out another cigarette and lit it. He drew in on it until the cigarette tip glowed red. "You're too critical of Kazimir."

"He's an imbecile."

"You should consider him in more favorable terms, daughter."

She gaped at her father in disgust. "Are you suggesting that I consider a romantic relationship with that lunatic?"

"Why not? Kazimir's as strong as an ox and as brave as a bull. What else do you need in a husband?"

"A few brains would be nice." Her eyes went to the side mirror. A moment later Anitchka made an appalled face. "Your idea of son-in-law material is out there in the rain being absolutely disgusting!"

"Better he relives his bowels outside, than in here."

"I mean, he's playing with his One-eyed Willie."

Nabatov blinked in confusion. "His what?"

She pointed at her crotch. "You know what I mean."

"Don't be ridiculous!"

"Go out and look, for yourself."

Pasha Nabatov snuffed out his cigarette and climbed from the car. Seconds later, he was back inside.

"Well?" she asked.

"I don't wish to discuss it."

"For years I've been telling you that man needs a rubber room. Now do you believe me?"

"I'll talk to him when we get back to Épône."

"Which means you'll do nothing."

"I said I would, didn't I?"

Kazimir climbed back into the car, softly humming. "Talk about relief."

"I'm glad you got your little problem resolved," she said, in a taunting voice.

"The pressure was killing me," the bearded Russian said, agreeably.

"I'm surprise that you didn't--"

"Let it go, Anitchka," her father cut-in.

"Let what go?" Kazimir asked.

"Your disgusting practices in the rain," she said.

"If I hadn't gotten rid of the hot sauce I'd have died."

She glared over at her father. "Have you never wanted to shoot him and put us all out of his misery?"

"This is not the time, daughter."

A taxi rolled past, pulling to a stop in the driveway of Cheng's villa.

Nabatov raised the binoculars to his eyes and studied the vehicle.

"Who is it?" Anitchka asked.

"I can't see them, yet."

A moment later, a man climbed from the car and trotted through the rain up to the villa's door.

"Bronstein," said the white-haired Russian as he lowered the binoculars, his voice filled with disbelief. "That damnable American is still alive."

A smile of delight spread across Anitchka's face. "Well, what do we do?"

"I intend to have a few words with him about that hot sauce," said Kazimir.

"There is nothing we can do," her father said. "Obviously, Bronstein still has the memory stick. Otherwise, he would not be here. Let us hope that Cheng believes the American when he hands over the memory stick."

"Six, two and even Harry pulls it off," she said.

Nabatov frowned at her. "What is that supposed to mean?"

"It's an American wager," Kazimir said. "Harry told me about."

"American men bet on everything," Anitchka added.

Her father's eyes narrowed upon her. "What did Harry Bronstein wager with you?"

"Nothing," she said, her cheeks pinking.

"Then why did this unique, American concept come up during conversation?"

"Harry was explaining how he holds the all-time record, at his fraternity, for removing brassieres." She made a vague movement with one hand. "He can unsnap one in less than two seconds with his right hand. But, if he's forced to use his left, his time drops by six."

"That impressed you?"

"I thought it was funny, Poppa."

Her father cocked one thick eyebrow. "And you think I should be worried about Kazimir?"

"You don't have to worry about me, Pasha. Not even if Shkarov stripped me naked and blew my whistle 'til my eyeballs popped out."

"What in hell does that mean?" Nabatov asked, looking back at the bearded man.

"I'm not sure, Pasha. It just seemed appropriate."

She cut in with, "The explanation is not fit for discussion when a father and daughter are together."

"Bronstein, again?" her father asked, scowling.

Anitchka's shoulders heaved. "Who else?"

Chapter 15

At the Villa's entrance, Harry Bronstein identified himself to an armed Asian man. The fellow was in his fifties with worried dark eyes in a worried round face. Then, Harry expressed a desire to see Yu-tung Cheng. To his surprise, the guard gave a complacent nod, and led Harry inside. The foyer was still and cool. It smelled of incense. The floor was black, polished marble, the ceiling high and domed. A black, enameled hat-stand with polished steel hooks stood just to Harry's right.

"Nice digs," the American remarked. "Lease or own?"

The guard spotted the pistol tucked behind Harrys' belt. Instantly, Asian complacency turned to heated Chinese aggression.

"*Gǒu zá zhong!*" The nervous man jabbed the barrel of his Kalashnikov sub-machinegun against Harry's stomach, next to the pistol.

"No need to get nasty." The American raised his hands. "I was just breaking it in on an enemy."

The guard jerked the pistol from behind Harry's belt and pocketed it. Then, with the Kalashnikov prodding Harry's spine, the two men strode off down a long hallway cluttered with black enameled chairs.

Nearly a minute later, the Harry and his guard strode into a big room with a high,-beamed ceiling. Polished mahogany paneled the walls. An ornately carved teak desk stood at one end. Seated behind the desk was a gaunt Asian with a waxy complexion. Thick, round spectacles rested upon his broad nose. He wore a dark blue suit and a gray tie. On each side of him was a young Asian male clothed in dark slacks and light-colored shirts. The choppy hair of the young men stuck out as if the strands were in the grip of a massive, electrical charge. One youth was chunky and flat-faced with dramatically slanting eyes. The other was angular with sharply arching cheekbones and a broad, sloping nose. A slightly sweet scent permeated the air.

The guard tossed Harry a warning look, before hurrying over to the desk.

On the wall behind the men dangled a gray, maroon, and gold tapestry. The huge work of art depicted an ancient Asian warrior cavorting with two young women. A silver-framed reproduction of Rembrandt's *Night Watch* occupied a portion of the wall, to the right of the desk. To the left dangled an abstract oil in the style of Barnett Newman.

The guard bowed and then spoke briefly to the man in the suit. A moment later, he handed over Harry's pistol. The suit sniffed the pistol's barrel. Then he nodded and set the gun down.

The guard turned on his heels and trotted out of the room without offering Harry another look.

"I've been expecting you, Mr. Bronstein," the suit rose to his feet. He offered the American a dim, wrinkled smile. "My name is Yu-tung Cheng."

"How is it you knew I was coming?" Harry asked, suddenly suspicious of his host.

"I have many sources."

Harry ran a nervous palm along the side of his jaw. "Do you know why I'm here?" He moved toward Cheng.

The Asian responded after a short pause, "I was told you had something to sell."

"What I have is a proposition, Mr. Cheng."

When Harry reached the desk, he could not help but stare. The Asian's black eyes looked blurred and bugged behind thick, spectacles. There were deep bluish bags beneath the orbs. Cheng's skin had the texture of glass.

"You smell like a dog that's been out in the rain, Mr. Bronstein." One of Cheng's waxy hands fanned the air.

Harry's tongue took a nervous trip across his lips. "I saw a Jaguar out front."

"It frightens you?"

"Its owner does."

"Shkarov isn't a friend of yours?"

"Not that I've noticed." Harry jingled coins in his pocket. "I have to ask... Do you work for him?"

"What gave you that idea?"

"Do you?"

The Asian offered a mocking smile. "You came all this way with that prospect on your mind?"

"You haven't answered my question."

"No, Mr. Bronstein. I do not work for Mikhail Shkarov."

The American started to laugh, as a wave of relief crossed his shoulders, but caught himself. "You haven't paid Shkarov, have you?"

"Paid him for what?"

"A camera's memory-stick. It contains Russian military information on the Irkutsk region."

"Assuming that such a thing exists, why would Shkarov offer it to me? Or, for that matter, why would I be interested?"

"I've seen your dance card, Mr. Cheng."

"You've what?"

"I know your business." Harry's eyes drifted down to the printed documents on the desk. Several were maps like those he had altered. He pointed at the documents. "Those are from the stick."

Cheng glanced at his cluttered desk, and then waved a thin hand at one of the chairs fronting the desk. "Please sit down."

Harry did as instructed, still uneasy.

"What's your interest in the memory stick?" the Asian asked, dropping his pretext of innocence.

"Shkarov's trying to scam you."

"How so?"

"The stick contains misleading information."

"Why should I believe you?"

"Because *I* altered the data."

Cheng hesitated, his surprise showing. Then he resumed his seat, the chair creaking under his weight. "Shkarov instigated your actions?"

"No. I made the changes before he got it."

"Why would you do such a thing?"

"The idea of revenge got the better of me. I thought I'd do a number on a guy named Kalandarishvili. I was hoping he wouldn't catch on and whoever he sold it to would cut his throat."

The Asian gave Harry a sly look. "Yes, I heard about him — and his death."

Harry jerked forward, defensively. "I didn't kill Kalandarishvili."

"Was Shkarov aware of the changes you made?"

"Not at the time I did it." The American wet his lips, getting his backside comfortable. "But, he knows now."

"How can you be certain?"

"I made an unaltered copy of the stick. Shkarov found out about it, and sent two people to get it. The idea being to kill me in the process."

"But, how could he discover such information?"

"Pasha Nabatov had a traitor in his organization. That turncoat fed Shkarov a steady stream of information."

"Who is the traitor?"

"Dr. Dmitri Popovitch."

"You can prove that?"

"If Galina Vishnevskaya is here, yes."

Cheng gave Harry a lofty, paternal look. "You still have the second memory stick?"

"I'm prepared to hand it over to you."

"What makes you want to be my friend?"

"My hope is that you will assist in resolving the Kalandarishvili situation in my favor."

"He who feasts upon hope will die of starvation, Mr. Bronstein."

"Hope is all I have left."

The Asian's face crinkled wickedly as his hand lightly touching the pistol. "My sense of smell detected recent usage of this weapon."

"It belonged to Popovitch." Harry crossed one leg over the other. "We fought. I had no choice but to kill him."

"There are always choices." Cheng tilted forward slightly. "Did this unpleasantness occur near here?"

"No. In France."

"Were you seen?"

"I don't think so."

Teeth glittered blackly in Cheng's widening mouth, as he eased back. "In regard to Kalandarishvili…"

Somewhere in the house, a telephone rang. The bell trilled twice and then stopped. A murmuring male voice followed. Then there was silence.

Harry took the memory stick from his pocket and placed it on the desk. "Everything's there."

"Obviously, I must have some way to determine the truth in your claims, Mr. Bronstein?"

"That's easy," the American said, pointing a finger. "Compare the dates on the files. On my stick, you will find the dates to be within a few seconds of each other, and several weeks prior to today." Harry reached out and pushed the memory stick closer to Cheng. "On Shkarov's stick, you will see a span of weeks between some of the dates, the latest being about a week ago when I made the changes."

The Asian picked up the memory stick. Then with the other hand, he opened a large ivory box of cigarettes. Cheng took out one and stuffed it between his lips. Then he shoved the box toward Harry.

"These are Zhongnanhai cigarettes, Mr. Bronstein." Cheng lit the cigarette in his mouth. "They are much more delicate than your American brands."

Harry shook his head. "Do we have a deal?"

"When your horse is on the brink of a precipice, it is too late to pull the reins. Fortunately, I have yet to ride to that far." He handed the memory stick to the young man on his left, exhaling a plume of blue smoke through his nostrils. "My people will examine its contents. If your claims are accurate, I'm willing to discuss your situation further. If not…"

"The access code to my memory-stick is: *Geronimo*," the American cut in.

With a glance, Cheng sent the two young men from the room. Then his body shifted within his suit as he renewed his interest in the American.

"You have the mannerisms of a man who is very new to this business," the Asian said.

"I'm not in your business, Mr. Cheng."

"You are now." The Asian taking another draw on the cigarette and exhaled. "Once in, there's no getting out."

Harry glanced toward the way he had come in. "Does Shkarov know I'm here?"

"Not yet." The Asian shifted in his chair and crossed his legs. "If you didn't kill Kalandarishvili, who did?"

"Innokenti Rakhmelevich."

Cheng's face twisted into a waxy grimace. "That does not surprise me." He hesitated, thinking. "How is it you became involved in this conspiracy?"

For the next five minutes, Harry explained his situation, including the details of his involvement with the Russian GRU.

"Where are the Russians, now?" Cheng asked.

"You've got nothing to worry about from them."

"I don't agree. Does Nabatov know you're in Port-Bou?"

"I'm sure he knows I escaped. He most certainly knew my intentions regarding you. But, he could not know that I've arrived."

"I expect he knows exactly when you got here and where you are, Mr. Bronstein. The question is what does Nabatov intend to do?"

The Asian pressed a button inset into the bottom of his desktop. A moment later two guards rushed in, brandishing machine guns. Cheng spoke to them quickly and sharply in Chinese. As the men hurried away, Cheng returned his attention to Harry Bronstein.

"It's odd that Nabatov's people didn't find your second memory stick."

"It was well hidden," Harry said. "Talk to Rakhmelevich. He searched me. He didn't find it."

"Experienced GRU operatives are not Rakhmelevich." The Asian fell silent, reflecting. "It is, also odd that you managed to escape."

"I was left alone with a guy named Kazimir Sokolof. He's a little on the slow side."

"Ah, yes. Kazimir." Cheng laughed softly. Then he spoke quietly but clearly. "Well, I guess that could explain it."

"There was a radio message and Kazimir left the room. That's when I legged it."

"He did not pursue you?"

"I didn't see him."

"You wouldn't. Why would the Russians help you after your ordeal with the Chechnyans?"

"They thought I'd partnered with Kalandarishvili in the theft of their intelligence. They also thought I could help them locate the Chechnyans."

"Did you help them?"

"I'm not sure. I told Anitchka Nabatov all I knew."

The Asian smiled crookedly. "I've been told she can be very persuasive."

The armed guards rushed back into the room. One of them hurried over to the desk and spoke with Cheng. He nodded and made a dismissive gesture, sending the men away.

"Nabatov and some of his people are parked down the road," Cheng told Harry.

Harry rose from his chair, shaking like an old man with one leg. "I didn't bring them here!"

"Regardless, they *are* here. And their presence puts me in an awkward position."

One of the young men who had been with Cheng, earlier, returned. He spoke briefly to his boss, and then hurried away.

"It would seem that you're a man of your word, Mr. Bronstein," Cheng said.

"Then you'll help me?"

"Unfortunately, convincing French authorities of your innocence is beyond my province."

"But, you must have political contacts in France."

"Of course."

"Then you can put pressure where it's needed."

"Even I cannot change a Magistrate's mind."

Harry tilted forward in a blast of emotion. "Why can't you force Rakhmelevich to admit responsibility?"

"Rakhmelevich would die rather than confess, Mr. Bronstein."

"Couldn't you supply witnesses? People who would swear it was Rakhmelevich who killed Kalandarishvili?"

Cheng smirked. "You complain about being falsely accused, and yet you ask me to help you convict a man with false testimony."

"I see no shame when it brings about justice."

"I don't think the French authorities would agree." The Asian inhaled deeply from his cigarette butt, and then snuffed it out in a large glass ashtray. "However, your suggestion brought another idea to mind. I might be able to provide witnesses as to your innocence."

"Then it's settled?"

"I said, 'might'. There is future business to consider."

Harry's face fell. "Once I'm out of this, I'm staying out."

"You'll never be out, Mr. Bronstein." Chang filched another cigarette out of the box and lit it. "Nevertheless, you are not the consideration. Shkarov is. I've done a great deal of business with him, over the years."

"More bad than good, I'll bet."

"Nevertheless, my assistance to you would disassociate him."

"Shkarov is trying to cheat you."

For a moment, Cheng looked thoughtful, as if precious memories were playing through his head. Then his face darkened, perceptibly, and his mouth drew down at the corners. "So it would seem."

Harry crossed his arms, becoming defiant in his frustration. "How can you trust anything he sells in the future?"

"You miss my point." The Asian coughed delicately as he snuffed out the cigarette in the ashtray. Then he took another from the ivory box and lit it. Afterward he returned his gaze to Harry Bronstein. "Questions will be asked by my superiors. They may assume that I've been negligent in my dealings with Shkarov. I could be recalled to Beijing for trial — and execution." He made a flourish with his cigarette, his lips and blackened teeth twisted together to form a gruesome grin. "This matter must be handled very carefully."

The words choked out of Harry's mouth, "So you'll do nothing for me?"

"I didn't say that."

A buzzer sounded.

"Please excuse me, Mr. Bronstein." Cheng got to his feet. "There is a pressing matter which I must address."

After the Asian left, Harry stood up and looked around the room. Built into the wall were a series of lighted cabinets displaying shelf after glass shelf of carved jade, in a spectrum of colors. Hung on the wall to the left of Harry was a copy of Van Gogh's Starry Night. A pair of display-cabinets holding porcelain: vases, cups, and sundry containers bracketed it. Several ornately carved wooden pedestals dotted the black marble floor. Atop these were huge, glazed, Asian vases.

The American went down to the cabinets, his eyes darting from one work of art to the next. What he'd first assumed was nephrite was actually the much more costly green and white jadeite. One shining example was a carved Chinese cabbage. The sculpture was an inset for a small enameled basin in the shape of a crab-apple blossom. There were spirit-fungi, chiseled from red coral, surrounding this. Adjacent to the jadeite were the usual dragon and duck statuettes, as well as several nephrite panels displaying a variety of pastoral pleasures.

Footsteps clattered on the marble floor in the hallway, drawing Harry's attention to the doorway. Galina Vishnevskaya stepped into the room and stopped. She wore a blue blouse and red slacks. A pink ribbon held her pale hair back, emphasizing her face's sculpted beauty. As she twisted, her huge breasts swayed beneath the cloth like a pair of giant soft-boiled eggs. When Galina spotted the American, her face went white.

"What happened to you?" she demanded, rushing over to Harry.

"I didn't like the deal you cut with Popovitch," he said.

"There was no deal with him!"

"What about that little, black box he gave you? Remember the deal, now? You were to inject me with something nasty."

She paled in shock. "How did you—"

"Voices carry on the wind," he cut in, with a smirk.

"It meant nothing." She swallowed thickly. "Popovitch gave me no choice." As her breathing quickened, her breasts rose and fell under the blouse, like living mountains. "If I hadn't agreed to kill you, he'd have killed me. But, I wasn't going to do it."

Harry cleared his throat. "You don't have to worry about the dear doctor anymore."

"What do you mean?"

"It wasn't easy to kill him." His eyebrows arched. "He was the one with the gun."

Galina crept forward. "We can still do the deal, Harry. I'll fix it with Cheng."

He shook his head from side to side. "I've already pitched my offer."

"You can't do this to me!" In a rage, she grabbed him by the shoulders, her long nail digging into his leather jacket.

Harry gripped her around the waist and gave Galina a shove. "It's done."

She rubbed the side of her face with one hand, her eyes blurring with tears. "Did you tell him what we had planned?" she asked, suddenly facing a grim realization.

"Scared?"

"You damn right I am!" Galina pressed her lips together, retreating several steps. "Shkarov is here," she said, her voice just above a whisper. "Without that money, I've got no place to hide. And if he finds out about our deal, he'll kill me."

"I've got nothing to gain by rolling over on you."

Shivering with uncertainty, Galina turned away. "How much is Cheng paying you?"

"Nothing."

"Nothing?" She whirled back, her mouth agape. "It's worth a million Euros, Harry! Don't be stupid, Harry. You'll need the money to get away."

"All the money in the world can't help me."

She laughed harshly. "Get it through your head, Harry. Shkarov will kill you for cutting him out of this deal."

"If things go as planned, Shkarov won't be a problem after tonight."

In the silence that followed, Harry heard Galina's ragged breathing. She sounded like a runner desperately trying to reach the winner's tape. "Things never go as planned," she finally said.

Several armed guards accompanied Yu-tung Cheng when he reentered the room. The guards kept an eye on Harry and Galina, as Chen went back to his desk.

"Has Mr. Bronstein been regaling you with his misdeeds, Galina?" the Asian teased, and sat down.

"We were admiring your pretty sculptures." She nervously faced the gaunt Asian.

Hustling footsteps sounded in the corridor. This time Shkarov and Rakhmelevich walked in, their dark suits splotched even darker by water stains.

"I believe you two know Mr. Bronstein." Cheng tilted his head in Harry's direction.

Rakhmelevich whirled toward the American and growled, "He's a man who's about to die!"

Shkarov looked over at Harry, knots forming along the Chechnyan's jaw line. He said nothing.

"Don't be hasty, Rakhmelevich." The Asian sat.

Ge uttered something in Chinese to his guards. Instantly, their weapons pointed menacingly at the two Chechnyans.

"Mr. Bronstein is my guest," Cheng continued, his eyes returning to Rakhmelevich. "Molesting him would be a fatal mistake."

"That bastard—" Rakhmelevich pointed at Harry.

"Let it be, Innokenti," Shkarov cut in, his voice low and worried. Then he walked stiffly to mid-room, his back to Harry, his eyes on Cheng. "Things are not as they seem, Cheng."

"Aren't they?"

"For starters, you can't believe a word Bronstein says." Rakhmelevich faced Cheng defiantly. "He's wanted for murder, in Paris."

"A murder you committed," the Asian said.

"That's a damn lie!"

The gaunt Asian scratched one ear, his bleary eyes staring coldly at Rakhmelevich. "You're calling me a liar?"

"That's not what he meant." Shkarov nervously fingered his crimson necktie.

Cheng pursed his lips, looking over at the other Chechnyan. "Then we are agreed that Rakhmelevich killed Kalandarishvili?"

"It wasn't planned that way."

Galina's eyes glinted with morbid delight as she watched the Chechnyans being grilled.

"I had no choice," Rakhmelevich protested. His left hand rubbed his right fist. His eyes were evasive. "The bastard tried to stab me."

"Nevertheless," Cheng said, "Your activities resulted in Mr. Bronstein being accused of the murder which, in turn, brought me under GRU scrutiny."

Harry looked, around behind of his chair and on both sides as if searching for a way out.

"I admit that mistakes were made—" Shkarov began.

"Mistakes?" the Asian cut in, his voice tart with mockery. "You and Rakhmelevich created an international catastrophe!"

"Damn it, Cheng!"

"Nabatov and his people are outside, Shkarov! As you must realize, their presence is not friendly."

"You don't have to worry about them, Cheng. Nabatov's after us, not you. When we leave after completing our business, they'll follow us and we will deal with them."

"Deal with them?" the Asian mocked.

"Because of Bronstein, we knew Nabatov and his people would be in Port-Bou."

"You knew, but you didn't warn me?"

"We tried to get a message to you. Ask your man servant."

Cheng's His answer came slowly, thoughtfully. "Something's wrong."

"No," shouted Rakhmelevich, "I talked to your man, myself."

"You miss my point," the Asian said, still thoughtful. "The GRU chased Kalandarishvili from Irkutsk to Paris. They knew that you would be selling the memory stick to me, so they came here." Cheng took his glasses off, polished the lenses, and then put the spectacles back on again. "And yet when they know you're in here offering it to me, they do nothing? Why?"

"Because the Russians know it's useless," Harry interjected.

"We didn't change it," said Rakhmelevich, pointing at Harry. "He's the one who did that."

The Asian made a taunting face at Mikhail Shkarov. "'You have my word, Cheng. The information is irrefutable, Cheng. There is no chance of a mistake, Cheng.' Wasn't that your promise?"

"We had no control over anything!" shouted Rakhmelevich.

Shkarov raised a hand. "Wait... Nabatov must know that Bronstein's here. He must realize that Bronstein brought you the second memory stick. So, whatever the reason for the GRU reluctance to act, it is not because of the information. Both memory sticks have valid data."

"So you admit you knew of Mr. Bronstein's malicious efforts?"

"There were no changes."

The Asian took a dramatic intake of breath. "Yes, there were. My people compared both memory sticks. They don't match. It is clear that the one you gave me is the altered one. I'm very tempted to terminate our association — with prejudice."

There were many moments of silence.

Then Shkarov said, "You and I have done business for a long time, Cheng."

"That is the only reason you're still alive," the Asian returned.

"All right. I should have been forthright about Bronstein's changes. But, consider who has spent that last ten years supplying you with the intelligence you find so profitable?" Shkarov said, his voice breaking. "We need each other, Cheng."

"So it would seem."

Harry set his teeth. The shit was about to go down the sewer, with him leading the stink to the sea, unless he turned the situation around. "No matter how Shkarov tries to spin it, Cheng, the bottom line is that he tried to cheat you. No matter what Shkarov offers in the future, you'll distrust it."

"You've made a valid point, Mr. Bronstein." Cheng took a moment to light a cigarette. "But, so did Shkarov." He took a deep draw on the cigarette and blew a stream of smoke toward the ceiling. "Perhaps what is needed is compromise?"

"I don't get you," Harry said.

"What if I supplied witnesses along with someone — someone other than Rakhmelevich — to take the blame for Kalandarishvili? You would be free. Your life, as you knew it, restored. Would that be agreeable?"

Harry, unhesitatingly, shook his head. "I want Rakhmelevich to take the fall."

"Like hell I will!" Sweat beaded along his hairline. He wiped at it with the back of one hand.

Shkarov's words came out dry and quiet. "Be careful, Innokenti." His eyes were on Harry Bronstein.

The Asian looked at his fingernails. "As you've just witnessed, Mr. Bronstein, Rakhmelevich would not be a cooperative player in your plan."

"I'd never be able to sleep knowing an innocent is paying for what Rakhmelevich did." Harry walked over to the desk.

"The man I have in mind is hardly an innocent, Mr. Bronstein." Cheng's flat-nailed fingers drummed on the desktop. "He is a murderer who's escaped punishment for many years."

"Then why would he be so accommodating?" The American's voice was thin and querulous.

"The man is dying. He has a large family in need of protection and support." The Asian's hands moved eloquently. "I would supply their needs, in exchange for his cooperation." His face broadened into a waxy smile. "Everyone would benefit."

"I still can't settle for that."

"Integrity and a dollar will buy you a cup of tea in Beijing, Mr. Bronstein."

The lips drew back from Rakhmelevich's yellow teeth, but he didn't say a word.

The American flushed. "I have a right to make Rakhmelevich pay for what he did to me."

"Mr. Bronstein, the lust for vengeance turned you into a fool once. Don't repeat your stupidity."

"It's Rakhmelevich or nobody."

Cheng looked over at Shkarov. "How much is Rakhmelevich worth to you?"

Innokenti Rakhmelevich's face took on a gray patina.

"Get that out of your head." The Chechnyan stiffened under Cheng's searing gaze.

Cheng said something in Chinese to his guards. Three of them rushed over to Rakhmelevich. Two of them grabbed the patch-eyed Chechnyan and shoved him into a chair.

The Chechnyan struggled, gasping.

The third guard shoved a pistol into the Rakhmelevich's mouth and cocked the hammer. An instant later, the guard's forefinger curled lightly around the pistol's trigger.

"I must pay my debt to Mr. Bronstein, Shkarov," Cheng said.

"Don't be a fool, Cheng!" Shkarov's eyes went white and wild.

The gaunt Asian shoved the pistol Harry had brought within easy reach of the American. "A dead Rakhmelevich becomes a good solution for both of us. You will have your revenge. I will deliver his corpse to Paris along with a raft of irrefutable witnesses in your favor: each vowing to have seen Rakhmelevich do the deed." Cheng nudged the pistol closer to the American. "Pick it up. Go to where he sits. Put the gun to his head."

"Cheng!" shouted Shkarov. His face swelled up with blood, as he tilted toward the Asian.

"Do not interrupt if you value your *own* life, Shkarov." The Asian's face twisted sourly, as he looked back at Harry. "Shoot him, Mr. Bronstein. Shoot him and all your worries will end. Shoot him and your hatred will be sated. Do it, Mr. Bronstein."

Harry's hand moved over to the weapon, his fingers spread to grip it, his breathing labored.

"That's it," urged Cheng, a sadistic gleam in his eyes.

However, a moment later, Harry pulled his hand back; empty. "I can't."

Galina let go a bray of laughter. "You gutless fool!"

"I'm disappointed." Cheng retrieved the gun and shoved it into a desk drawer. "What say you, Shkarov? Are you willing to do the deed? Or should I leave it to my people?"

"You push me too far, Cheng," the Chechnyan cried out hoarsely.

The Asian lifted his hands from the desk, mated the fingers into a steeple, and then touched the tip of the steeple to his chin. His elbows hit the desktop, supporting his arms. His eyes locked upon Mikhail Shkarov.

"If Rakhmelevich is of such value," Cheng said, "our business dealings are over — and you both will die."

Spots of color appeared in Shkarov's cheeks. "Now, who is being the fool?"

Harry said to Cheng, without energy, "May I leave?"

"I pay my debts, Mr. Bronstein," the Asian said. His fingers folded and then meshed. He put his hands flat on the desktop and rattled the fingers up and down. "I look forward to seeing you, again."

"You can't let him walk out of here," said Shkarov.

"You should know when you're beaten." Even to him, Harry's voice sounded flat and discouraged.

"Your lives still dangle at my whim," Cheng told the Chechnyans. "Keep that in mind as we continue this evening's events."

Harry Bronstein's stride lengthened as he followed the long hallway to the door of Cheng's villa. It was over. There was nothing left except to face the fury of the French courts. Assuming, he could evade Nabatov's mob. Why didn't he have the stomach to kill Rakhmelevich? He had thought about it often enough.

Outside, Harry Bronstein trotted down the asphalt drive to the road fronting the villa. The rain had stopped. Crickets chirped. If only he had not come to Paris. If only he had not taken the ferry to Calais. He moved out onto the gravel and started running down the road, oblivious to everything around him. If only he had agreed to let Kalandarishvili come to his hotel. If only he...

"What in hell were you doing in there, Harry?"

The familiar female voice jerked Harry Bronstein out of his self-pitying thoughts and he skidded to a stop. Anitchka Nabatov was moving toward him from a clutch of bushes. She carried a stubby weapon he recognized, from his military service, as a PP-19 Bizon submachine gun.

Harry felt his knees begin to wobble. He was a dead man. Reluctantly, he raised his hands in submission.

"Go ahead and shoot me," he told her. "You'll be doing me a favor."

When she reached Harry, Anitchka grabbed him by his jacket and prodded her gun against his belly, backing him toward the ditch. A few seconds later, they were off the road and behind a thicket.

"Do you not understand the trouble you've caused?" she demanded.

"I asked for your help but you refused."

"Is Cheng going to help?"

Harry shook his head. "The conditions he made were too tough."

"What conditions?"

"He wanted me to kill Rakhmelevich."

"Cheng must've taken a real shine to you."

"I couldn't do it."

"Why not?"

"I — Let's just say I've done my quota of killings."

"What happened to the second memory stick?"

"Cheng has it."

Her voice softened slightly, and she let go of him. "Did he believe what was on it?"

"He believed."

Anitchka smiled. "You did good, Harry." She tilted forward and kissed his cheek.

He looked at her askance, completely surprised. "Good?"

"Where are you headed?"

"If I can catch a ride, I'll take the train back to Paris. What do you mean by 'good'?"

"Don't be foolish, Harry. French prisons are horrid places. Come away with me."

"I don't think your father would approve."

"Poppa's too worried about finding the mole to concern himself with you."

Harry blew breath out in an amused blast of air. "I thought you people knew everything."

"Meaning?"

"Your mole *was* Popovitch."

Anitchka blinked in surprise, her mouth dropping wide.

"I saw him and Galina Vishnevskaya, together. They both work for Mikhail Shkarov."

"Popovitch?"

"You don't have to believe me." He pointed back toward Cheng's villa. "Ask Galina when she comes out."

"Popovitch is in there?"

"He's dead."

Again, she blinked in surprise. "You killed him?"

Harry nodded. "It wasn't part of my plan."

She was silent, her eyes on his face. "Where's his body?"

"I left it across *A-75* from the petrol station, just before the border. The ground slopes down into a wooded area. It's in there."

"Come on," she said, nudging him back toward the road.

The words twisted past his lips as if uttering them hurt, "I'm all done running, Anitchka."

"There won't be any more running."

"Does that mean you'll hand Rakhmelevich over to the French authorities so I can get out from under this mess?"

Her dark head wagged. "He and Shkarov will be taken back to Moscow to face execution."

"In that case, I've still got a date with a French Magistrate."

Anitchka took his arm and tried to pull him along. However, Harry jerked free.

"I won't spend the rest of my life on the run, Anitchka."

"You won't have to. I'll get you a new identity. You'll be able to do whatever you want."

"I won't be able to live as myself."

"Not your old self. But, you could become a new man, a better man."

"I like the old guy." He moved passed her. After a few steps Harry stopped and looked back. She was still watching him. "In spite of my romantic fumbles I was playing for keeps." Then Harry turned hurried off down the road.

Anitchka broke into a run in the opposite direction.

When her father and Kazimir saw her hurried approach, Kazimir shoved the Alhambra into gear, and roared up to meet her.

"Cheng believed Harry," she gasped, through the side window. "He has the memory stick."

"Excellent," her father said, with a smile. Then his brows furrowed into a frown. "I hope you didn't let Bronstein in on what we were doing?"

"Of course I didn't."

"I mention it only because you've got the face of a little girl who's lost her first love."

Her cheeks warmed with embarrassment. "If you will stop reading empty assumptions into my words, it might interest you to know the identity of the mole."

"Mole?" Kazimir said.

"Who?" her father demanded, sharply.

"It's Popovitch," she said, climbing into the Alhambra's rear seat. "The bastard's working for Shkarov."

"That's crazy," Kazimir said. "He's going to help Golovkin dismantle the electronics for the move to the new safe-house."

"We can get confirmation from Galina Vishnevskaya."

"Bronstein told you this?" her father asked.

"Harry said he heard Galina and Popovitch plotting."

At that moment, a beige Jaguar roared onto the roadway from the villa, heading in the same direction taken by Harry Bronstein.

"It's Shkarov," Kazimir said. "Tits on a stick is driving. Rakhmelevich is in the rear compartment."

"Trail them with your lights off. Stay well back until we have them to a secluded area," Nabatov instructed. "Then we will make our move."

The Alhambra roared off, giving chase.

Before they could close the distance on the Jaguar, it slid to a stop on the road. The doors immediately opened. Then, Shkarov and Rakhmelevich jumped out. They dragged Harry Bronstein into the car's rear compartment. A moment later, the jaguar roared away.

"We have to stop them before they kill Harry, Kazimir," Anitchka pleaded.

"I'm doing my best. But, that Jag's got a lot more horsepower than this piece of Spanish shit."

When the Jaguar reached a bridge, it skidded out of control and plunged through the railing.

"Oh, Harry," she groaned.

Kazimir slid the Alhambra to a stop on the bridge. The three of them got out. Then, Anitchka ran over to the ruptured railing and stared down into the swirling canal.

"Come on, Harry," she said, to the black water.

However, after ten minutes of waiting, no one came to the surface.

"They're all dead," the bearded Russian said.

"You and Kazimir go back to Paris," Nabatov instructed, clearly satisfied with the outcome of the night's events. "I will remain behind to claim the bodies."

"What about Popovitch?" Kazimir asked.

"I will notify Moscow. They will have someone take him into custody when he makes his rounds, at the embassy."

"Popovitch is dead, Poppa." Anitchka ran her tongue over her lower lip. "Harry killed him."

"Can't that American do anything right?" Nabatov's arms rose and fell with frustration. "Why in hell…"

"He did get the memory stick to Cheng," Kazimir interjected.

"I don't suppose Bronstein told you where he'd left the body?" her father asked.

"It's across from the petrol station, near the border," she said, still staring helplessly into the water.

Nabatov was silent for a little while. "You and Kazimir take the car and recover Popovitch's corpse. I want it delivered to our Paris embassy." He looked at his watch. "Make sure the press doesn't get onto his death."

Chapter 16

Lt. Damien Fournier was a big, chunky man with a dark, heavy face gloomy from decades of seeing the horrors inflicted upon humanity. He had sagging jowls, and very thick fingers. At the joint of each knuckle was a dimple. His graying, dark hair was combed straight back. He wore a brown suit and white shirt. Black, plastic spectacles rested upon his beak-like nose in front of dark, beady eyes. His low voice wheezed when he spoke.

"Stop lying!" he shouted. His dark-brown eyes bulged. "It took three months to extradite you from Spain. Since then the Magistrate has questioned you, I have questioned you. Even our psychologist has spent days questioning you."

"I didn't mind the shrink's questions." Harry Bronstein grinned. "She's built like my favorite fantasy."

The two men were in one of the soundproofed interrogation rooms, sitting across from each other at a narrow, Masonite-topped table. Video and sound equipment recorded what transpired during Harry's questioning, at 11 rue des Saussaies. A panel of switches embedded in the tabletop allowed Fournier control over these devices. For Harry's part, his face had healed, leaving him nearly as handsome as before his run-in with Rakhmelevich.

"She saw through your filthy lies!" Fournier shouted.

"I have to tell you... I hear the lie, thingy a lot. Usually it's from women who've read more into our relationship than was intended — at least by me." Harry sat in a chair clothed in orange prison garb, shackled hand and foot.

"Who helped you get to Spain?" exasperated Fournier.

"As I told you, and everyone else, nobody helped. I hitchhiked part of the way. Then some woman took pity and gave me a lift."

"A woman whose name you cannot remember! Whose description is beyond your recollection. Driving a car, the make color and model of which eludes you. How convenient!"

"Memory lapses are a bitch, considering my situation."

"You murdered Alexi Kalandarishvili. That is your *situation*." The lieutenant took a pale, spotted cigar from inside his suit. "When you fled

France to avoid arrest, you had a choice of Portugal, Morocco, Andorra, and the UK. Why did you select Spain?"

"Innokenti Rakhmelevich was headed there."

The cigar wrapper broke between the police officer's fingers with a sharp crackling sound. "Do you really think I'm stupid enough to believe that terrorist is still alive?"

"Actually, I was counting on it," Harry said, impulsively.

Fournier leaned back in his chair, nipping off the end of the cigar with his incisors. "Do you know Galina Vishnevskaya?" He spat the bit of tobacco onto the floor.

The question caught the American off-guard. Harry knew, of course, she was dead. However, he had assumed her remains were long-since fish food. The American swallowed thickly, his mind blank, his eyes wandering evasively up toward the ceiling.

"I didn't catch the name," he said, stalling.

"Galina Vishnevskaya. The name doesn't ring any bells, Mr. Bronstein?"

"Sounds Russian."

A broad smile spread Fournier's fat face wide, like a basketball. He gripped the cigar between his teeth, at one corner of his mouth; his fat fingers forming a mesh atop his big belly. "Does it?"

"Is Galina a friend of yours?" Harry said slowly, with half-closed eyes.

Fournier smiled and took the cigar from his mouth. "I thought she might be one of yours."

After a period of mute concern Harry said, "I've never taken much interest in women."

"There's no need to compound your lies." The lieutenant's face became grim as he tilted across the desk toward Harry. "Yesterday morning, Port-Bou police found part of her skeleton along a beach."

"Which part?"

"Enough to identify her."

"How does one identify *bones*?"

Fournier's breathing wheezed and the flame from his lighter crackled against the cigar. "Forensic science can perform miracles, these days." He puffed smoke. "But, if the truth be told, there were three simple things that pointed to the skeleton being that of Galina Vishnevskaya." He shifted the lit cigar to his left hand and held up the forefinger of his right. "First, there was an engraved bracelet encircling her left radius and ulna. It carried the name, Galina Vishnevskaya." The index finger popped up, adjacent to the raised forefinger. "Secondly, there was a belt attached to a monogrammed buckle etched with Galina's initials." Another digit jumped upward. "Thirdly, divers found a woman's purse in the front seat of a submerged Jaguar. It contained numerous personal items including a passport and driving license for Galina Vishnevskaya." Fournier stopped speaking, waiting for Harry to make a comment. When that did not happen he said, "You're not the least bit curious about the Jaguar?"

"I'm a Moped type of guy." Harry raised his eyebrows a little. "But, I get the feeling you think I had something to do with Galina's death."

Fournier nodded his head, grinning. "She drove the vehicle." He tilted back, again, drumming his fingers on his belly. "The seat was positioned to fit someone of her height. But, I am convinced that you were in the Jaguar."

There was another interlude of silence. Then Harry asked, "Why do you say that?"

"When you were arrested, you were barefoot."

"Somehow I don't see the relevancy."

"Perhaps, this will clarify the situation," said the police lieutenant. "A man's shoe was on the sand not far from her remains. A matching shoe was in the Jaguar's rear compartment. Spanish authorities sent both shoes to their Madrid forensic laboratory for DNA extraction. The results haven't been determined, yet. I am willing to bet my next year's salary that the same man owned both shoes. Further, that those shoes belong to you."

"Even if those shoes are mine, they don't link me to her death."

"They put you with her when she died. What's more, your lack of interest in how she died tells me that you know."

Harry did know. Rakhmelevich had tried to shoot him, and one of the rounds struck Galina in the back of the head. This, of course, was the reason the Jaguar ended up in the canal.

"Normally, death's unpleasant variations hold little allure for me," the American said. "But, considering all that's happened... How did she die?"

"A pistol round passed through her skull."

"Sounds painful."

"Just for an instant."

Harry cleared his throat, feeling more and more uneasy. "Was the gun found?"

Fournier let go a grunt of delight and sat erect, as if he was anticipating a fleshy feast. "Now, that question is extremely relevant."

"I was afraid it might be."

"Spanish investigators found it inside the Jaguar." He tapped the clump of black ash from the end of his cigar into the ashtray.

"Clever of her killer to leave it behind."

"Nevertheless, it was there." He took a draw on the cigar and blew a cloud of smoke toward Harry. "But, this is the good part. Madrid forensic scientists lifted one beautifully preserved print from the pistol." Again, the detective paused. This time he looked upward at the corner of the ceiling, waiting for the American to respond. When Harry made no remark, Fournier said, "They identified it, of course." Once more Fournier paused. Once more, Harry said nothing. "Aren't you the least bit curious as to whose fingerprint it is?"

"Fingerprints don't really do it for me."

Fournier smirked. "It belongs to you."

"You're just full of surprises."

"Now, listen to me, you murderous shit." The police officer's face twisted in rage, his voice a wheezing hiss. "You're going to tell me exactly what happened in Port-Bou."

"Would you believe I was kidnapped? Threatened by gun-wielding terrorists? And when I tried to take the damn thing away from Innokenti Rakhmelevich, the gun went off and killed Galina?"

"No, I wouldn't believe it!"

Harry shrugged. "I took a shot."

The homicide detective stuffed the cigar into one corner of his mouth and crossed his arms, grinning, showing his yellow teeth. "When you finish your sentence for killing Kalandarishvili, you'll be delivered back to Spain to answer for the murder of Galina Vishnevskaya."

A young, uniformed police officer entered the interrogation room without knocking. "Lieutenant…"

Fournier switched off the recording equipment. "I was not to be disturbed!"

"I'm sorry, Lieutenant, but it is the *Préfet de Police.*"

"Are you mad? The man's newly appointed. He's up to his ass in paperwork, his wife is a lunatic, and his mistress is pregnant." Fournier leaned reached over to the ashtray and revolved his cigar in it, smudging out the coal. "Impossible!"

"It is him, Monsieur. And he insists upon speaking with you — about M. Bronstein."

The Lieutenant jumped to his feet and raced over to the telephone, hanging upon the wall by the door. "Hello? This is Lt. Fournier."

"He's out in the reception room, sir. He came, here, at the behest of the Prime Minister."

Fournier returned the handset to its cradle and faced the gendarme; his mouth gaped in shock. "The *Préfecture de Police* is here? Sent by the Prime Minister?"

"He is quite agitated, Sir."

"Keep an eye on Bronstein." The Lieutenant quickly he straightened his tie. "If he so much as breathes wrong, shoot him until you run out of bullets." With that, the Lieutenant of Police stalked out of the interrogation room.

"I think Fournier dislikes me," Harry said.

"He hates you more than any other man on earth," returned the young officer.

"Because I fought extradition?"

The gendarme shook his dark head. "You shouldn't have attempted to seduce the police psychiatrist."

"I did more than *attempt*." Harry scratched the end of his nose, smiling.

"So, Fournier assumed."

"Why would Fournier care?"

"The psychiatrist happens to be his wife."

Harry's brows shot up in shock. "She never mentioned it — either time."

Raised voices erupted from outside the interrogation room.

"Fournier sounds pissed," Harry said. "Is it possible he's irritated because the *Préfecture de Police* has more than one mistress? One with psychiatric leanings?"

"I'm quite certain *you* are at the crux of the discussion."

The angry shouts continued for several more minutes. Then Fournier stormed back into the interrogation room.

"You are free to go, Mr. Bronstein." Lt. Fournier turned to the other police officer. "Take him to the property room. Have him sign for his possessions. Then escort him out of the building." Fournier returned his attention to the American. "I would suggest you get the hell out of France... as quickly as possible." His voice choked with fury.

"Not that I'm staring a gift horse in the mouth," Harry said, looking from man to man, "but why is God being so good to me?"

"Because he's never met you. If he had, he would strike you dead after nailing your balls to the ceiling. However, the Prime Minister thinks differently. He telephoned the Prefect of Police ordering him to have you released." Fournier muttered a series of curses. "And to think I lied to his wife in order to protect that idiot!"

"What about Spain?"

"That is between you and Spain."

Harry stood up and extended one hand toward Fournier. "Say goodbye to your wife for me?"

Fournier's face and neck turned crimson, as he turned and stormed away.

Thirty minutes later, Harry Bronstein walked down the sidewalk adjacent to rue des Saussaies. His suitcase was in one hand. His camera bag was in the other. Over one shoulder hung his laptop-case. Snow was falling. The wind howled. His ears were going numb. However, nothing concerned him. In fact, he was grinning as if he had never grinned before. Surely, his release had been a miracle.

A black Peugeot pulled to the curb and the electric side-window rolled down.

"Harry?" a woman called from within the vehicle.

He stopped and looked over, his stomach knotting at the sound of the familiar voice.

"It's Anitchka," she declared. "Come."

"No thanks," he said, cautiously. "I've got a plane to catch."

She leaped out of the car and rushed through the slush forming on the sidewalk. "You don't have a choice," Anitchka said, when she reached Harry, "Now, get into the damn car."

"I'm not going anywhere except to the airport."

"We'll go together."

"Thanks, but I'll catch a cab."

A pistol appeared in her hand. "That's not an option, Harry." Her voice was low and deadly.

He gulped, choking on his words. "I won't say anything about anything to anybody!"

"I can't take that chance, Harry."

"Anitchka, I swear. Not one word. Not if they cut off my legs and take me dancing."

"The proverbial fan is about to receive an overload of shit, Harry, and you're the reason." She grabbed his jacket with one hand and shoved the barrel of the pistol against his groin. "Now get into the damn car or I'll shoot One-Eyed Willie."

"Considering your romantic history, have you never considered therapy?"

"Move, Harry!" She prodded him over to the car with the gun and opened the rear door on the passenger side. "Drop your things in the back, and then get into the front. I'm a crack shot, Harry. If you try to run, you won't make ten feet."

He climbed into the car feeling angry and frightened.

Anitchka closed the doors, and hurried around to the driver's side. Then she crawled behind the steering wheel, and started the Peugeot's engine.

"Are you taking me back to Moscow to stand trial?" he asked.

"No trial."

His eyes widened in terror as he looked over at her. "You mean you're just going to execute me?"

"Tomorrow evening, you'll be on the front page of every newspaper in France," she said, putting the car into gear. As the vehicle merged into passing traffic, she set the pistol on the seat between them. "The *police nationale* will be hunting you. Interpol will be hunting you. The FBI will be hunting you. The entire world will be hunting you."

"Just for grins, could you skip the tingly afterglow and back up to the foreplay part of this orgasmic tale? I think I've missed something."

"Fournier did not meet with the real Prefect of Police. That man was actually an actor hired by my father: a dead ringer for the real Prefect of Police. Tomorrow morning, the real Prefect will receive Fournier's report on the efficiency of his department in carrying out orders to release you. By tomorrow afternoon, Fournier will face an embarrassing demotion and you will become a worldwide, criminal celebrity."

"No! This can't be happening to me." The American moved an impatient arm. "Not after all I've been through."

"Life is tough, Harry." Anitchka glanced over at him. "Did you and One-Eyed Willie have sex with Galina Vishnevskaya?"

"My life just went from arching in the heavens down to the seventh level of hell, and you're worried about who I'm having sex with?"

Anitchka smiled out of one side of her mouth.

Harry turned his head very slowly and looked out the car's side window. "I've got to tell you, Anitchka… You've ruined the best day of my life."

"The Embassy flight to Moscow leaves in forty minutes. You and I will be on it."

"Not a chance." Then he turned back to her and picked up the pistol. "I'm going to kill myself."

"Don't be ridiculous." Anitchka reached over and took the weapon from him without a struggle. "I've arranged a new identity, for you. Everything will work out if you do as I tell you." She pocketed the pistol. "I saw you dragged into the Jaguar. How is it Shkarov didn't kill you?"

"Rakhmelevich held a gun on me. I knew if I didn't get hold of it, I'd be dead. So, I made a grab. He squeezed the trigger three times, trying to shoot me. One of the rounds hit Galina. That's when the car went off the bridge." He held up a finger and studied it. "After the water rushed in, Rakhmelevich was too busy trying to survive to concern himself with me. That's when I got out and swam as far and as fast as I could underwater. Then I crawled out onto the shore, and hid among the weeds. When the sun came up, a cop working the beach stopped me. There had been some burglaries in that area. I was taken into custody when I couldn't produce any form of identification. It didn't take them long to match me to the wanted flier Interpol had put out."

"What happened to the Chechnyans?"

Harry shrugged his shoulders. "They might be dead. They might still be alive." Tears puddled in Harry's eyes, and he batted at the wet. "Right now, I could cry."

"Suck it up, Harry," she said, her concentration on the slushy road ahead. "We have too much to do."

"Anitchka, I'm whipped." His arms rose and fell in defeat. "I've got no more fight in me."

With one hand, she reached into her purse and pulled out a Russian passport. She tossed it into his lap. "That's your new identity. You'll be able to do whatever you want — after you've assisted me with one or two small matters using your dialect recognition skills."

"Skills? I have no skills! Look at me. I'm nothing but a shit-for-brains twit who is living a never-ending nightmare."

She lifted one corner of her lip. "Shit for brains twit is an oxymoron."

"I don't care what it is!"

"Relax, Harry. You're nearly dead."

He made a dry noise deep in his throat. "What in hell do you mean, nearly dead?"

"In a few months your embassy, in Moscow, will receive news of a sea accident. They'll hear how you died; how your body was not recovered."

"Is this more fiction? Or are you foretelling my future?"

"That's when the entire world will stop looking for you."

Harry gave one earlobe a nervous tug. "Lucky me."

"Stop worrying. By the time spring rolls around, you and I will be in Berlin."

He looked at her squarely. "I thought we were headed for Moscow."

"That's our first stop. You'll do a few months of training, there."

"What training?"

"You're going to KGB school."

"I didn't think the KGB still existed?"

"It doesn't. But, the school does."

"KGB school... Berlin..." Harry made a gurgling sound in his throat. "Wouldn't it be easier to let me shoot myself?"

"The Chechnyan terrorists have gone into partnership with Berlin's Neo-Nazis. You and I are going to sort out who is who. It's a simple job, for someone of your skills."

"Anitchka, have you cleared this with the head of the *Glavnoye Razvedyvatel'noye Upravleniye?*"

"Of course. We're going to run you as an independent agent. It happens all the time in this business." She smiled at him. "Isn't that better than being dead?"

"In case you don't know, just the thought of those Chechnyans sends One-Eyed Willie's looking for a place to hide. And, the spot he keeps picking is very uncomfortable."

"You and One-Eyed Willie will be in no danger."

Harry opened the passport and looked at the photo. It matched the one from his American passport. Then his eyes drifted down to his new name. At first, nothing registered. Then realization set in and he gave Anitchka a disbelieving stare.

"Hitler?" Harry blurted. "My new name is Harry Hitler?"

"He was a much revered man in Germany. He still is, by many."

"But, why Hitler?"

"That name will guaranty you a place within the Neo-Nazis movement."

"Neo-Nazis? Have you forgotten that I'm a Jew?"

"It's only a name, Harry. If it bothers you, we'll change it." She glanced over at him. "How does Goebbels sound?"

"That's not funny." He closed the passport, and fell silent, studying the passing scenery out the side window. After a few minutes he said, "I won't work against my own country."

"You won't have to, Harry."

"How long will we be in Germany?"

"A year or so." Her voice was calm, serious. "My father, I, and Golovkin are already posted there."

He looked over at Anitchka in surprise. "What happened to Kazimir?"

"It was terrible."

"My God! Was he shot because I escaped?"

"Worse. He married Anais."

The American screwed up his eyes. "You mean Kazimir quit the GRU to get married?"

"He didn't quit. Anais is expecting their baby. She refused to leave Paris until the kid is born."

"I'm glad his numbness got cured."

"He credits everything to you and your hot sauce." She smiled at Harry. "Did you invent some sort of aphrodisiac?"

"It's more of an attention getter." He hesitated. "Hitler... My mother must be rolling in her grave."

"Wait until you see our apartment in Berlin."

"You said *our* apartment?"

"We're posing as man and wife."

Harry gave her a crooked grin. "You mean I finally got to you?"

"From the moment I first saw you, Harry."

Chapter 17

"I hate Berlin." Innokenti Rakhmelevich was bundled in a parka and looking over the balcony railing of Shkarov's apartment on *Wichertstr* above *Café Voland*. "Look at that damn snow."

"It's the middle of February," Mikhail Shkarov said. He looked at his partner with an uncurious gaze. "What did you expect? Rosebuds?"

"I miss Paris."

"Paris is out of the question." Mikhail Shkarov sat at the small table on the patio, dressed for a blizzard, sipping coffee. "Berlin is the only place the Russians will never look for us."

"Are you blaming me for the screwing Cheng gave us?"

"We lost a million euros because of you." He picked up a week old edition of *Moskovsky Komsomolets* and then slammed it down on the table. "And if you hadn't shot Galina she wouldn't have lost control of the car and nearly killed us." He gave his left wrist a painful shake. "My wrist aches every time the barometer drops."

"That was Bronstein's fault. If he hadn't tried to take the gun from me..."

"Are you sure you killed him?"

Rakhmelevich spread his hands. "I shot him twice, just before the car went off the bridge."

"But, are you sure Bronstein's dead?"

"I heard him groan." The patch-eyed Chechnyan paused to think. "I must've hit him at least once. Why?"

"Because this morning when I came out of *Café Voland*, after having breakfast, I could have sworn I saw Bronstein get into a taxi." Shkarov picked up the newspaper and slammed it down, again.

"Have you heard anything from your mole?"

"Popovitch is dead." Mikhail Shkarov tapped the newspaper. "It says so, right here."

"What happened?"

"According to this article, Popovitch was arrested on charges of treason. Apparently, several months ago. He died during a lengthy interrogation, but the news was not made public until, today."

"Leave it to those torturing GRU bastards!"

Shkarov snorted, "Officially, Popovitch committed suicide."

Rakhmelevich rolled his good eye. "How many times did he shoot himself?"

"Seven. Listen to this…" Shkarov picked up the newspaper again, and began reading, " 'According to the lone witness at the detention center in the basement of the Russian Embassy in Paris, Kazimir Sokolof, the prisoner suddenly produced a pistol and did the deed before he could be stopped. How Popovitch came into possession of the gun is a mystery. Equally baffling, is where the weapon disappeared to after Popovitch died. The Russian Ambassador to France was not available for comment. However the Ambassador's First Secretary suggested that Popovitch's suicide was the Doctor's way of avoiding the expense and embarrassment of a trial and execution.'"

Rakhmelevich have his head a weary shake. "I'll never commit suicide."

Shkarov checked his watch. "Come on," he said, getting to his feet. "Now that we are using Berlin's National Party as our cover, we don't want to be late for the swearing in ceremony of the latest Nazi members."

"Those Nazis are all a bunch of traitors."

"Traitors who hide us, Rakhmelevich."

"For a price. We have to cut them a piece of everything we take in."

"Never mind that. What did you think of the credentials on that new Russian recruit?"

"Not many Russians speak English, French, and German."

"I'm thinking we should put him on our payroll."

"I'll take him aside, tonight, and see what he has to say."

"Also mention our commitment to expediting his rise through the Nazis party's leadership."

"He probably knows it'll be a cakewalk for him. I mean, how could the Nazi membership not want a Führer named Harry Hitler?"

Books by Michael Paulson

Cherem
Dead On*
Deadly Age*
Deadly Sting*
Deadly Trade*
Deadly Turn*
I, Philibert Q. Winslow
The Van Gogh Deception
Who Killed Michael Douglas

*Deacon Bishop Detective series

www.ingramcontent.com/pod-product-compliance
Lightning Source LLC
Chambersburg PA
CBHW071006280626
47160CB00015B/1419